THE LEFT-HANDED TWIN

THE LEFT-HANDED TWIN

A JANE WHITEFIELD NOVEL

THOMAS PERRY

THORNDIKE PRESS
A part of Gale, a Cengage Company

Copyright © 2021 by Thomas Perry.
Thorndike Press, a part of Gale, a Cengage Company.

ALL RIGHTS RESERVED
Thorndike Press® Large Print Core.
The text of this Large Print edition is unabridged.
Other aspects of the book may vary from the original edition.
Set in 16 pt. Plantin.

LIBRARY OF CONGRESS CIP DATA ON FILE.
CATALOGUING IN PUBLICATION FOR THIS BOOK
IS AVAILABLE FROM THE LIBRARY OF CONGRESS.

ISBN-13: 978-1-4328-9450-4 (hardcover alk. paper)

Published in 2022 by arrangement with Penzler Publishers/The Mysterious Press

Printed in Mexico
Print Number: 01   Print Year: 2022

As always, for Jo.

While the religious system of the Iroquois taught the existence of the Great Spirit *Ha-wen-ne-yu,* it also recognized the personal existence of an Evil Spirit, *Ha-ne-go-ate-geh,* the Evil-minded. According to the legend of their finite origin, they were brothers, born at the same birth, and destined to an endless existence.

— Lewis H. Morgan, *League of the Ho-de-no-sau-nee, or Iroquois,* 1851

1

Night had fallen on the western end of New York State. Carey McKinnon, MD, was still at Buffalo General performing an emergency surgery on a boy who had been hit by a car after school. McKinnon's wife, a tall, slim woman with long black hair, came out of the back door of their old stone house in Amherst, walked to the carriage house that had served as the garage for as long as there had been cars, got into her Volvo, and drove to the west to get on the Youngmann Expressway.

Jane McKinnon had chosen this time for her errand partly because it would give her mind something to occupy it while Carey was fighting for the boy. Jane was a person who wasn't good at not thinking, and she knew that was what Carey would be doing — fighting for him. She had known and admired Carey when they were in college, and when they had met again years later, after he had become a surgeon, she had not been surprised that he had found something important to do with himself.

What had surprised her was that he had come to find her again because he loved her. The name Jane McKinnon was about the role and the relationship she had chosen — maybe acquiesced to — when he had asked her. For the thirty years before that she had been Jane Whitefield, and occasionally she was again. That was the name her parents had given her for daily use. It was distinct from her real name, the very long one that was in Seneca and not really pronounceable in English, the one her clan had used many times, for a girl in each generation, and would again after she was dead.

Tonight she was on the way to her old house, the one her great-grandfather and a few of his friends had built just after the turn of the century in the small city where he and his wife had moved from the Tonawanda reservation. After that the Whitefields had lived there for around a hundred years. Jane had always loved the secret parts of the place, the basement made of big local stones set with mortar, the floor beams that held the house up, still rounded because they were made from the trunks of whole trees. She had been the last Whitefield to live there, and she had stayed until she'd married her husband.

Jane had not lived there in years, but it was a place that came with special responsibilities and she knew she could not sell it even now. The house was a place where people with certain needs used to come to find her, and when she had thought of selling it she'd had warnings in dreams that there might still be new people who had heard it was their one last safe place to go. And there had also been a few very bad people who had found their way to the house. Until she was sure the victimizers and hunters were all dead, selling the house to some unsuspecting family would be inhuman.

When Jane took the exit into the town she drove along Erie Street to Wheeler Street and over the railroad tracks past the old closed-down fiberboard factory. It had been empty of workers for so many years that it was starting to look like an ancient ruin. Weeds had grown up through the parking lot where cars used to be parked through all three shifts. Nearly all the windows of the main buildings were broken. The openings had let the weather in, and now there were plants, even saplings, growing out through a few of the frames.

Three blocks before the Niagara River she turned right. Her house was the fourth one in a row built so close together that it took skill to drive a modern car up the narrow driveway to her garage.

First she drove past the house as she used to when she had lived here so she could study the building from the street before she approached on foot. The house looked dark and quiet from this view, and that reassured her. She could see that beyond the front window of the house next door to hers, a reading lamp was on, and she could see the bluish glow of a television screen on the ceiling. That reassured her too. The house belonged to old Jake Reinert, her father's friend since they'd been children. She was always glad to see that he was there and being borne along by his routines.

She turned the corner and went around the block looking for cars that might have someone sitting in the driver's seat, for any kind of van or enclosed vehicle, particularly with tinted windows, for any vehicle with license plates that were obscured or made unreadable by plastic covers or mud, and for any vehicle that seemed to be paired with another — one at each end of a block, for instance. She also looked for a car with any after-market device, such as a spotlight or an antenna.

What Jane had done when she'd lived here had been dangerous and illegal, too, so law enforcement vehicles would be as menacing as stolen ones. Because this was her old neighborhood and she still visited regularly, she was familiar with most of the cars parked on the streets. The only two she didn't recognize were an underpowered compact that neither a killer nor a cop would want, and a pickup truck with a soft front tire.

Jane parked a few houses away between two big old sycamores instead of under them. In the early spring sometimes they self-amputated limbs and she didn't want one hitting her car. As she passed Jake Reinert's house she went up on the front porch and looked in the window. He was watching a cable news show and reading a magazine at the same time. She rang the doorbell and stood back from the door so he could see her through the peephole. The door opened, and Jake was smiling. "To what do I owe this honor, Madam?"

"I just happened to be passing by, peeping in the neighbors' windows, and saw you reading a magazine. Since you usually don't let my mail pile up, I figured it was probably mine."

"Not this time," he said. He held it up and she saw it had a family on a new boat roaring across a small lake.

"Yeah," she said. "The women in my magazines usually have more clothes on."

"I'll ignore the misplaced innuendo. Did you bring that quack you married with you?"

"Not this time. He's working, or so he says. But I know he'll ask about you. Have you been doing okay?"

"Still living the dream. I do have some mail for you, though." He went across the room and brought back a stack of envelopes held together by a rubber band.

She took it. "Thanks, Jake. See you."

"See you, Janie."

She walked around to the back of her house, scanning the windows she passed to be sure none of them had been broken in an attempt to get in. She went up the back steps and unlocked the kitchen door, then opened it to go in.

She stopped. The air smelled wrong. There was a faint scent. She quietly closed the door, set the mail on the counter beside her, and remained motionless as she teased her nose with the air for a few seconds. It was very subtle, but it was a floral aroma. Perfume smells didn't belong here. Even

14

now, years after Jane had retired, she never wore perfume or used products that were scented because an enemy could use the smell to detect her presence in the dark. She always carried a perfume bottle in her purse but it contained concentrated juice of the roots of water hemlock plants, not perfume.

What worried her most was that women and girls were not the only people who liked to smell good. The faintness and subtlety of the smell might mean she was detecting aftershave or a man's hair product.

Jane stayed where she was. The person could have come and gone. But if someone was in the house with her now, he might have heard her unlock the door and be waiting for her to step into the open to attack her. She decided to outwait the enemy she imagined, to baffle his notion of how long a person standing in a dark room would do nothing. She had to be sure the other person moved first.

She stood with her back against the wall opposite the doorway, still sampling the air to gauge the strength of the scent and listening for movement. The electric clock on the wall she could see was a favorite from the days when she'd lived here. It had a bright white face with clear black numbers and a case that was a ring of red plastic that always made the kitchen seem cheerful. Because it was old, the two hands and the twelve numbers had been painted with dots of radium. She could even make out the positions of the glowing hands in the dark. 9:07.

She had left the clock here as one of her hostages to future safety. Nobody would move away and leave such a joyful, friendly kitchen clock. If a clock like that was still here, she must be too. 9:09.

She had left a number of other hostages too. There was a set of three solid iron skillets of the sort that was hard to find anymore, a nearly complete set of antique silverware, clothes in the closet of her old room, and even some framed photographs. 9:13. The photographs were snapshots of a real Haudenosaunee family. It didn't happen to be her family or one from her reservation, but they were real. The house was full of furniture and books.

Footstep. Jane heard it and knew the exact spot and had a notion of the weight of the person. As Jane moved past the refrigerator, she swung its door open in front of her to block a gunshot and dropped to her belly to reach under it and jerk the person's ankles toward her.

"Aah!" the voice screamed as the person hit the floor in the hall.

The refrigerator light was enough for Jane to verify it was a girl. As Jane slithered on top of her she quickly ran her hands up and down the girl to be sure there were no weapons, and then held her forearm across the girl's throat. "Who are you?"

"I'm looking for Jane Whitefield."

"One more try. What's your name?"

"Sara Doughton."

"Very good. And what makes you think this is the place to look for Jane Whitefield?"

"My lawyer told me this would be my best chance."

"Why do you have a lawyer?"

"I had one. She was a court appointed attorney in LA. Her name is Elizabeth Howarth. I was involved with a man named Albert McKeith and we were both arrested."

"For what?"

"Murder."

"Did you do it?"

"No. But he did."

"What did your lawyer tell you to do?"

"Take the deal. Tell the prosecutor everything I knew and then testify to it."

"What did you do?"

"Just what she said. It was bad advice."

"Why was it bad?"

"Because the jury didn't convict him. He sat there in court for days listening to me telling everything he did. The jury said 'not guilty.' So now he's free, and he's coming for me."

"Tell me what Elizabeth Howarth looks like."

"Long hair."

"Color."

"Gray. Almost white. She wears it tied in a ponytail or a single braid most of the time."

"About the same height as you?"

"No. Taller than you, even."

Jane said, "Tell me why you want Jane Whitefield."

"She told me that Jane Whitefield could help me disappear."

"I mostly stopped doing that years ago."

"I thought you had to be her," the girl said. "You're the way she said you were."

"How's that?"

"Tall, dark, not sweet, no bullshit."

"Why should anyone help you?"

Jane could see in the refrigerator's light that the girl was pretty, and she had a soft, soothing voice. "I did what I thought was right, so I could make a clean new life, maybe help other —"

"Stop. Never lie to me," Jane said.

The girl hesitated. Then she said, "I did what they told me would get me free. They said they knew I had not done anything. If I would cooperate they would drop any charges against me. They made up papers that said so and Elizabeth told me to sign them and live up to the deal. They kept me locked up in County while I told them everything I knew or saw. When the time came I testified against Albert. The day after I testified they let me go."

"Where did you go?"

"I didn't have much money or a place to sleep, but I knew some people I had met working in a coffee place a few years ago. One of them, a girl I used to be friends with, told me she would let me sleep at her place for a couple of days.

"I had mentioned this girl one time while I was in jail. She was the only local reference I could think of who wasn't a creep. I guess Elizabeth must have seen the tapes of my interrogation and remembered the name. One day she drove there. When she found me she told me how the trial had ended. Albert McKeith got off. I said 'How could that be?' She said, 'It happens.' I guess it must, because there sure are a lot of rotten guys with serious records walking around loose."

"How did she tell you to get here?"

"She bought me a plane ticket and then made me memorize the address. She said you would kill me and then her if she wrote it down."

"Well, you're here," Jane said. "Do you know enough to be sure that nobody followed you?"

"I think so."

"So does everybody else who gets followed. Is the car you drove the white pickup or the PT Cruiser?"

"The PT Cruiser."

"You did okay. There was nobody watching it when I got here." She sighed. "I'll try to do what I can for you."

"That's a lot to do. You must be really close to Elizabeth."

"Right now I hate her. And there are some things you'll need to know before I do anything for you."

"Like what?"

"I won't help you get revenge against anybody — Albert McKeith or the judge or whoever didn't help you. If you want revenge, go back and get it yourself. And I won't try to get you justice. I don't always know what justice is, but the rest of us do without it, so you can too. If you want to run away, you come to me. That's all."

20

"Okay."

"You already know not to lie to me. I know that's a hard one, but you'll have to resist. Lies waste my time and the truth might tell me something that will keep you alive."

"Yes," she said. "No lies. Anything else?"

"Just a warning. I've been taking people away from the messes they've made of their lives for a long time. Everybody who has come to me had somebody who wanted to kill him. Most of those killers are still out there looking. What most are looking for right now is the person who took their victim away. So the most dangerous thing you've done so far is to come near me. Before anything else happens, take time to think about that. I'm going to put some money on the table. If you decide to leave before I come back tomorrow, keep it. If you're still here we'll start making plans."

Jane reached into her purse and put a thick sheaf of hundred-dollar bills on the table, turned, and walked out the door. She locked the door and stepped off the concrete steps and walked the rest of her circuit around the house. She found the place where the girl had entered the building. It was the old opening that had originally been the small door in the outer wall where the

21

milkman used to put the bottles when he made a delivery. The opening was barely big enough for a child to slither through, but this Sara was as skinny as a model. She had used something to pry the latch up, but at least she hadn't broken anything.

Jane walked to her car, got in, and drove back around the block to check the girl's car once more. Then she turned toward home.

2

It was almost eleven when Dr. Carey Mc-
Kinnon drove off the highway into the
driveway in Amherst. The lights were on in
the living room so he could see the stone
fireplace through the front window. All that
light was unusual at this hour unless there
were visitors. He noticed the lights were also
on upstairs, in the master bedroom. Jane
was a very modern woman who had been
earning a serious degree at Cornell —
economics and history — when he met her,
and she had turned out to be one of the
brightest of his friends. She thought about
the planet the way a scientist did. What he
hadn't known at the time was that she also
thought like a Seneca woman. She was
grateful for the earth and its animals and
plants, but she also was grateful *to* the earth
and its animals and plants. She was not a
person to leave lights burning without being
conscious that it created heat and caused

fuel to be consumed heating water to turn turbines. Waste was incompatible with gratitude.

Carey drove his BMW up the driveway around the old stone house to the carriage house in back. He pressed the remote control and the doors opened horizontally, two mechanical arms pushing them outward to permit him to drive in. Carey's father and grandfather and the McKinnons of their century had always gotten out of their cars to open the doors, but Carey had noticed that the same motors that opened and closed some gates were perfect for the carriage doors, too.

Carey got out of the car and walked to the kitchen door, unlocked it, and went inside, then pressed the indoor remote control on the counter to close the garage. He was still wearing scrubs tonight because after his surgery there had been another hour and a half before he was ready to leave the hospital.

He walked through the kitchen and the living room looking for Jane. She had heard him and was waiting for him at the top of the stairs. She was wearing a long robe made of a thin layer of soft white cotton, the belt cinched tight at her waist.

"Hi, honey," she said. "Everything go okay?"

"Robert Winston Machevsky, soon to be known as Babe Machevsky or maybe Rocky Machevsky, or maybe even Maestro Machevsky, is no longer in danger. Unfortunately he has some bones that are held together with titanium pins, but I'm pretty sure even those are going to be a dim memory. Maybe when he travels to the Nobel Prize ceremony in a few years he'll set off some metal detectors, but otherwise he'll be fine."

"Great," she said. "I knew you would fix him right up. You look like you could use a drink and a bath."

"You're right."

"What would you like to drink?"

"Do we own any martinis?"

"At this moment they're only potential martinis, but they can be assembled in minutes."

As he came up the stairs and she came down they sidestepped to each other and kissed, then went on.

Five minutes later she appeared in the doorway of the big bathroom by their bedroom where Carey was soaking in the oversized bathtub. Jane set the two martinis on the counter between their two sinks, shrugged off the bathrobe and reached up to hang it on the hook, then turned around and looked into his eyes.

"Well, that's my first wish, already granted," he said. "I wonder if the genie will give me two more."

"No, but I will," she said. She handed him the two glasses and then stepped into the tub and sat down beside him. They sipped their drinks and talked and kissed and caressed each other and talked less and less. After a while Jane stood and stepped out onto the soft rug and they dried each other with thick bath towels. Then they walked into the bedroom.

Much later the soft breeze through the upper window was cooler, and they lay side by side and held hands.

"When are you leaving?" Carey said.

"I'm sorry it was obvious. I hope it didn't ruin homecoming for you."

"I had noticed you had lights on downstairs so I wouldn't come in to a dark, empty house, and I guessed that the light up here was because you were packing. I hoped you weren't, but then things got so good I knew. I don't mean you haven't been pleasant company on some other night. But this time you were making sure I would get the message."

"There's probably some truth in that. I wanted you to know how I felt. But tonight was also about giving myself a memory to take with me that would remind me what my life with you is like. And I wanted the memory to include me knowing what I have and showing you. And that's what I think kept us up so late."

He craned his neck to see the clock on the nightstand. "It is late. Time kind of got away from me."

"And already here we are again, lying here looking at the ceiling and listening to the owls telling each other it's time to get back up in the tree before the sun."

"I don't suppose —"

"This has been perfect. Beautiful. And as soon as we're back together we'll be here again. What a huge day you've had, Carey. You saved at least one person's life and fixed his injuries so they'll heal right. And I remember you said you had three surgeries this morning, and those probably went well, too, but you already forgot about them, right? I thought so. And I don't know what else you did before you came home and reminded your wife why she married you, and then why she's always finding an excuse to lure you up here again. Right now, it's time to close our eyes. I'll be back with you as soon as I can." A few minutes later she leaned over and looked down at him and listened to the deep, strong breaths of his sleep.

3

Jane walked into the carriage house at four thirty A.M. She knew it was best to get away from the McKinnon house before her husband woke up, and that would happen a half hour from now. The only way she could not hear the man she loved say "Don't go" was to be gone.

She started her car's engine while the carriage house doors were still shut so he wouldn't hear the starter, then opened them to avoid accumulating carbon monoxide and let the car drift out of the carriage house, gaining speed silently because of the driveway's slope. When she coasted past the end of the house where the master bedroom was, she pressed the button to close the carriage doors. She saw it happen in the corner of her eye as she pulled out onto the highway.

Jane drove to the house in the town by the river. This time she pulled all the way into her garage, took her bag, got out, and closed and locked the combination lock on the garage. She had no idea how long she might be gone, so she had a battery charger in the trunk. She was also not certain which of her current possessions would still be with her when she returned, so she kept the key with her until she was in the kitchen and could store it in the freezer.

She opened the basement door and descended the steps with her bag still on her shoulder. She walked to the old workbench near the far wall, took the stepladder that was leaning against the wall, and carried it to the old coal furnace that had been left there years ago when the oil furnace had replaced it. The old furnace used to feed hot air into several round ducts just under the first floor that ran up to brass grates set in the hardwood floors. Jane climbed the stepladder and separated two sections of one old duct, reached inside, and took out a metal box. She took out ten thousand dollars in banded stacks of hundred-dollar bills, put them in her shoulder bag, and returned the box to its place. Next she reached into the other duct and took out a pair of Glock 9mm pistols and two spare loaded magazines and added them to her bag. She took out a lady's wallet, and then examined several business envelopes, found one that said "FC21–26," which stood for "female Caucasian age 21–26" and took it. She fitted the two heating ducts together again, took the ladder back to the other end of the cellar, and went upstairs. She left her bag near the door and climbed to the second floor.

She found Sara Doughton sleeping on a pair of couch cushions and a blanket in the closet of the bedroom Jane had occupied as a child. "Wake up," Jane said.

Sara sat up. "Is it daytime already?"

"For us it is. It's best to get on the road before we're too easy to see."

"Okay." Sara got up, folded the blankets and put them in the cedar chest, and then put the cushions on the old chaise.

Jane said, "That was a smart place. You don't want somebody to be able to find you in the dark."

"I learned that in a hard way."

"I'm sorry. Where did you get your car?"

"Elizabeth bought me plane tickets. I took one as far as Salt Lake City and turned the other one in for cash. With what I had it was enough. It's not a great car."

"Does anybody who might be looking for you know about it?"

"No."

"Then it's a great car."

"Did you bring anything into the house that you want to take with us?"

"My bag is in the trunk."

"Then let's go join it."

Carey McKinnon awoke at his usual time of five A.M. and looked at Jane's side of the bed in case she had changed her mind. No. She was gone. She had set the alarm on his cell phone, so he turned it off before it could ring. He sat up but didn't bother to search for a note. She was not a person who left notes.

He swung his legs off the bed and stared through the open doorway and down the long, straight hall. He felt the misery settling on him. The McKinnons had only one long-standing disagreement but it sometimes made him feel that their marriage had never been free of this argument, just had extended truces.

He couldn't complain that he hadn't been warned. Years ago when they were friends from college just getting together romantically, before she would even talk about marrying him, she had told him her secret.

The secret was that she had spent her time during the years when they had been out of contact acting as what she called a "guide."

She didn't mean any normal sort of guide. People who believed that they were about to be murdered found their way to her. She conducted them away from the places where they were in danger to new places where nobody knew them. Then she taught them how to be new people. She was guiding them out of the world.

She had worked rarely at first, using methods she had developed from the experience of working as a skip tracer during college summers. She had learned how people who didn't want to be found traveled, obtained and used false names and identification and references, got themselves places to live, landed jobs, even paid taxes. The time came when a friend of both Jane and Carey had reason to disappear and Jane had realized that she already knew how to make him vanish, so she did. Only a few people had known, and Carey had not been one of them.

Of course, the time would come again when someone else needed help. That time the victim was a woman who was being stalked by a deranged admirer. Jane took her away too. Once people knew that Jane could make a person vanish, the information never stayed put and stopped circulating. Somebody's father borrowed money from the wrong people, a classmate had a fight in a bar and hurt his opponent too seriously.

Jane had always refused payment for what she did. She even refused to let the person she was helping pay any expenses. She would say to him, "When I put you somewhere, you're going to need all your money. I can get more, and I'm not running from anything."

People didn't know it, but Jane's instinct always led her to the customs and habits of her family, which were part of their Seneca culture. Senecas were not very interested in wealth. A person was respected because of what he brought to society, not what he kept for himself, and people didn't automatically translate effort into money. Instead of invoices and contracts, Jane gave and received presents, did favors, and honored responsibilities to people because they were human beings.

What she had told some of her earliest clients — she didn't even use the word "clients," but called them her "runners" — was "Today you feel awful. You're scared, tired, lonely, and desperate. One day, maybe a year from now, or maybe ten, when you're feeling safe and happy, you'll look back and remember how you felt. If you still feel like it then, you can send me a present."

By the time Carey and Jane were negotiating their marriage, this had been going on for years. People had sent Jane many presents, and still did. Two women who were working in a county registrar's office in Ohio had sent her a package of genuine birth certificates, at least fifty in the first batch and more later. Other presents were equally unexpected. A man who had the skills and the equipment sent her three semiautomatic handguns for which he had made the receivers and bought the rest as spare parts, so there were no serial numbers, model numbers, or brand names.

There was also Rhonda Eckersley. When Jane met her, she was married to an abuser working his way up to killing her. The day before Jane had made her disappear her husband had chained her by the neck to a ring in the floor and invited some friends over to help him punish her.

A couple of years later Rhonda had a new name and had married a new husband. She had been sending Jane an unsigned card each fall around the anniversary of her disappearance, usually one that celebrated the season — pictures of colored leaves, migrating birds, harvests of vegetables. The new husband was apparently rich, because the year she remarried, the card was inside a wrapped package. That year and every year after, the rest of the package was money. There were other runners who had thought the same way, probably because they knew that Jane would use their presents to pay to take some new runner away from his troubles. Eventually she had formed a corporation in which Jane ostensibly provided professional consulting. That gave her an excuse for receiving money and banking it.

She had explained it all to Carey before she would think of marrying him. He had discussed with her the fact that state and federal laws prohibited the use of false identification, documents, and cards, obtaining false driver's licenses, marriage licenses, or other official papers, depositing or withdrawing money under false names, and nearly everything else she did.

Jane had been guiding people beginning in junior year at Cornell through the two remaining years of college, his four years of medical school, and his five years as a surgical resident. In other words, on the day when he had arrived at her old house to see if she was still living in western New York and might be interested in renewing their friendship, she had already been a serious criminal for over ten years.

He had accepted her offer to stop being a guide. She had made an effort. He had been afraid that a day might come when a new runner would arrive whose need would be more pressing and important than her promise. After a time, he had understood her way of thinking. She had been perfectly aware that what she was doing was almost suicidally dangerous. She was the one who had been doing it. She didn't think it would be fair or right of her to present herself to him and then be killed. But there was also another factor. She knew that it would be insane to be a guide if they had children, and she had wanted children.

As he had feared, there had been a few times in those years when she'd had to go on a trip to preserve a life. He had not approved, but he had decided not to make her miserable if she had to go. He had considered it a relapse when it happened.

But then, years later, the day had come when he had learned that one of the most important and admirable people in his life was in that kind of trouble. He'd told Jane that he had to ask her, just this one time, to help the older surgeon who had taught and mentored him. She'd saved his old friend and teacher. But then she took on other runners.

He was sure the fact that they had not had children yet had changed things too. They had the sort of infertility that was most frustrating to him as a physician — the idiopathic, unexplained inability to have children. They'd been examined and tested and retested, and Jane had been given hormones and medicines of many sorts. He remembered that one day she had simply gone into the baby's room and taken down the antique Seneca cradle board from the wall, wrapped it up in museum-quality tissue and a protective box, and put it away.

He missed her already, and he knew she was putting herself in danger. There was no reason for anyone to ask her for help if they weren't in danger. And he knew that she had felt she needed to take on the weight of somebody else's troubles and try to give them a future. He wished, but he didn't even know what solution was available to wish for.

4

Jane said to Sara, "I assume that you've either thrown away your cell phone or at least taken the battery out."

"Thrown it away. The only thing I used it for was talking to a bunch of people I'm doing my best never to see again. They all have my number and would have tried to use it to locate me."

"Good." Jane reached into her purse and took out a new cell phone. "Here. This is for you."

"Oh my God. This is the newest iPhone. That's a lot of money."

"Right now it's for show. It's exactly the phone women of your age and description have, if they can afford it. One way to keep from striking people as not right is to never surprise them."

"Thank you," Sara said. "I'll leave it turned off."

"For the moment, that's right. But I've

loaded it with the usual apps, including a few that use your location to give you information, like maps and directions. But it's on the setting to block that for now. It also has some unusual new ones."

"Like what?"

"Some people at the University of Chicago invented one that messes with facial recognition devices. When somebody tries to identify you, these devices measure the size of your features, the space between your eyes, the exact color of your hair, and so on, and compare it with whatever picture of you they have. But it also does something we don't see. It compares to be sure that the pixels on the new photo are the same as the ones on the second photo. This app substitutes a couple of pixels on the new photo, and that makes the recognition device fail to recognize it. So you have a picture that looks like you to any human, but not to any machine."

"It doesn't sound very practical. It only does one thing."

"One thing can be a lot." Jane smiled. "But getting out of the world doesn't depend on using one thing. It's more an attitude, an awareness that you don't do things that could put you in danger, and you never miss a chance to mislead a hunter.

If you always shopped at three particular clothing chains before you ran away, you never shop at those stores again. You do an inventory of all of the brand names you always bought in your old life, and you switch. You change the color of your hair, buy glasses and scarfs, and so on. If you always loved Chinese food best, a person looking for you can go to any new city and ask someone for the names of the five best Chinese restaurants and begin looking for you. Think hard about who you were and what was predictable about you, and change it. Before long, you'll be very hard to find."

"Do you think I can do that?"

"I think so. But I don't know you, and it's not easy."

"But you can teach me, right?"

"I can tell you what you need to know. And I'll help you get settled in a place that's pleasant and where you can do well. But you'll have to do some very hard and sad things."

"Like what?"

"If your mother is living, the people searching for you will find her and watch her because she's somebody you would be sure to get in touch with. After her, they'll look for a father, sister, brother, best friend. If you want to disappear you have to cut yourself off from the past, and everybody you knew there. That's hard and sad."

"Maybe not so sad for me," Sara said. "My father left when I was about six. That was sad. I used to cry about him for years. I would tell myself he remembered me and he was just waiting until I was old enough so he could take me away from my mother. She had custody of me, and I thought that meant my father had to wait a certain number of years. I swear I think that idea came from her. But she always said she only had to be related to me until I was eighteen, so I could have thought that's what it meant. After I was with Albert, I went to visit her in Chicago once. She was remarried for about the third time, and was dressing about half her age. She made it clear she was not happy to have me turn up. I was a bundle of bad memories and things she had to explain to the man she was with at the time." Sara shrugged. "Right now, I don't think she'd know anything a killer could use, and Albert wasn't with me when I went to see her. How do you know about the things that killers do?"

"I've taken a lot of people out of the world. They don't have much in common with each other, but the people hunting them do. A person whose first idea of how to solve his problems is to stop somebody else's heart has already crossed some lines. After the first person he's killed, what he honestly comes to feel is that no other person's life is as important as a little inconvenience to him. Some of them are very good at understanding other people's feelings, but it's a predator's skill, used only to find ways of controlling or using or manipulating victims. They tend to find the same ways."

"That's just like Albert. He loved to control everybody, especially me. Now I guess he'd just like to kill me. But I'm sure he's thinking of a way that will be fun for him. Have you ever killed anyone?"

"Yes," Jane said. "That's not something I like to remember. But I try not to lie to people who need the truth from me."

Sara squinted and looked at the back window. "Wow. That car's headlights are terrible. Blinding."

"That's the car I've been watching for a while. The black Range Rover. He showed up right after we got south of Buffalo."

"You've been watching that one car all this time?"

"Not exactly. I've been watching the road behind us all this time. The car wasn't surprising at first. It's just that he's stayed with us a long time."

"It's not even that dark anymore. He doesn't need his headlights at all."

Jane said, "It's possible he turned on his high beams now because he was trying to get a good look at us. Have you seen that car before?"

"No."

"You said before that you drove from Salt Lake City. Is that where you bought this car?"

"Yes."

"Did you buy it from somebody you already knew?"

"No. After I got off the plane I started looking in my phone to find some cheaper way to make the rest of the trip. I ran across this car in an online ad. The girl who was selling it had just got married to a guy who had two better cars than this. She figured if she sold it she could get most of her buying price back because it was already depreciated, and save the insurance premiums and license fees. And she had to park this one on the street. Why are you interested?"

"Because I want to know if this is somebody looking for you, or somebody looking for me. If he didn't follow you from Salt Lake City, then it's likely that he had found my house and saw us come out and get into this car."

"What do we do?"

"Give him a chance to show us which it is," Jane said. "Can you reach over the seat and get my bag?"

While Sara leaned over the seat and pulled the bag over, Jane watched the car in her mirrors. Sara set the bag between them. She looked hard at Jane. "Are you just doing this to show me I have to stay alert?"

"I hope so." She kept looking in the mirrors. "When you're trying to switch from an old life to a new one, you're like a crab changing to a better shell. You're in the most danger when you're between shells. If this guy behind us is a cop, he could be working with a partner in another car and talking on the phone. Sometimes one of them follows you for a while and drops back, and then the other one pulls forward to take his place. That way you don't feel like one car has been behind you too long. Unfortunately, a killer working for your former friend Albert might work with a partner the same way." She looked in her rearview mirror and kept her eyes there for a minute or two. "And there he is."

"Who?"

"The black SUV just dropped back. A silver SUV about the same size and shape is pulling forward to take his place. Can't tell the make yet. Can you open my bag, please?"

Sara opened it. "Holy shit. I never saw so much money."

"I try to pay most expenses in cash. Have you ever fired a pistol?"

"Somebody took me to a range once."

"Good. There are two pistols in there, identical Glock 17s. They're loaded. Carefully hand me one, holding it by the barrel."

"Here."

"Thank you. Now. Do you feel you could contribute to our defense if this turns ugly?"

"Probably."

"Then pick up the other pistol, also carefully. It's also loaded. You don't have to search for a safety catch. They have one that's built into the trigger assembly. Be prepared to either hide the gun or open the window, point, and shoot."

Jane drove aggressively, trying to add speed as she could. The car seemed to need springs and a wheel alignment, because when the speed was high enough there was a bit of shimmying and a sensation that the car was bouncing so much that the wind rushing under it might cause the front end to rise off the pavement.

Sara said, "The silver one is in front and

the black is nosed up right behind him."

Jane glanced in the mirror. "It looks like he's drafting, trying to get the car in front to pull him forward into its vacuum."

"Does that work?"

"It seems a little odd, when either one of them can outrun us alone. But I guess they don't need me to tell them how to murder us," Jane said. "I'm still hoping they're just behind us, not after us." Jane's right leg was straight, pressing the pedal to the floor now. The car's engine didn't seem to be able to go any faster, but running at such high rpm, it sounded smoother and more even, if higher pitched.

A sign flashed past on the right. "There's the sign. Hold on. I'm going to get off up there at the park entrance." She stared ahead as though transfixed, her face immobile, until the entrance appeared on the right side of the road ahead, and as they approached it the entrance appeared to enlarge like a mouth opening. Jane only moved the steering wheel a tiny bit to divert the car onto the drive. Then they were on a long, straight pavement. On their right was a row of painted parking spaces. Jane glanced to the left. "The silver car is staying on the highway." As soon as she'd said it, the second Range Rover, the black one, took the opening behind her.

"Get the gun ready, but do not use it unless I tell you to."

"What do I do — aim at their tires?"

Jane said, "No. If I tell you to fire, every round goes for the driver's head. If you miss, you'll make a mess of the windshield and even that may save us."

She glanced in the rearview mirror again. The black Range Rover was already almost abreast of them on their right, its tires going over the long row of empty parking spaces. Jane made a very slight change in the car's trajectory, and the Range Rover's driver adjusted to keep from touching her car and fell a couple of feet back.

Jane could see that the driveway continued straight to the end of the long row of parking spaces, and then re-entered the highway. As she watched, the silver Range Rover coasted off the highway to the far end of the parking lot where it met the highway, and stopped. The car drove forward, then back, putting its side across the exit at the far end of the lot.

"Oh, my God," Sara said. "What are we going to do?"

"Let them decide. I'll just make the choices clear to them."

She sped up again, gradually. What she

was doing now was not steering, but aiming. The car was heading precisely toward the driver of the silver Range Rover. Jane did not allow any variance in the path of the vehicle. It was a projectile that had been launched and Jane was changing nothing. If the driver of the silver Range Rover didn't move in a few seconds the engine block of Sara's car would plow into the side door of his vehicle and kill all three of them.

Sara began to whisper, "Please, please make this —" But she didn't say it.

The black Range Rover was pulling up abreast of their car again. Sara said, "Jane."

"I know. He's where I want him."

The driver of the black car seemed to make a decision. He moved closer, as though to nudge Jane out of her trajectory, then corrected his course. Jane glanced in his direction and a faint smile appeared on her face. He had been bluffing. Jane was not. She sped up some more, heading directly for the driver's door of the silver car.

The driver of the silver car stared. His mouth opened, and he seemed to be saying something aloud. At the last possible moment he threw his vehicle into reverse and spun his tires to pull back fast. His movement opened the exit onto the highway for

Jane, but Jane veered to her right before she flashed past his front wheels and roared up onto the highway.

Jane's sudden shift to the right made the driver of the black Range Rover jerk his wheel to the right to avoid her, so he missed the exit entirely and drove deep into a jungle of four-foot-tall shrubbery that had concealed an unimproved surface of rocks, stumps, and trash.

Jane accelerated again as soon as she felt four wheels on the highway. She kept glancing in her rearview mirrors to see when the two cars would come up out of the parking lot. A minute went by, and then another minute and she had traveled too far to see the opening from the lot anymore. The road curved and an intersection appeared ahead, so she took the road that met the main highway. She didn't slow down much, even though the road was narrow and had a rough shoulder made of coarse stones.

Sara was holding her head in her hands with her eyes closed. Jane said, "Are you all right?"

Sara looked up. "I know something I didn't before."

"What?"

"I saw one of the drivers — the one in the black car. I know him."

Jane nodded. "That's valuable information. Who is he?"

"He's a friend of Albert McKeith's. His name is Jason DeLong."

"Did he see you?"

"Yes. I'm pretty sure. He was on this side of the car."

"Okay. The main thing is to get as far from them as we can while they're still stuck in the weeds." Jane began to accelerate again.

Sara saw the rate at which the trees appeared and disappeared in the headlights and felt the car going faster. She said, "Can I ask you a question?"

"Sure."

"How did you know that guy in the silver car would move?"

"I didn't."

5

As the sun rose higher in the sky it lit a beautiful spring day, with a steady breeze that was just enough to make the leaves on the trees flutter and give off glints of reflected sunlight. Jane kept them south of the New York State Thruway, moving through small towns that had grown up on secondary footpaths that the Haudenosaunee had plotted through the forests that once covered their longhouse-shaped territory from the Hudson to the Niagara. Jane saw a shopping mall in the distance. She drove to its lot entrance and kept going until she reached the ramp leading to an underground parking garage. She parked far from the other cars.

"What are we doing here?" Sara asked.

"Two cars pulled up behind us a while ago. I have a theory about how they managed that, and I have to check it."

"What's the theory?"

"I think at some point after you bought this car, somebody placed a GPS tracker in, on, or under this car. A place that's below-ground and surrounded by concrete is a good place to do it because our transmitter's signal will be hard to pick up while we're here. For the moment we're probably invisible."

Jane got out and took the keys. "Search the inside of the car. Look under the dashboard, the seats, mats, glove compartment, everywhere."

"What am I looking for?"

"The transmitter. It will be a rectangle, probably black plastic, about two-and-a-half inches by two, or smaller. But anything you find, show me. Some of them are round, like a coin. They're almost always magnetic."

Jane opened the trunk and crawled into it to see and touch every surface, lift the rugs, examine the spare tire well and every inch of exposed steel. Then she lay on the concrete floor of the lot and checked the chassis and wheels, the underside of the gas tank, and then the bottom of the engine compartment. She stood and opened the hood and studied everything she could see or feel.

After a few more minutes, Sara called out, "I think I've found it."

Jane got back into the car and looked at the small black box in Sara's hand, then took it and studied it closely. "Very good. Yep, this is one. Where was it?

"It was plugged in under the dashboard." She showed Jane a wire with a small plug at each end.

Jane reached into her jeans pocket and showed Sara two more small black boxes.

"There were three?" Sara said.

"I think that we got them all," Jane said. "They're pretty good ones. The two I found operate on a lithium-ion battery, but a charge lasts at least two weeks. The one you found is even better, and more expensive. It must be nearly fifty bucks. That model plugs into the car's OBD2 outlet, the place where a mechanic plugs in his computer to scan the engine, so the transmitter will use the car's power and keep transmitting your location until a mechanic finds it. Nobody else looks there."

"How are Albert and Jason getting the results?"

"Does either of them have a cell phone?"

"Everybody has a cell phone."

"That will do it."

Jane took the three small black transmitters and walked to a row of cars in the more crowded part of the underground lot. She stopped behind a pickup truck that had a gun rack in the rear window and stuck a transmitter to the underside of the cargo bed, then walked to another car about fifty feet away, saw the small red sticker with the Marine eagle, anchor, and globe on the back window, and bent to stick the second transmitter under the gas tank. On her way back to Sara's car she dropped the plug-in transmitter on the concrete, stomped on it, and then picked up the pieces and dropped them in the nearest trash can.

When she got back into Sara's car, she held her phone out. "Here. Take my phone. I don't want you to use yours yet. When we get up aboveground get driving directions to Cantrell Falls, New York. It's roughly in the middle of the state."

"What's there?"

"Somebody we're going to need."

Jane and Sara drove past Chautauqua, Cassadaga, and Cattaraugus, went over bridges to cross the Allegheny and the Genesee, the heart of Seneca country. The names of places and rivers were all in the old language, Onöndowa'ga Gawe, so they felt easy for the muscles of her tongue to form. They had only the right phonemes — soft vowels between the consonants N, T, D, K, W, H,

G, or Y. None of the words ever had M, B, or P, so a Seneca speaker's lips never touched.

Jane and Sara stopped in little towns where they could park the car away from the main streets and the shops and walk in the back doors of the small casual restaurants past the kitchens. Jane chose booths and tables that were back from the front windows, but facing them so they could watch the street. When they had eaten and used the restroom, Jane would pay in cash and they would go out the back way again, study the area around their car before they approached it, and then drive on.

They stopped near Syracuse and Jane took out her cell phone and made a call. "Hello. My name is Rose Williston. I have a young woman visiting me from Stanford University in California. She's got an interview tomorrow morning at Syracuse University for graduate school and she needs her hair styled. Yes. Desperately. She'll need the works — wash, cut, and color, and whatever you recommend after your stylist has spent some time with it. Also, if you don't have a manicurist in your shop, I hope you can give us a recommendation. Yes. And I do understand that just popping up like this should cost more. I know that asking people to stay late isn't easy, but maybe it will help if you tell them I'll double their usual rate. I want to make it clear that this girl isn't one of those awful spoiled princesses. She's a hardworking, brilliant, and unassuming person. I'm the awful spoiled princess." She laughed. "Yes. Mathematics. That's wonderful. When? Four thirty. See you then."

Sara stared at her. "What was that?"

Jane said, "I made you a hair appointment."

"Why?"

"It's part of the process. It's got to be one of the first things we do, and it's necessary."

"Is it?"

"If you don't want people to find you, then you have to change the way you look. A little while ago one of the hunters saw you. If there are old pictures of you on his phone or Albert McKeith's phone, then there's at least one he can pick out that looks exactly the way you look today. He can show it to people he's asking about you. 'This is my sister, and she suffers from terrible depression. Any information you remember about her might save her life.' Or the cops. 'This is the escort who stole my credit card while I was asleep.' He can send the picture ahead of you to people in any new town you go to."

"Oh, shit. You're right, of course. I just feel like I've got no control over anything and I don't know what's happening."

"I called a hair salon that's well-known in this part of the state for very high quality work from expert stylists. This isn't LA or New York, but people who have worked in LA and New York are often interested in living in central New York State for a while because of the Finger Lakes and all the colleges. You and I are primarily interested in a transformation, but we'll also be going for very high-end work and beauty. Nothing keeps the supposedly random forces of the universe on your side as much as being attractive, unless it's the impression that you're rich, and this will give you both."

"Did you tell them my subject was mathematics? I don't know a thing about it."

"Neither will she, at least not enough to talk about it with a graduate student. If the subject comes up, the conversation will die from lack of oxygen. Even people who know lots about it don't want to talk about it. If you say you're in art or literature or sociology or political science, she might have opinions and expect to hear yours. Math? Not a chance.

"I've got to warn you," she continued. "This is just the beginning of the changes.

They're going to have to come fast. Changing your looks has to come first because we're going to need to get pictures of you for your identification cards and documents. Also, the time to make changes is before you go to the place where you want to stay. It's best to show up as the new person who already looks different from the old person and has never heard of her."

"You're saying I have to change everything?"

"Short answer? Yes."

"So nothing about the new me can be real?"

"At least two of the people searching for you know you already, right?"

"Well, yes."

"Then my advice is that you should change everything you can. It's not that anything about you now is bad, but it can get you recognized, and recognition can get you killed. Getting killed is bad."

The salon was empty when Jane and Sara entered. One female stylist was sitting in her barber chair drinking a cup of coffee and talking to another stylist in the next chair. A skinny woman wearing skin-tight black leggings that made her look like a pen-and-ink drawing appeared from a back room and charged toward them. "Hello. I'm

Marissa Kent." The two stylists stood up and set aside their coffee.

"I'm Rose Williston," Jane said. The surname was one that Jane had used occasionally in the Syracuse area because there were some businesses associated with people with that name and a couple of Williston Streets. "And this is Mandy, the client I told you about."

Marissa Kent shook hands with Sara and held on with her right hand, staring at Sara's hair. Her free hand went up to Sara's head and fiddled with the hair, running her fingers through it and then holding some between her thumb and forefinger and flicking it so it would fall naturally. "Yes," she said softly as she scrutinized it, and then put her hands on Sara's face and lifted it so she could stare into Sara's eyes and feel her cheekbones like a sculptor planning to reshape them. "Yes, I see," she whispered to herself. Finally, she said to Sara, "Mandy, you're lovely, and we can make you pop so everyone can see you." Sara looked at Jane uneasily as Marissa Kent led her to the chair. "Sit!"

She watched impatiently as Sara settled into the big chair. "Are you allergic to any hair products that you know of?"

"I don't know."

"Peroxide? Ammonia? Arsenic? I was kidding about the arsenic."

"Never used them, except the arsenic."

"Then you're not allergic." She went to a round table in the middle of the salon where piles of women's magazines were fanned out. She selected one and came back with it, leafing through the pages. She stopped at one picture of a woman with hair that was light brown with blond highlights, as though she had spent time in the sun. "That's your color."

"Pretty. It will bring out the golden retriever in me."

"Put your finger on the length you want it."

Sara pointed at a spot a half inch above the shoulder.

"Good girl," said Marissa Kent. She turned to the two stylists. "Lauren, you do the cut. Mimi, you do the color." She took the magazine from Sara and handed it to Mimi. Lauren the haircutter began bustling around collecting and arranging scissors and Mimi headed for the back part of the salon, where the dyes presumably were kept.

Sara watched as Marissa Kent stepped over to Jane at the window. Marissa Kent stared at Jane's head and reached out to touch a few strands of long black hair.

"There are women who would kill for hair like yours. Where is your family from?"

"My mother was Irish, and my father always said he had ancestors from Asia a long time ago."

"It's beautiful. I would have guessed South America."

"There could be some of that too. You know how people are. They can't leave each other alone."

While Sara was waiting for the hair coloring to work, the manicurist did her nails. A couple of hours passed before she noticed Jane counting hundred-dollar bills into a pile in front of Marissa Kent at the register. A few minutes later the colorist handed her the magazine and spun her chair around to face the big mirrors. She looked like a young cousin of the woman in the magazine. Jane gave each of the women a hundred-dollar tip.

A few minutes later they were back in the car. Jane said, "You can lose all the politeness now. They know you're a nice, appreciative person — maybe the best mathematician they've ever styled. What do you really think of it?"

Sara said, "It's different. I've never looked anything like this, with shorter, conservative hair. But it's not, like, ugly."

"Right. I think you look good." Jane started the car. "Of course, the main thing is that you're different. You don't look like the person they met a few hours ago." She pulled out onto the street and took the turn onto the highway heading east.

"What else has to be changed?"

"Whatever can be," Jane said. "Your name, of course. Your clothes. We'll get you a few kinds of glasses and sunglasses. I didn't notice any tattoos. Do you have any?"

"Only a small one that doesn't show."

"A flower? A design?"

"A name."

"You don't sound happy with it. They can be removed. Whose name is it?"

"His."

"Albert McKeith?"

"He asked. I guess it was to show other men he owned me but show me he didn't trust me."

Jane glanced at her and saw that she had tears in her eyes. Jane said, "You should tell me whatever you think I'll need to know to keep us safe. If there's something we have to change or fix or hide or lie about, I want to know it. Anything else is only your business."

"I think I have to tell you this." She swallowed. "It seems best to tell you now, while we're alone in the dark and nobody else can overhear it."

"Okay."

"I was just out of high school, working as a barista at a coffee shop. He came in one day. He was kind of good looking. He wasn't particularly tall or striking, but he was well-built, like he lifted weights. He didn't, but he had square shoulders and a thin waist without doing anything. His face had a friendly, approachable look. And you know how some people look smart?"

"Sure," Jane said. "I think it's something about the eyes."

"Exactly. His eyes were smart, and that was what made me curious about him. When you looked at them, you could see he was already conscious, looking back, aware of you. He had already thought about you a little bit.

"He seemed to be about my age, but it turned out later that he was older by about four years. Working as a barista is always either frantic or boring, and either way you think about the customers who come in for coffee. He used to come in for coffee around eleven o'clock every morning. He would walk in tired, but not tired like yawning. It was tired like he had just been up all night doing something great and he hadn't

64

crashed yet. He was happy.

"He talked to me, and called me by my name. Obviously, he was just reading it off the name plate pinned on my chest. It shows you how stupid I was that I knew it and it still impressed me that he bothered to read my name. He must be trying to tell me that he likes me enough to remember it. He must think I'm really hot, because he's never seen me before and I haven't said anything but 'What would you like?' I even took his reaction to my saying it as a sign, because he took a second to look at me and smile to himself before he said he wanted espresso.

"We were supposed to ask the customer's name so they could read it off the order and write it on the cup. He said 'Al' and then gave me his credit card. I read his whole name before I stuck the card in the reader. I look back on it now and can't help thinking it's harder to get a dog to like you than that."

"There are worse creatures to be like than dogs."

"There sure are," Sara said. "I guess I'm telling you how I got to know some of them. He kept coming in, always late in the morning, and always a little bit disheveled. I mean in a cute way — not sloppy and certainly not dirty or anything, but maybe his hair would be a little wild. Once he had a five o'clock shadow like he just got up and came out without shaving. That was about two weeks after he'd started coming to me."

"Coming to you?"

"For his coffee. I forgot to mention that. After that first morning he never got into the line for somebody else's register. If my line was long, he might pick up one of the newspapers on the table or check something on his phone screen. He'd end up in my line. That morning when he got to the front he saw I had noticed the unshaven look. He gave me this little smile and pointed at his face. He said, 'Well, what do we think? Do we like it, or do we hate it?' "

"That was pretty skillful," Jane said. "Combining you into a 'we' and giving you a say in how he should look, as though whatever you said was what he would say."

"Of course it worked," Sara said. "I reached out and touched his cheek and ran my fingers over it. I said, 'It's not you.'

" 'It's me,' he said. 'I grew it.'

" 'It's not the you that we like.'

"He said, 'Okay, we hate it,' and went to pick up his coffee while I took the next customer. The next day, when I took his order, he asked me to go out with him. I said yes. He took me out for a drink at Chateau Marmont. It was odd. The place was full of people I vaguely remembered seeing on TV, and other people who looked like they should be on TV. I don't remember eating anything.

"We left when more glamorous people were still arriving. Albert had an old Corvette. I thought he'd bought it out of a sense of irony and sophistication. It seemed smaller than the newer ones, and its upholstery was worn. One thing I didn't realize at the time was that it was made before a lot of safety regulations and advances, so he was driving us around in LA's nighttime traffic in a car that would behead us if it rolled over, and that had a fiberglass body that could break in two if it got T-boned. It wasn't old enough to be an antique but it was a hell of a lot cheaper than a new one.

"I got my first glimpse of his world that night. He was a person who had turned being a deadbeat and a hanger-on and a suck-up into a profession. All I could see was that people let him into parties where I saw celebrities. The one that night was in the the hills above Hollywood. It was in a house the size of a department store, built on three levels anchored in a steep slope, like steps, so each level was open to the sky.

I remember the lowest level had the pool and some big sunken Jacuzzis, the middle level had the dance floor, the band and the DJ and the entrance to the main interior floor. The top level was devoted to food and tables and chairs, and more dance space.

"The party was incredible. We danced a little, mostly as a way to get across the crowded dance floor, and we went to the top floor so he could talk to some guys he knew. I was barely eighteen, but I had a drink and that helped it all feel so beautiful and dreamlike, and the alcohol made me dance better and feel better. It was all insanely good — the music, the glimpses of faces I had seen on screen, the food. And I swear to you, none of it was my imagination.

"When we went down to the lower level I got a close look at the people hanging out in the pool and on the deck. These people — both men and women — were the kind who looked so hot that they wanted to always be seen in their bathing suits. Nothing I saw at that party was less than miraculous. The night air was sweet far above the city, and it was always the perfect temperature.

"And then the crowd began to move like water in an emptying bathtub. The music got quieter and stopped. Down at the street level there were people waiting for the valet parking attendants to bring their cars. Hours earlier when we'd arrived Albert had spotted a morning newspaper still in the driveway of a house nearby and had parked his car there, so we didn't have to wait.

"We got into the Corvette and Albert drove it down the winding roads out of the hills. I understood a whole lot all of a sudden. It was about four A.M. I knew what he had been doing all of those nights that left him tired but smiling and looking for coffee. And I know now that what I'm about to say will sound like ego, but it's true. I knew that a very big part of his good time that night was because of me. I had been fun and pretty in a fresh-faced, too-young kind of way. He really liked looking at me, but he also liked having me on his arm. It had brought him a lot of the kind of attention he craved. Other guys wanted to know where he had found me, as though there were a bunch of us somewhere, and some very attractive women who knew him came around to say hello, and they did it in a way that made me realize that my being with him had raised his value for the moment, maybe even made a couple of them jealous.

"But I have to admit that I sensed something else right away too. It was that the world represented by the party wasn't just something he had. It was also something that had him. And I felt a twinge, a little stab of fear that if I came back, or stood too close, it would have me too."

"What happened then?"

"The sex. By then it seemed obvious, inevitable, the only part of the night that still had to be checked off. He just drove the car to his place and we went in and started taking our clothes off. Afterward I fell asleep. When I woke up around eleven in the morning it was both of us at the coffee shop trying to revive ourselves with caffeine. My friends who worked there with me had covered for me. When Albert left, I worked the rest of the day and stayed late to help clean up and worked really hard at it.

"When I was done, Albert showed up and said, 'Come on.' I asked where we were going and he said he was taking me home so I could get a few hours of sleep before the party. I said, 'Where's the party?' and he said, 'You don't know them.' I slept, got up, and went to the party with him. The next day I quit my job."

"How long did your relationship last?"

"I guess it was four years. It's odd. Usually I've kept track of things like that — how long I've lived somewhere or known someone or whatever. I stopped because it didn't mean anything. All of a sudden, I wasn't working during the day. I had saved some money at the coffee shop, but I hardly spent any of it because he was always there. If I went to buy something he would whip out his plastic because he needed to have a part to play in everything that happened. I was still working, in a way. It was like my job was 'girlfriend.' We would start to move around at eleven, get coffee, and then at around one thirty he would start communicating. We would drive around town and talk to people all afternoon. While he was driving, he would be on the phone too.

"He would talk to somebody and hear about a party. Sometimes he would be talking to the person who was paid to be in charge of the party, and he'd get invited. In return he might ask if he could help this party organizer get something for the party or solve a problem. It would be something like that the caterer wouldn't supply the right kind of champagne for the party. Albert would say he'd pick up a case or two of the right kind, like Cristal. Or the conversation would go all strange, almost in code, and I would know it was about drugs. Albert would say he'd scrounge up some and then he'd usually have to make an arrangement to pick up some money from the person on the other end. Once in a while the guy would want his party 'dressed up' or 'populated.' That meant he wanted Albert to invite more women."

"How did he profit from all this?"

"You have to understand that he wasn't talking to the person whose party it was. The richer and better-known the person who gave the party, the less that person had to do with the party. There would be a party arranger who was paid to make the party happen. He would rent a big house in the right neighborhood, hire the band, the caterer, a DJ, a security company, a party furniture rental, and whoever else was needed. He was given a ton of money. He would make the best deals he could because the money left over ended up in his pocket, whether that was the deal or not.

"I went to years of parties and heard a lot of Albert's conversations. People would start calling him around one thirty or two in the afternoon. Some of them would be calling to find out if there would be a party that night. Albert would say 'I'll put you on the list.' But then he would say, 'One thing. Can you bring a case of Cristal?' or it might be some particular drug. If it was a woman's voice I heard on the phone, the next thing he would say was, 'I'll put you on the list. You can bring three or four girlfriends. Just text me all of their names. Maybe a picture, too, just so they don't get to the checkpoint and find out somebody else got in using their name.'

"At first I would think he was just endlessly talkative and everybody knew him and knew he could offer access to that insider world. But in time I realized that he was working. If he volunteered to bring five cases of Cristal, then during the day he would talk five people into bringing a case of Cristal. Sometimes ten people. During the party he might tell the party giver — the pro, not the celebrity — that he'd gotten him a deal. Cristal is usually about twelve hundred for a case of six. But he'd say he had picked up five cases for thirty-five hundred. And the guy would reimburse him the thirty-five hundred. Sometimes he'd also get a commission of five hundred or so."

"He got away with that?"

"Nobody complains if everybody's happy. The party guy has saved a few hundred bucks on the champagne deal. Each of the people Albert invited who brought a twelve-hundred-dollar case as a gift got to go to this celebrity's party and it only cost him a gift, which he thought the celebrity knew about and would feel thankful for. The woman who got invited and got to invite six of her friends — because she was sure to stretch the number to make more girlfriends grateful and owe her a favor — to this incredible, epic party will be happy. The friends are happy because they have fun and meet all the semi-famous guys.

"I overheard a host thanking Al for bringing seven hot young women. This time I had seen them arrive, and the car only held six, and I had counted six. And then I realized the host had counted me as number seven. I noticed that Albert didn't correct him. And Albert had boosted his status, made a lot of money for one day, and ensured he'd get invited to any party this party giver would organize for the next year, at least. Everything that Albert could control or appear to control became a source of income for him, a commodity."

"Were the women commodities?"

"Not in any illegal or financial way. But to bring a few very attractive young single women to a party full of men who were either rich or pre-famous or friends of famous guys, with killer music, held in a beautiful house, how do you suppose the evening ended for a lot of them? What Albert got was credibility and future access to more parties."

"Albert sounds like a con man."

"He was. But everybody there those nights was selling something. For the celebrity host, the party was a way of showing the town how successful and important he was, and that kept his name current and helped build or protect his reputation as a generous, hip guy, a ladies' man, and so on. A glamorous reputation gets people bigger jobs. A lot of the attractive people of both sexes were trying to get discovered, employed, and befriended. The bands wanted to be heard by big people who could hire them again or get them a recording career. The caterers, bartenders, security guys, and party rental companies all wanted more work so they could pay their debts, expand, and put their competitors out of business. All that stuff was accomplished by being known. To get that, a lot of them would make sacrifices. None of them that I ever saw objected to the little that Albert cost them."

"What did you want?"

"I was not a precocious eighteen-year-old. All I knew enough to want was that things wouldn't end. What reached my eyes were beautiful places and people, what reached my ears was music, what I ate was delicious. What I felt on my skin was sunshine when I woke up and sexual touch before I slept. So it was to keep things the way they were."

"It's hard to blame you."

"But you do."

"It didn't end well."

"No, it didn't. I lived in a wonderful bubble. I woke up each day next to a handsome guy who had turned me into his adoring girlfriend with about an hour of effort spread over a couple of weeks. I didn't question anything. I loved the nights best. Sometimes we would leave one party and drive to another a couple of miles away, so it felt like one party that moved with us. I lived on hors d'oeuvres during the evening. If I was hungry in the daytime I knew Albert would buy something, and I would pick at his plate, like an exotic pet."

"I guess you didn't aspire to be a feminist hero."

"Nope. I loved every single day of it. I'm sure you think I'm an embarrassment for wanting that. But life was great. What I was doing required no more justification than dancing."

"What ruined it?"

"What ruined it was me."

"How?"

"By getting too comfortable. This was kind of like Adam and Eve. Maybe every relationship is a little bit like Adam and Eve. Adam is going along, living this life in a paradise, and Eve comes along. And we were two practically new people who didn't know each other before and didn't know much about anything, really. And what you do in that situation is try to stick together and try to make a place for two in this paradise and don't fuck it up. You know instinctively that if you could do everything right and never get lazy or stupid, things would probably stay perfect. You just have to not let the snake in. Over time you would get even happier and love each other more and more until you died. The problem is that the snake was there at the beginning. The snake is you.

"What happens to people is that whatever is going on in the world they're in, they burrow in deeper and deeper. Once I knew that Albert was living off the parties, I looked for my role in the scheme. I was pretty, and soon I was wearing sort of edgy clothes. It was a hot summer — all summers are hot in Southern California — and it was night most of the time while I was awake, and nobody's grandma was around to be critical. Albert's income opportunities depended on his reputation for being hip and in demand. I could help him just by being as attractive and sexy and good-natured as I could be, and clinging to him all the time like a parrot perched on his shoulder. It made other men respect him. And I'm sure that you've noticed by now that nothing attracts women to a guy like having another woman showing she's with him. I didn't know why then and I still don't. It may be because they think if he already has a woman who likes being with him he can't be a homicidal psycho. Maybe they like being around a troublesome, risky guy because he's energetic and fun, but since the emotional stuff he needs is already being taken care of by somebody else, there won't be any expectations or entanglements. And there are some other women, of course, who just see everybody else's guy and start trying to take him away because they're mean. So Albert could attract and deliver a lot of party people, and I could add a few. And he would use every moment of contact with them to increase our income or his influence or his access. His mind was open for business all the time.

"People gave him drugs to show their

friendship and he would respond with an introduction or an invitation to some event. He would give small hits of the drugs to people at the party to seem generous and fun or trade big samples to other people who had things he wanted. He kept track of the best caterers and served as an intermediary who would be sure they were available on the right date at a cut rate because he was their close friend. He would get a kickback from the caterer and a commission from the host. It was the same with bands, valet parking companies, security people, and party guests. Whatever he did was intended to bring money, and he got paid every day.

"I was good. I got invitations to a few parties before anybody knew about them so he could begin pulling schemes right away. I listened to gossip. People I told things told me things, and that extended our reach. Eventually I met some people who were interested in the parties as a way to popularize clothing and makeup brands or jewelry or shoes. They would give me stuff to wear at parties. After a while they started to pay me to wear them at parties so the right sort of people would notice them and start wearing them too.

"Albert was good at learning who was

about to be semi-famous and getting to know them. Then he would find party givers who would pay him to guarantee they'd be at their party, and he would persuade the semi-famous people that getting them an invitation to that party was better than nominating them for a medium-level award. Some way or other, each of these contacts would pay Albert."

"Where was all of this going?" Jane said.

"I didn't know. Albert wouldn't have admitted it, but he didn't either. Albert was bringing in a lot of money and paying out a lot of money at the same time. I couldn't have told you if we were getting rich or going broke. If you took a snapshot of him at any moment, his hands held a lot of money. For the moment that was enough."

"How did he come to kill somebody?"

"That's the hard part. But I can't explain without telling you all of it," Sara said. "Things went on for about three-and-ahalf years. That's like, a thousand mornings when we woke up together and spent the day doing Albert's schemes and hustles to keep up our credibility and access. And as I told you, after a while it was both of us that had names people knew and contacts and acquaintances. At some point I had grown beyond being part of the scenery. I was modeling clothes and accessories, first just to interest the other wildlife, but then to a wider group. The people pushing the fashion would take videos of me wearing them at the parties, walking and dancing and talking to other women, or once in a while, to a man. They'd put them on their companies' websites and TikTok and Instagram and on people's fashion blogs. And one night I was in the middle of one of these strut-and-spin sessions at a party and Tommy Talton came up and got on camera with me and started clowning around, hugging me and saying things to make me laugh. A couple of hours later somebody showed it to me and told me it had gone viral. He looked great and he was having fun and he was not camera-shy — why would he be? It was a regular performance.

"I was suddenly a person that people had seen. For about a minute I got to be one of those women that people wonder about. Who was I and what was my name? Was I somebody that people like Tommy Talton knew? A secret girlfriend or something? Tweets and comments started coming across people's screens. People who do most of their living online have their brains connected to so many sites that they know things happen or exist in seconds without knowing anything *about* the things. So there were comments like the theory that I was Tommy Talton's secret daughter and his appearing with me was a coded signal to his fans.

"Albert, whose mind was always open for business, wanted me with him even more than before, but now we had so much to do that we had to split our time and be at two places at once. I would agree to model something and take a rideshare, or somebody from a fashion site would give me a ride while Albert drove around town in his old Corvette. I was getting disoriented, confused and blinded by all the new people and the invitations and one-afternoon jobs. One of the things that made it weirder was that a common way that people got access to you was to say they knew you from some party. When you saw them you couldn't remember them, but you still had no idea whether you'd seen them before, or they really didn't remember you either or got you confused with somebody else. A couple of times when someone said that I said, 'You lied. I never met you,' and the person would say, 'But you know me now.' And there was a bad truth to that. I knew them about as well as the people I thought I knew.

"I went to a photo shoot at a house in

Sherman Oaks with a photographer named David. He was working for a designer, the woman who actually owned the house. There were a bunch of clothes there, and she had them all hung up in one of the bedrooms that I was supposed to use as a dressing room, and the shooting was on the balcony a few feet away. David was sweet, and he was handsome, and you know how they can be. You're posing and they're arranging your clothes to look good, and moving this and tugging that and pretty soon they go to the rack and bring you the same jacket in a different color and they're helping you on with it to speed things up and then off with it. You just kind of get careless or maybe even tired of contorting yourself to keep him at arm's length and not seeing anything much. And then too much comes off, but the first time he doesn't seem to notice, and no harm was done, but pretty soon instead of posing on that couch, you're having sex on it."

"Is he the one that Albert killed?"

"Oh, no. That was still a year off. David was just the one I was with when I took the step that changed everything. At first, I had been in that life because that was what Albert was doing, and I wanted to be there with him. I was happy being his girlfriend. I still wanted everything to be the way it had been, but when I was in the car on the way home after that photo shoot I realized I had obliterated that. I couldn't go back to being just the devoted, adoring girlfriend anymore. In the first place, it's a role that's pointless and impossible if you're cheating. You can't be that. The second thing I had become aware of without pondering it was that I had grown bigger and more important in that world than Albert was.

"Albert was a little con man scrambling around doing errands and keeping the change, essentially. He lived by skimming money off deals, fooling some people into including him, or paying him to include them. He'd been doing it in front of me for a long time, so it wasn't Albert that ruined things. I ruined everything by realizing that if I wanted to I could make more money and go to even better parties, maybe be an influencer. I didn't take a big step and lose my innocence. I just opened my eyes and saw it was gone.

"After that I behaved as though everything was the same. I made him think it was, but for me it couldn't be. I saw us both at once for what we were, and it made me restless. When I felt tempted, I cheated with men who were — what? Better? No. Not even better looking, usually. They were just bigger fish. They had higher status.

"Eventually I got caught. I was overconfident. That day Albert was out making his rounds and pitching his current schemes, and I was spending the afternoon firming up and maintaining some friendships I had been cultivating. The most important was a woman named Posy Chalmers, who is a really talented and rising singer. There was a music promoter who was helping to produce an album with her. He had set up an afternoon meeting with her at his house and said she should bring some friends. I had the suspicion that he had in mind some kind of photography that would use her friends as free models looking like the other people at a party or hanging out or something like that. Her girlfriends were also people I considered promising contacts too, and then there was the promoter.

"I had heard of him before. He was supposed to have a lot of invisible juice because he had some very powerful friends, not only in music, but also in movies and television. When I met him I wasn't smitten. He was very nice, and all that. But he was like, forty. He was wearing jeans and a Hawaiian shirt for his conference with Posy. I could see he had a very hairy body, but the hair on his head was already retreating along the top. I kept catching him looking at me. I was wearing dark sunglasses, so I guess he couldn't tell. Their talk was going on for a long time, and I thought about him. I wondered what — if I was willing to lead him on a little, maybe just flirt with him for a while — he would do for me, to make me like him."

"Did you find out?"

"One of the secrets of the world where I had been living for about three years was that the best part happens at night. Drinking in daylight is always a mistake. I made that mistake. One of the women there told somebody else, and they told somebody else, and then the story got to Albert. About a month after that, the promoter was dead."

"Did you see it happen?" There was a pause, only a second, but that was too long, so Jane looked at Sara. Tears had formed in her eyes. Jane waited.

Sara said, "I was with Albert in his car, thinking he was going straight to the party we were scheduled to go to, and he took a little detour. He drove to the promoter's house and dragged me with him to watch him shoot the man."

"Did you call the police?"

"No."

"Then how did you get to court?"

"People who knew that I had slept with the victim were happy to mention it to the police. They arrested both of us."

6

It was late night when Jane drove Sara's car to the central New York town. The outskirts hadn't changed since Jane's last visit. The highway that ran past the last few farms became smoother and straighter as it neared the town, and there were businesses. One sold farm machines, mostly green John Deere tractors and the wheeled contraptions they pulled — plows, harvesters, deep trailers, and flatbeds. On the other side of the entrance were several yellow machines intended for digging and construction — bulldozers, backhoes, and a couple of cherrypickers. The property on the right side of the road was a gas station, closed for the night. As they came closer to town there were more businesses — a furniture warehouse and a couple of fast-food franchises with outdoor tables. The next sign said, "Welcome to Cantrell Falls."

Jane touched Sara. "Wake up."

Sara stirred and sat up, but didn't speak. She looked out the windows.

As the car moved into the town there were a few offices and stores, and then old houses under tall shade trees, and they passed a couple of churches and then older houses under taller trees.

Stewart Shattuck's house was on the circular street that embraced the town's central park. Like the others in that area it seemed to date from around the time of the Civil War, two-story redbrick structures with wooden trim, all built right up near the curb so ladies didn't have to walk many steps to get to the family carriage. Two of the houses still had the slab at the curb that a person could step on, and two others had stone hitching posts with iron rings. Jane drove on the streets around Stewart's, keeping her distance for the moment. She studied the vehicles parked in the neighborhood, as always, and then parked on the next block and walked with Sara. She directed their walk to take them past the two biggest vehicles, a van and a truck, and took the time to look in the side windows to see if there was anything on the seats or dashboards to worry her.

She and Sara stepped up onto the front porch of Stewart's house and gave a quiet knock. The door swung inward immediately, pulled by a small woman, who kept her body half-blocked by the door as she looked past them to study the street. As soon as Jane and Sara were over the threshold she pushed the door shut and slid a thick bolt into its receptacle in the woodwork.

As the woman turned away, Sara saw that she had been holding a short black all-steel rifle with a pistol grip. She raised it and set it on the shelf beside the door. She smiled at Sara. "Just a precaution, honey. You don't want anybody following you inside."

"No we don't, Molly," Jane said. "It looks clear out there tonight."

"If you're the one who says it's clear, it's clear. But as Stewart says, 'Some day the asteroid won't miss, and all the dinosaurs will die.' She hugged Jane. "How have you been, Jane?"

"Good, and you?"

"Better and better." She looked at Sara. "And who is this?" Sara said, "My name is —"

"Stop." Molly held up her hand. "I don't need to know what you've been called, and telling people won't make you safe. Stewart will give you a new name anyway. I'm just asking what we're up against."

"She needs the works. I had her hair cut,

dyed, and styled this afternoon, so it doesn't look the way her chasers will remember it. One of them was her boyfriend for four years, so he knows a lot. She saw him commit a murder, so we know he's up to it. She's twenty-two, so we should give her a birthday near the right year, but not in it."

"We'd better get started. I'll take you to Stewart."

She walked to a staircase, climbed it, and stopped at the top, where there was a broad landing with four doorways that led to four large rooms. One was a photographic studio with lights and reflectors, backdrops, and clothing racks. The next had three rows of tables set up as computer workstations, and the last had several big drawing tables with projects clipped to them. The fourth was a spacious room with heavy Victorian-looking furniture. She led Jane and Sara into the room with the drawing tables.

Behind one of them stood a gray-haired man in his fifties, big and built like a football lineman. He looked around the drawing table when they entered. "Janie," he said. "It's always a pleasant surprise. I'm glad to see you made it again."

Jane said, "I try to be hard to find. I'm glad to see you're still here."

"A man who doesn't go out much and

minds his business has certain advantages. You weren't followed?"

"No. We were chased by two Range Rovers, and she saw one of her chasers in one of them, but we lost them, and we might have damaged one of them in the process. That was south of Buffalo."

"That's far enough from here. What do you need?"

"Ideally, I would like two levels of identification. I've got some IDs I grew myself that would fit a young woman. The birth certificates are real. Somebody planted them in the records of a town in Ohio. I went to take the driver's tests for the licenses, and paid a couple of years of bills on the credit cards. So they're pretty good. I just need to have you make them have her picture and fiddle with the magnetic strips and some of the art so it fits her. I'd also like a premium set of credentials. I'd like a real passport and a real driver's license and a few cards that will bolster the main identity.

"And here's the big problem, I think. She's been making money and getting attention on social media. She's worn clothes and accessories to show them off for small fashion companies. She's even been in shots with a few celebrities. I've been hoping you could do something with that. Do you have the Chicago facial recognition app?"

"That and a couple of modifications of it, and a few other things. I love it when geniuses are generous. Maybe I can clean up some of the pictures of her that are out there, misidentify some, and watch for chances to do more. But you know how the Internet works. Once something is posted, it goes everywhere and stays in the world forever. All I can do is try. It's easier to change her than the Internet, so let's start. Moll?" he called.

"Yes, Stewart?"

"Can you get going on the pictures?"

"Yes, Stewart."

Molly led Sara into the photography studio. "Before we start let's talk about eyes," she said, "You have green eyes."

"I'll admit it," Sara said.

"It's sort of a bad choice when you're trying to disappear. Forty-one percent of the people in the country have brown eyes. That's the best. The worst is purple, like Elizabeth Taylor had. There are so few that nobody can put a statistic on it. But green is second worst. Only two percent of people in the United States have green eyes. But they make contact lenses that do nothing but change your eye color. If you want we can give you some brown ones and put

'Eyes: Brown' on all your papers and things."

"Do I have to?"

"Jane thinks you ought to change everything you can. And what you really don't want is to have anybody running some program to make a list of all the people whose licenses or some other records say they have green eyes and have it pick you out."

"Isn't there some other way?"

"Well, Jane had to put her physical stuff on the paper when she took the tests for licenses and things, and her eyes are blue. We can put blue on everything else and give you blue contacts. Seventeen percent of people in the country have blue eyes. That's not great, but it beats green by over eight times. And because blue and green are close, you could go with no contacts. Most people don't notice the difference, and the ones who do will probably think some dumbass official saw your eyes, thought they were blue, and wrote it down."

"All right."

Molly handed her articles of clothing for the photographs. She took a sweater off the rack and said, "Let's try this for a picture taken in winter." For the next photograph she gave her a businesslike white blouse and a black jacket. For each photograph Molly made a couple of tiny changes to her hair or makeup so it would look as though the pictures were all taken on different days. She also varied the lighting, the backdrops, and the poses.

In the studio, Stewart said to Jane, "Is she going to be alive long enough to make all this effort worth the money?"

Jane shrugged. "I hope so, obviously. If she isn't, I probably won't be either, so I won't need money."

"She's got a little bit of an edge. It's often a sign of toughness, and she'll need that, but it's not the survival trait that some people think it is."

"That's true. It's hard to stay alive if you're the only one who cares if you do. But I think she's just scared and tired right now. One good sign is that she's been thinking a lot about how she got into this predicament and the name that keeps coming up for blame is hers."

"You're the expert, Janie," Stewart said. "I just see them for one night. You stick with them long enough to know them."

"They're not all perfect. A lot of the people in danger of being killed did things to make enemies." She reached into her purse and took out the envelope she'd brought from her house that said "FC 2126" and handed it to Stewart. "Those are the licenses and things for the identifications. For the moment three good fake identities will do. Later I'd like one of them to become her single perfect one."

He looked into the envelope and fanned the credit cards and licenses out on the desk and read them. "Anne Preston Bailey, Michelle Tobin, Amy Hughes Fuller. Good names. I've begun to forget them already. And you've got a good start on the licenses and certificates. I can do what you need by morning."

"Good," Jane said. "What about the perfect ones for Anne Preston Bailey long term?"

"As you know, real passports require prying them loose from the federal government. That means sending them perfect supporting documents to apply — birth certificate, a Social Security number that won't set off alarms, and so on. Fortunately you have some here. It's riskier every year, and the time is running at about six weeks."

"What will it cost me?"

"Before we're done it will probably add up to about twenty thousand. If it all goes well they'll send the supporting stuff back, so she can use it again. If it doesn't go well, we'll have other problems."

"I don't have twenty thousand with me. Can I pay in a couple of weeks?"

"Your credit is still good with me. All the times you've paid me buy you that much. Pay me three grand in the morning for the okay versions of the three names. Send the rest when the passport arrives in six weeks or so. By then I'll have the rest of the identification."

Jane reached into her purse and took out three banded stacks of bills and handed them to Stewart. "Thanks, Stewart. I'll check with you in about six weeks to see whether the masterpiece is ready."

"Good idea," he said. "If the FBI answers, that means it's not coming."

When Jane went into the photography studio Molly was just shutting down the lights and putting the equipment away. Sara looked worn out. Molly heard Jane come in behind her and turned. "You may as well get some sleep. Stewart and I will be busy all night." She pointed up the hall. "You remember the two bedrooms down at the end? And there's still a back stairway too, in case you need to get out without saying goodbye."

Jane and Sara went up the hall. Jane opened the door at the end and stepped inside. The room was plain, but extremely neat. Jane said, "Does it look okay to you?"

Sara said, "When Elizabeth came to get me after the trial I was sleeping on the floor under a table."

"This should do it, then. I'll be in the room next door. That way any visitors will probably run into me first." She reached into her purse and took out one of the two Glock pistols. "Put this where you can reach it. If you hear a commotion go down the back stairs. But expect to see a second man waiting outside the back door to grab you. Look for him before you step out."

"Okay."

"And tomorrow will be a long day. Sleep until I come for you in the morning. And don't shoot me when I do."

"I'll try to remember."

Jane went into the next room and opened the window two inches so she could hear the approach of a car on the quiet street outside. She set the second pistol on the empty side of the bed and lay down without undressing. She closed her eyes and lay still, letting her other senses, hearing, touch, and smell, explore the air surrounding the house. In minutes she was asleep.

The altitude of the bedrooms, two and a half stories up among the canopies of the trees, and the absence of menacing sensations let her body stay still with its muscles at rest and her mind sink into empty darkness for hours.

When it was ready her mind began to dream. She was in a forest, but not the kind she knew best. This wasn't like the forests of the Northeast, where she had grown up, with deciduous species like maple and white oak and hickory and red elm and chestnut at low altitudes or the pines that grew higher up the mountains. This forest was the wild mixture of exotic trees and other plants that she had seen in Southern California — date palms, coconut palms, sego palms, short and barrel-shaped or tall and narrow, swaying with the slightest movement of air, eucalyptus trees seventy feet tall with shredding bark trunks or the other kind with bark so smooth they looked like human skin. There were magnolias with white flowers the size of soup bowls, purple-flowered jacaranda trees and live oaks entangled with bougainvillea vines with flowers of bright magenta, red, orange, looking like splashes of an artist's paint.

"Yeah." She recognized the voice. "Everything grows here better than it grows wherever it evolved. You have to be careful in this place because if you drop a seed by accident it will sprout." As he spoke she heard his footsteps coming on a gravel path. He was slow, but she recalled that he had seemed old when she'd met him.

As she thought it, he said, "That's right. And you don't get younger just because you're dead."

"Hello, Harry," she said.

Harry Kemple emerged from the trees. He had been one of Jane's first runners after she had begun helping strangers. Seeing him was not pleasant. "I'm sorry," she said.

He wore the only sport coat she'd ever seen him wear, a lightweight gray fabric that had tiny checks that the eye didn't distinguish unless he was very close. It hung loosely over his bony shoulders, and the elbows were worn from leaning on years of poker tables. The gray pants were worn as much as the coat, the fabric on the backside shiny from sitting.

He frowned. "I've told you a million times to stop apologizing to me. It happened quickly. He jerked my head back and brought the blade across both carotid arteries in a second. I didn't see it coming, and I had only a few seconds of knowing I was bleeding out, and then blackness. John Felker was a pro. Just like a surgeon. We all die, and that wasn't bad as deaths go. A lot of people suffer in pain for years."

"I'm still sorry," she said. "You were my mistake, and it was a stupid one. I had already taken you to a safe place. He made me trust him and I actually thought that the fact that he knew all about you proved he really was your friend."

"Right. Who ever dreamed that would happen? And who knew a forger would keep a list of customers? He might as well write a confession and keep it in a drawer."

"I should have thought of it," Jane said. "I should have been smarter about people."

Harry shrugged, and it made the slash across his throat open a little so she saw the wet pink skin inside his trachea. "It's part of the ecology of the planet. If nobody ever got careless or didn't think far enough ahead, none of them would ever die, and you wouldn't have room to walk around for the crowds. It's just lucky you only got me killed, and not both of us."

"That's true."

"And it all gets taken care of. The right-handed twin Hawenneyu, the Creator, and Hanegoategeh, the left-handed twin, Destroyer, have always kept the world in balance. On one floor of the hospital the left-handed twin makes a man hemorrhage in surgery and die, and on another floor Hawenneyu the right-handed makes a woman give birth to a healthy baby girl."

"Why are you in my dream tonight?"

"Maybe because California was where you hid me and he found me. Sara came to you from California, right?"

"Maybe, but that wasn't what I want to know."

"And I don't know why I'm in your dream. It's your dream, meaning it's what's playing on your brain tonight. I'm a product of your brain, probably just a small stray charge that shortcircuited a synapse that should have been left open and unused while you're asleep. If you don't know something, I don't either."

"But you asked a serious question."

"No, you did."

"That's exactly what you would say if you were a spirit guide sent to help and advise me. You're making me wonder if the one I'm helping to run is the one who's innocent. Who is Sara?"

"Same answer as before. I know what you know. I'm partly a memory of a real man, a gambler who used up his last bit of luck and died years ago, and partly an image that got triggered because you associated it with making another mistake."

"Has she been lying to me?"

"Yes, she must be. That's the first thing all cops learn after the academy. Everybody lies."

"I don't mean just leaving a few things out because they don't reflect well on her and maybe she hasn't been able to admit them to herself yet."

"And sometimes they're lying to manipulate you into being defenseless when it comes time to cut your throat."

"Which is it?"

"What do you know, actually know, about her?"

"I know that men are tracking her who mean her harm. I saw them and played chicken with them. I know that the authorities arrested her with him for a murder, and decided he was the one they should charge, not her. But I also know that the jury didn't convict him. I know that if Elizabeth told her to run from LA she believed she was in danger from him. And if Elizabeth told her how to find me she believes she can be trusted.

"I also know, because she admitted it, that she went on a first date and stayed for four years. When she realized that he was a con man living by pulling micro-swindles, she didn't move on, but learned to do it too. The cause of the murder was her cheating on him."

Harry said, "Well? What's the conclusion?"

"I don't have one."

"Then all you can do is watch and listen."

He walked up the gravel path through the trees. Jane followed, and at the top was the white expanse of the huge modern house that Sara had described as where her first party had been held. Harry walked up the grade a bit and entered the lowest level through a rounded wooden door in a white wall. He left the door open and Jane stepped in after him.

The large pool that Sara had described was straight ahead, lighted by underwater floodlights, and beyond it Jane could see the sunken hot tubs bubbling. Harry walked to the near end of the pool and kept going without a pause. He began to step down the broad steps into the water. Jane could see his gray pants darkened as they were soaked, first to the calf, then the knees, thighs, waist. His arms were extended to both sides to keep his balance as he walked against the resistance of the water.

He looked over his shoulder at her and said, "Eyes and ears." He kept going as the water reached his chest, his ears, his temples, and covered the dome of his skull.

After a moment the surface of the water calmed and became mirror-smooth again. Jane stepped closer and looked at the bottom of the pool. She was not surprised that he was not there.

7

Jane woke before dawn when the first car motors turned over and the cars backed out of driveways along the street and made their way around the park and accelerated. Presumably they would be heading for the highway that would take them to the New York State Thruway and jobs in Syracuse, which was far enough away to require an early start. Her first thought was, "Why didn't she call first?"

Jane reached for her purse, picked up the gun from the bed, put it away, and took out one of the burner cell phones, then sat up. She dialed the number of Karen Alvarez in Los Angeles. Karen was the friend who had been at Cornell with Jane and had seen her take her first runner out of the world when they were juniors. A few years later, Karen had become a defense attorney with an innocent client who was about to be convicted of a murder and given a very long sentence, probably without the possibility of parole. She asked Jane to help him. Since then, they had spoken a few times — once when Jane wanted Karen's help sneaking another innocent man out of the Clara Shortridge Foltz Courthouse in downtown Los Angeles.

Jane listened to the signal that was supposed to sound like the phone on the other end ringing, then Karen's voice. "Hello."

"Karen, I'm sorry to call in the middle of your night."

"Hell you are," she muttered.

"I am. But I'm not going to be alone for long, and then not again for a while, maybe not at all today."

"What is it?"

"I have a runner."

"I thought you weren't —"

"Well, I am for the moment. She's twenty-two. She testified against her former boyfriend in a murder trial, but he got off. She said Elizabeth Howarth was her lawyer, and that she was the one who sent her to me the day after the verdict. She had the right address."

"I'm especially eager to get mixed up in another totally illegal life-threatening scheme at" — Karen paused to look at the time on her cell phone — "three fifteen

A.M." She sighed. "What do you need?"

"I'm getting a strange feeling about this. Can you find out whatever you can for me? Was there really such a case? His name is Albert McKeith."

"Spell it."

Jane did.

"Got it."

"Did Elizabeth really send her to me? If so, why didn't she call me first?"

"Why not call her at three sixteen after I hang up on you and ask her?"

"I tried calling when I first heard this story. She wasn't in her office and I couldn't leave her the number of a cell phone I hadn't bought yet. I'm not at home so she doesn't know how to reach me, and you have access to legal records. I assume the name of it is State of California versus Albert McKeith. And if that doesn't work, Elizabeth knows you, too."

"I'm too tired to argue with you. It's too much like work. Give me your cell number." She listened while Jane read it off the display on the phone. "Okay. I'll let you know what I find out."

"Thanks, Karen," she said. "I'll be eternally grateful."

"How about a little bit guilty for waking me up?"

"No," Jane said. "I don't think so." She hung up.

Jane got up, brushed her teeth and her hair, and walked down the hall to the center of the house. She could see there was light coming from the doorway of the computer room. Stewart and Molly were sitting at one of the long tables in front of a row of machines, looking at images of documents on screens. "Good morning," Jane said. "I didn't want to sneak up and startle you."

"It's okay," Stewart said. "We've been up all night, so we've worked most of the startle out of ourselves."

Jane looked at the nearest screen. "Is this what you've been working on?"

"Some of it," he said. "You've seen some of this equipment before. A person can't use an original forgery or a painting for identification, so we scan the artwork and then transfer the scan to plastic blanks. There are embossing machines down on the next table that produce raised type and apply holograms, logos, and photographs of your client. Another computerized machine programs the information we want on the magnetic strip on the back and the embedded chip."

"Do you know roughly when it will be ready?"

Molly said, "Yours is done. This is somebody else's order." She walked down along the table to the end, picked up three envelopes that were lying there, and handed one of them to Jane.

Jane accepted it and put it in her purse.

"Aren't you going to look at them?"

"Didn't you?"

"Of course."

"Then I know I don't need to. You've kept a lot of runners of mine alive for a long time. I'll just wake up my new one and get moving before first light."

"Be safe," Stewart said.

"We'll try. I'll see you in about six weeks. I'll call first."

She went back along the hall to Sara's room and knocked on the door. She knocked again, and finally heard her sleepy, hoarse voice say, "Coming." After a moment she opened the door.

Jane stepped in and handed her the envelope. "Good morning. Get dressed and we'll leave before it's light out. It's safer for us and for them if we come and go in darkness."

"What's this?" She held the envelope up.

"That's your three new sets of identification, the primary one and the two backups in case the primary gets burned. Starting

110

now you are Anne Preston Bailey, and the sooner you get used to it the better. Think about the name and try it out in your mind. Give me your purse."

"What for?"

"So while you're getting dressed I can stay occupied by replacing your Sara Doughton identification. I'll need anything you have that has that name on it or an old address or phone number or anything that leads back to your old life."

"Why do you want those things?"

"I don't want them, but neither do you. I've learned that runners are stupid about these things. They sometimes hide old licenses and credit cards and things instead of destroying them. It's not like you were going to be able to do anything with them again."

"If I buried them in a sealed plastic bag, do you think Albert and his friends would find them?"

"No. I think somebody would find them, though. A year passes. Mary Magdalene Rossi is walking her dog in the woods. Her dog has a nose that can practically track butterflies. The dog alerts on the spot and digs it up. What does Mary do with it?"

"I don't know."

"The world is mostly inhabited by pretty

good people. When they find something like your identification and credit cards, they try to get in touch with you at your phone number right away. I'm not saying Albert will be there to answer your phone, but he might have a caller ID set up on your number. If Mary doesn't reach you or him, she'll either write to you or skip that step and mail your cards to the address on your license to give them back to you. Her letter will mention where she found your stuff. Albert will know one place that you've been, and that's a big step. If he feels like it he can use your credit cards to get skip tracers after you." Jane stopped. "Do I need to go on?"

"Here's my purse," she said. "Take whatever you find. And my name is what again?"

"Anne Preston Bailey."

"The feeling is strange, but it's not a bad name."

"Keep repeating it in your mind until you believe it. When you're dressed, I'll meet you at the top of the stairs." Jane took the envelope and the purse.

Jane stepped out, sat on the steps, and went through the purse, checked the burner phone she'd given her to see if it had any numbers in its memory. It didn't. She checked the iPhone to see if it had been used. It hadn't. She went through the wallet and removed every card, and then placed the Anne Bailey cards in the appropriate spaces, the license in the plastic window, the credit cards in the slots where the old ones had been. Stewart had thrown in a few other items that would help make the wallet seem real. There was a library card for the city where the license said she lived, a couple of loyal customer cards that gave discounts for groceries. Jane took all of the cards that had come from Sara's old life. She decided against destroying them in that house, because she knew that at some point, there was a strong chance that Stewart's house might be found and everything in it given close, tireless examination.

Jane was sitting on the top step when Anne Bailey joined her. Jane held out the purse for her and she took it. Then Jane started down the stairs and she followed.

"Aren't we going to thank them and say goodbye?"

"I took care of it. They've gone to bed. They work nights, so this is when they sleep."

"How did you pick the name Anne Preston Bailey?"

"I thought about you and I looked at the identities I had on hand. That one seemed closest. The name has to sound the way you look, not just ethnically and so on, but by feel. Haven't you ever thought when you were introduced to somebody that he didn't look like his name? 'He can't be named Howard Stanhope. He doesn't look like a Howard. Maybe it's his middle name or something.' "

"Yes. I have."

"Well, most of the time other people feel the same way about it. It bothers us because it's not the name we think fits. It makes us study the person and think about him to figure it out. We don't want people to think about you and study you. We want them to accept you and move on. For me, Anne Bailey works. I don't think it will startle anyone. Do you?"

"No," Anne said. "It shouldn't be hard to get used to."

"It also happened to be the best of the three identities that seemed to fit. The driver's license is one I went and applied for a few years ago, and renewed once. Stewart replaced my picture with yours. The height, weight, date of birth, and so on fit you. In a couple of months, we should have the masterpiece version of that set, with everything we can get included."

"Thank you," Anne said. "You're amazing."

"Stewart is amazing," Jane said.

They were on the ground floor now, and Jane had moved to three different windows to assure herself that the world outside was still empty and benign. She turned off the light in the foyer, opened the door, and stepped out. She held the door long enough for Anne to follow, then closed the door and made sure it had locked. Then she set off on foot.

They didn't meet anyone on the way to the car. There were no pedestrians on their route, and the only cars they saw were a few on the main street heading for the cities to the north. In another minute they were in the car Sara had bought in Utah, heading for the highway.

Jane drove east for two hours while her runner dozed. She finally stopped at a diner in a small town that wasn't much different from the one where they had spent the night. "Breakfast time," she said. She watched her companion sit up, blinking and rubbing her eyes. "What's your name?"

"Anne Bailey. What's yours?"

"Maura Slater. I decided to switch for a while. Do you like places like this?"

As they walked toward the diner Anne

turned her head to look around. "I was born and grew up in a town about this size in Indiana. As soon as I could I left to go to Indianapolis just because it was bigger and my mother wasn't there. I got a GED a year early and went to a community college there so she would think I was doing something and send money once in a while. I found that wasn't big enough either. But I stayed until I got a diploma before I went to look at bigger places."

"Interesting. What was your diploma in?"

"Liberal arts. It qualified me to serve coffee if somebody else brewed it and put the little milk-dribble design on top."

"Probably you can read and write coherently. Probably you had to know how to find out about a topic and discuss it. Did that stuff stick with you?"

"Some. I can even balance a checkbook without using my phone. Of course the numbers in my checkbook weren't high."

"Did any of the experience suggest a career you'd like to have?"

"Nothing that comes to mind now. Why are you asking all these questions?"

"To learn how to keep you out of the hands of the people who want to kill you. If all you're doing is hiding, it gets unpleasant fast and pretty soon it's hard to make the effort. What you want to do is be living a life. Disappearing requires you to give up everything left from your old life, and it's heartbreaking. But sometimes it's not entirely bad. If you can't be who you were, it gives you a motive and a license to decide who you really want to be."

"I haven't thought much about that. I just am."

They reached the diner, and Jane said, "Let me check it out first. Pretend to be checking your phone." She opened the door and stepped inside to look for threats. She saw that the place had people of a range of ages at tables and counters having breakfast. She spotted a couple of unoccupied booths. She went to the door, beckoned to Anne, and went to claim one.

Jane waited until a woman came and gave them menus and silverware and then left. "Right now all of our attention has to be on getting you to a safe place. But then you should think about what I said. Decide if you want to be an airplane mechanic or a doctor or a goat milker."

"Those things require training. Even the goat thing."

"True. But every career has a path, a way to get into it. Whatever you want to do is possible. And I can get you started."

"What if I'm not qualified?"

"You probably aren't right now. But if you're close enough, I probably have a way of lying about it or finding an alternative."

"Why would you do that for me?"

"That's what I do. Elizabeth told you that much, right? When I was younger, I realized that I wanted to do something that made sense to me. Hardly anybody is bad enough to deserve to be murdered. Therefore, keeping a person from being murdered almost always made sense."

When they came out of the restaurant Jane handed Anne the car keys. "You drive for a while."

Anne got into the driver's seat and started the car. "Where do you want me to go?"

"East. The sun has moved enough so it shouldn't be in your eyes. Remember while you're driving that the thing that matters is keeping us alive. And if you drive through a place where you think you'd like to live, stop and wake me."

"I'll do that."

While Anne drove, Jane took a nap. After two hours she sat up and looked at the sights on the road. "Hi, Anne."

"Hi."

"Have you got anyone following you?"

"I doubt it. I haven't seen anyone."

"Have you been looking?"

"Not really. I don't know how they could find us after all this time."

"Well, they managed to use GPS trackers to find your car while it was parked near my house or they couldn't have followed us down the road along Lake Erie. What if, along Lake Erie, there weren't only two cars chasing us yesterday? If there were a third one that was holding back, he could have been in touch with the others by telephone and then taken over when the others ran into trouble."

Anne sighed. "You're right. I should have been thinking about what could happen and watching for it."

"Good idea. And suppose you had looked in the rearview mirror and seen them, do you know what you'd do?"

"It would have to depend on where we were when I saw them."

"Where are we now?"

"What do you mean?"

"If it happened right now, what's in front of us?"

"I don't know."

"You have a cell phone with a GPS and a map application. You've never used the phone yet, so nobody can identify its number as yours and use it to track you. If you turn on the app you can know what's ahead all the way to the Atlantic and what the traffic is like, all the turns you could make, and where all the roads lead."

"None of that occurred to me."

"To be honest, I never expected it to. You would have been the first. Most people don't grow up expecting to have to lose a pursuer."

"I'm trying, but I'm afraid I'll never remember all this stuff."

"I'm pretty sure you will. You just have to remind yourself that you came this far for a good reason. The man who is after you thinks you caused him to commit a murder and then betrayed him and testified against him."

"He wouldn't be exactly wrong."

"He doesn't want to tell you off. He wants to kill you. He really, really wants to. And now he's got a taste of it. He also has reason to believe that he can get let off if he gets caught. Those things make him more dangerous. Allow yourself to be scared. That usually works, but you also have to learn to recognize danger and know what you'll do about it."

"I'll try."

"It's pretty simple, really. Don't ever do anything risky if there's another way. Never miss a chance to hide your trail or mislead a pursuer. If changing something makes getting caught five percent less likely, do it. If you do that every time you can, the odds move dramatically in your favor. We've changed your name and changed your looks a little bit. Good start. We can do much more. But the change in your mind is what counts. Sara went to big, open parties, so Anne Bailey doesn't. Sara slept late. Anne wakes the birds up, and that's when she prefers to go out. Sara liked edgy, barely-there clothes. Anne doesn't. Sara probably wore spike heels. Whether she did or not, Anne chooses shoes that she can run in. They also change her perceived height."

"It sounds awful, hiding and looking over your shoulder, scared all the time. I know, I got myself into this position, so I should just shut up and listen."

"No. I want you to talk, because you have to listen and think to do it. It is awful. What you have to do is imagine a new life that would make you happy. You don't want a disguise or a role. You want a life. Picture the woman you would be if you hadn't made any mistakes or wrong guesses in your life, never slacked off or taken the easy way that turned out to lead into a swamp. Then start being her."

"It sounds so lonely."

"It is at first. But that will end too. You've got plenty of things that will make it easier. You've got a pretty face and body. You won't have to worry about finding men. They'll find you. But you will always have to choose carefully and be sure what's happening is what you want. A guy who takes you to a dive bar where there are fights or people are taking drugs in the bathrooms is endangering your life. You can't afford to get arrested or have to go to the emergency room. A guy who takes you to big open parties will get you noticed. He thinks he's giving you a good time, but getting you noticed can be fatal. It's better to get a job and socialize with the people who are part of the world you choose. Make as many decisions as possible ahead of time."

"How will I know when it works?"

"You'll like your life again."

8

"Hey, Alberto," the deep voice above his head said. Albert turned to see the tall, wide shape of Max the Bouncer silhouetted in the bright overhead lights of the tennis court. "Nobody's seen you in a while. Is everything okay?" Club music was playing from above, from unseen speakers higher on the property. The music was still just recorded stuff meant to attract people like a beacon before the party started, so Albert could still hear Max speak.

"It's been a hard year, Max," Albert said, "I haven't been out much." He pointed to the man behind him with his thumb. "Do you know my friend Jason DeLong?"

"Can't say that I know him. I've seen him." He held out a hand that seemed to be the size of a catcher's mitt. "Hey, Jason. I'm Max."

Jason reached for the hand, which instantly closed on his to give it a single shake.

"You're not going to cause trouble if you're with Alberto, so welcome to the party."

"Thanks," Jason said.

Max elbow-nudged the man beside him, a black man about his size wearing the same T-shirt with "SECURITY" on it. He was wearing sunglasses, so it was difficult to see where he was looking. "This is my friend Cosimo. This is Jason DeLong. Jason, this is my friend Cosimo."

"Pleased to meet you." Cosimo's hand was not as thick as Max's, but his hand squeeze was as convincing, surely capable of breaking bones. Cosimo shook once and then said, "Hey, Alberto. Good to see you." He waved a few people past and then stepped into Albert and gave him a quick bear hug and released him.

When Albert was free he and Jason went past onto the lighted tennis court. People, many of them dressed in expensive, fashionable clothes, were streaming across the tennis court to the narrow door in the high fence that surrounded the court. Albert knew that Max had already known all about the nature and cause of his recent troubles. All the gestures of welcome and affection had given Max and Cosimo time to study him and Jason, examine them for weapons, and verify that Albert and Jason weren't on some violent mission. Albert supposed that now that he had murdered a man, he should expect to get special attention from bouncers and bodyguards for the rest of his life.

He looked over his shoulder and saw that Cosimo was on a cell phone. He bet himself that he was letting somebody up near the house know that Albert was here and that they'd checked him and let him in. He supposed that the fact that he hadn't killed Bobby Robinian at a party had weighed in his favor. He hadn't spoiled anybody's good time or wasted anybody's efforts or investment.

As they walked toward the house the music grew louder, going up by a few decibels every hundred feet. The house was one that Albert had been to before. Some very rich guy from he didn't remember where — Japan? England? — owned the place and rented it out for parties, weddings, or whatever. The house was in demand because it had all the right features for parties. The ways in could be easily controlled, there were several large, flat spaces for people, and the house was opulent but not fragile. There were dramatic views of the city, a few surprising architectural features that helped it fit into the hillside, but no antiques or famous paintings. No party giver wanted to have to insure or guarantee anything like that. The tennis court, the big, paved patio a bit farther on, and the lawn served as party zones for the people who didn't qualify for admittance to the inner courtyard at the back of the house. Those who were not semi-famous, on the rise toward being well-known, influential partygoers, or physically stunning, were able to dance, drink, eat, meet each other, see things, and experience pleasure under a clear summer night's sky, and many would do so without thinking much about the party in the inner court-yard. They got glimpses of the privileged coming and going, so they felt like part of the same party. They could see the band beyond the inner courtyard wall and hear it, and feel the pleasure of being where things were happening.

Probably half the guests weren't aware that there was an inner party and an outer one, and those who knew felt that the distinction was all right, simply the natural hierarchy and a way of keeping the band and the other almost-celebrities and the getting-known protected and unmolested. They knew the world was populated by a few insiders and many outsiders. Society was a meritocracy, but it was based on the new and the fresh, so that any of the outsiders might make the right connection on some random night and instantly become insiders too. This crowd was drawn from the Valley and the Westside, so everybody had friends who went to acting or singing classes but so far hadn't been beautiful enough or talented enough or lucky enough, and others who wrote screenplays or songs that were almost the same as ones that had made somebody rich and, for the moment, well-known.

Albert and Jason made their way through the growing crowd of partygoers, most of whom had only learned of the party online. A few of the partygoers probably knew that they were important too — not individually, but certainly together. They were the ones who made the party big and were the audience and witnesses to it. They represented the customers for the products — the recorded music, the newly designed clothing, the movies, the television shows, the tequila, champagne, or vodka. They were the ones influenced by the influencers. If a song, show, movie, shoe style, or personality blew up into a success by word of mouth, it was their mouths that said the words. They were the ones to see or hear it and each tell the next ten people about it over the next few days. They attested to the hotness of the hot, the greatness of the great.

Albert and Jason walked past people they knew and greeted them with false but convincing smiles, chest bumps, cheek kisses, or hugs, and kept going. They were on the way to the second gate and the second set of gatekeepers, and the others were not.

Albert reached the door in the white wall around the inner garden patio and saw that the professional party maker Nate Blount was a few yards away. He was looking down at a piece of paper under one of the lights along the edge of the house's roof.

Albert stood patiently and watched Nate Blount. When he had finished reading, he took the ballpoint pen in his hand and scratched out a couple of entries, refolded the paper and put it into his back pocket. He looked up toward the doorway and his eyes fell on Albert as though he had just noticed him. He walked to the opening.

"Alberto," Nate Blount said. He had to yell to be heard over the music. "I heard you had some drama. Are you out on the loose again?"

"At least for now," Albert said, but he realized it hadn't been loud enough, so he just yelled, "Yes!"

"Max texted me that you were here. Want to come through?"

"Sure."

"Let him in," Nate said to the security men just inside the wall.

"And my friend Jason too?" He pointed his thumb at him over his shoulder.

Nate let a frown appear for a half second, but it passed, and the two security men stepped back to let them in, then stepped to block the opening again.

The back of the house featured glass sliding doors, and the center ones had been rolled aside to make a thirty-foot opening. The living room was the size of a hotel lobby, and some of the most favored guests were coming in and out freely. Albert recognized some of them, but didn't know them well enough to speak to, so he didn't. When Nate headed toward the opening Albert and Jason followed. Nate was one of the party arrangers who had known and dealt with Albert for years. When Nate had needed more women to even out parties, Albert had invited some. Nate hadn't considered it his business if Albert had charged the women admission fees or made some other independent deal with them. Albert had also helped Nate get some party supplies at deep discounts, because he knew people who made money taking things off the trucks that made deliveries to stores. He had been helpful enough times that Nate wanted to keep the relationship alive, at least for now.

Albert said, "Nate, have you seen Cornell arrive? Is he here?"

"He's here. I saw him over there and around the corner. Look for some big couches."

"Thanks, Nate."

Cornell was Cornell Stamoran, the host of the party, the man who had given Nate some money and told him to make it happen. He was legendary in the music business. Like many very successful people he had been overpraised. His compositions had been compared to the work of classical composers and to the most pure and time-burnished old folk ballads and been called "incomparable." He was holding the party to celebrate the release of a new album, maybe the seventeenth, Albert thought, but wasn't sure. He was sure that the money for the party had come from the record company and not from Cornell Stamoran.

Cornell Stamoran was also a man known to have connections with some dangerous, shady people. When he was younger, he had cultivated the image of a former gangster.

His clothes, his manner and expressions, had made that history seem possible, but he had never admitted or denied anything of the sort. He had simply changed the subject. If he was asked about it in an interview, he ended the interview.

Albert had known him before his rise to fame, when he had been a bar musician who put together groups to showcase his writing, and disbanded and changed members about once a month. He had lived by being a freelance part-time drug salesman. Albert had sometimes bought from him if the discount was sufficient, and sometimes referred other customers, either for the drugs or the music. Albert had never been sure how deep the criminal ties went, but it was not possible to go to a Cornell Stamoran party and not see a few men who were carrying firearms and looked the part. He had even been at the legendary party when a group of three men and a group of four opened fire on each other, and the only people hit by bullets were women.

He said to Jason, "Wait for me between here and the doors so I can find you."

Jason nodded and drifted to the wall where he could see who came and went without being in the way.

Albert went around the corner to the less

traveled part of the big space and saw the couches. There was Cornell Stamoran in a white suit, flanked by two pretty young women. He was six feet seven inches tall and inclined to sprawl to straighten his legs. After a second Albert sorted the parts of what he was looking at and realized the two women were sitting on his lap, one on each thigh. They were chatting to Cornell Stamoran, who seemed to have persuaded each of them that he was listening to her, and it occurred to Albert that Stamoran was so smart that maybe he could do that.

As Albert took a step toward the couch, Cornell Stamoran's eyes widened slightly and then narrowed as he smiled. All he said was "Alberto." Stamoran gave his knees a little shake and the women dismounted to let him stand. "Excuse me, ladies." He walked to meet Albert but, as he reached him, he put his long arm around Albert's shoulders and kept walking with him. "I'll bet you want to talk to me."

"I do," Albert said, "But so does everybody else. I can wait until you —"

"Now is fine. In a little while it'll be so crowded you won't be able to tell if you're scratching your ass or somebody else's, and you won't hear yourself talk." He ushered Albert into a small sitting room with a few easy chairs at a window looking out over the city. The walls on both sides had built-in aquariums, and Albert was slightly disapproving because fish tanks were passé.

Stamoran said, "I heard you had troubles. I'm sorry."

"You don't have to be, but thank you."

"I always had you in my mind as a peaceful guy."

"I think I was. Until Sara made me so jealous I had to shoot him in front of her."

"You must have been really hurt."

"I was. And it got worse later. When she testified against me at the trial as an eyewitness, I couldn't believe it."

"Yeah, man. How did you get out of that?"

"My lawyer. Somehow, he picked out three jurors he could pay off. He helped pick the jury, so maybe he knew them. But he was sure they'd take the money and hold out against the nine that wanted me dead. One by one, the nine got homesick or something and gave up. The three didn't."

"Wow," Stamoran said. "Can you give me his name, just in case?"

"Millisander. Robert Millisander." Albert took out a pen and wrote it on a bill from his wallet, and a phone number. He held it out.

Cornell Stamoran held it up and looked

at it. "Amazing." He folded it and put it in his pocket. "But you need something from me, right?"

"Maybe some advice, maybe just a name. I don't know. After the trial she took off and disappeared. My friend Jason DeLong started tracking her lawyer right away to see if she was going to hide or something. A few days later I was out of jail and he called me to tell me she had gotten sent to a woman in the east who makes people disappear."

"That's something I never heard of," Cornell Stamoran said. "Finding people, yes. Losing people, no."

"Then that's it," Albert said. "It was a long shot, but I knew you know a lot of people, and have a lot of friends, so I thought I'd ask."

"I just said I never heard of it. That doesn't mean nobody has. I know a man. If I ask him he'll probably talk to you. He's not somebody you want to get to know a lot about, but he has connections."

"What kind of connections?"

"He's a Russian, and he knows other Russians. Let's leave it at that. Would you like me to ask him what he can find out?"

"That's more than I could ever ask, Cornell. Thank you."

"Well, you're a genuine badass now, Alberto. A killer. He'll probably like you better than he likes me. His name is Porchen."

"Portion, like this is only a portion?"

"It sounds like that, but it's not."

"How does he spell it?"

"In Russian."

9

The day started with a loud rap on the front door. Albert sat up and looked around, and saw that it was nowhere near eleven. It was barely eight. He lay back down in the bed and felt relieved that it had only been a dream. As he closed his eyes he heard the scrape of a key sliding into the door lock, then the thump of something hitting the door and then the door opening.

He opened his eyes again but lay still. Any of the people who might open the front door and invade his apartment was capable of shooting him — police, gangsters, home-invasion thugs. Lying flat with both hands in sight was the best strategy for living until afternoon.

The two people who entered were none of the things he expected. The first was a tall man, about thirty, with peach-fuzz hair. He was wearing a thick leather jacket, a pair of black boots with a strap and buckle, and a wide black leather belt. He stopped at the foot of the bed. "You invited us. Why didn't you open the door?"

"I don't know," he said. "I was asleep."

The second one was a woman in her early thirties wearing a leather jacket much like her companion's and a pair of tight spandex pants with a jean stitching pattern printed on them. Albert wondered if they had come by motorcycle, and why he hadn't heard it. "Was it because you're naked?" she said. "I've seen lots of dicks before, nicer than yours, I'll bet." Like the man, she had an odd way of speaking. It wasn't severe enough to be called an accent, just a way of emphasizing unexpected parts of a word.

"I'm not actually naked," he said. He sat up and swung his legs off the bed. "I just assumed you were a dream." He was wearing boxer shorts.

The man said, "You asked to meet Mr. Porchen. Do you still want to or not?"

Albert remembered his conversation with Cornell and became fully awake. "Yes. Yes, I do." He snatched the pants he had left on the chair last night when he had come in. He zipped them up, buttoned the waist, then pulled a shirt on and stepped into a pair of shoes. "I'm ready."

"She'll go with you in your car to show

you the way."

While Albert went to his dresser to pick up his wallet and keys the man walked out the front door. Albert followed him out the door and found him on the small concrete porch, looking both ways, then dancing down the stairs and getting into a plain sedan and driving off.

Albert turned and looked at the woman behind him. She had the pale skin of another night person and dark hair that was tied tight in a bun. He took a step down and then she did, too.

She said, "What are you stopping for?"

He went the rest of the way to the sidewalk and then stepped to the passenger side of his old Corvette. She said, "This is cute." He opened the door for her and she sat down and brought her long legs inside. When he got in and started the engine, he reached up to release the black fabric top from the chrome frame of the windshield.

"Don't. Just go."

He refastened the top, looked into his side mirror and then pulled out onto the street.

She said, "Get on the 405 South and take the Santa Monica Boulevard exit."

"Okay." He drove toward the freeway entrance and got on the southbound side. They had both been silent for a while, so he said, "What can you tell me about Mr. Porchen?"

"Nothing."

"Nothing?"

"You asked to see him. You must know something about him that makes you want to talk to him."

"I'm sorry," he said. "I was just talking to make the time pass quickly for you."

"Not necessary. I'm a grown-up. I will tell you two things that will help you with him. Don't waste his time, and don't ask questions about things you don't need to know."

He drove on, paying full attention to his driving. He left the freeway at the Santa Monica Boulevard exit and drove toward the ocean until she said, "Turn right up at the light."

He followed each of her instructions until she said, "Park up there on the right in front of the black building." The building looked like a glass cube, but the glass was tinted black, so nothing could be seen inside. As he stopped the Corvette at the curb a young man in jeans and a sport coat came out the front door and down the five steps to the sidewalk. He stopped beside Albert's door and said, "Leave the keys in it." Albert got out.

The man sat behind the wheel and drove

Albert's car to the corner and turned right, out of sight. Albert was surprised that losing touch with his car frightened him more than the time he had spent with the people who had come to fetch him. He had lost his means of escape.

The woman stood on the sidewalk while he stared down the empty street after his car. She said, "Go in. Or don't." She spun and walked to the steps, and then climbed them.

Albert walked quickly to catch up and opened the black glass door for her. Inside was a large waiting area with a polished concrete floor and a four-foot-tall reception desk. The front surface of the long, high desk was an undisguised and unembellished rusted sheet of iron. Albert noticed that there were three round holes in the iron, and then it occurred to him that the holes were of a size to make good gun ports, and he hoped it was just an idle thought. Waiting behind the counter was the man who had opened his door with a bump key.

The woman said something to the man in Russian and he responded. She said to Albert, "You can sit right there if you want." Her eyes indicated a leather couch. She kept going past the end of the counter and into the hallway beyond.

A minute later a man about sixty years old with short, bristly gray hair and a sport coat stepped into the hallway and waved him in.

Albert got up and followed him to the open door of an office. The man closed the door and said, "I'm Oleg Porchen. Cornell said you wanted to talk."

Albert realized he had to say what he was going to say quickly, or his time would be up. "Yes, sir," he said. "I've been searching for a woman who used to be my girlfriend. She cheated on me, so I killed the man she'd had sex with. She betrayed me and testified against me as an eyewitness at the trial."

Porchen nodded. "I see." Albert noticed that he didn't say "But you were guilty," or "Maybe she was afraid you'd hurt her," or any other stupid thing. He was a man, so he saw.

"My friend and I found her a week ago near Buffalo, New York. She got away, and we couldn't find her after that."

Porchen was clearly irritated and impatient. "You could hire private detectives. They find runaway girls every day."

"Later on they would be able to prove they found her for me, and when her body was found they'd tell the police. And that's if they could even find her. She has professional help."

"What kind of professional help?" Porchen looked wary, but curious.

"When we caught up with her, she was with a woman who was helping her. We caught up with her while we were driving two Range Rovers. The other woman was driving her in the old compact car she'd bought. When she took an exit off the highway onto a parallel road, we got ahead of her and pulled across the road in front of her. When she saw us she didn't stop or try to turn around. She drove toward my friend, speeding up. When he was sure that she was too close and coming too fast to be able to stop, he pulled his car back out of the way."

"What then?"

"He was looking at her and not in his mirror, and he backed into a ditch and got stuck. She still didn't slow down. She went past him and kept going. We never caught up and never saw that car again."

"How hard did you try?"

"Very hard, and I had advantages. She was my girlfriend for four years. I had all her information — her Social Security number, all of her credit card numbers, her phone, the passwords for her computer accounts. I had pictures of her. None of it helped. Once she met that woman, she never used any of those things again. She just disappeared."

"Did you see this other woman?"

"I saw her for a couple of seconds. My friend was staring at her through her windshield for at least ten seconds while she was driving straight toward him. She's between thirty and forty, has long black hair, and she's tall and thin."

"Like her?" He pointed, and Albert turned to see that the woman who had guided him here was inside the office leaning on the door behind him. She reached up and pulled a bobby pin out of her hair and it unraveled and fell straight into a cascade onto her shoulder.

"Yes. A lot like her."

"And this was outside Buffalo, New York? Which way was she going?"

"South. We were on a highway on the shore of Lake Erie, going toward Pennsylvania and Ohio."

"Is that all the information you have?"

"About her, yes. I still have all the information about my ex-girlfriend. It's on my phone right now."

"Give your phone to Magda."

The only one who could be Magda was the tall woman who had come here with him. Albert felt reluctant to let the phone out of his possession, but he moved quickly to step into the hallway, where she was waiting. She took his phone and walked to another open room on the hallway. Albert went back to join Porchen.

Porchen said, "I like Cornell Stamoran. I think he's a genius, and he said you're a friend of his. That doesn't make you a friend of mine, but I'll see what I can find out about this woman. It could take some time, but I'll be in touch."

"Okay." Albert realized that he had to do better than that. "Thank you very much, Mr. Porchen." He stood and began to back toward the door. He caught himself nodding his head twice in an almost-bow. He heard, or possibly felt, the door open. He looked over his shoulder and saw Magda holding out his telephone. He took it, muttered "Thanks," and followed her out of the room.

She stood outside the office twisting her long hair at the back of her head into the tight bun again, pinned it, and said, "What are you waiting for? The phone is copied."

Albert said, "I don't know." He looked at the glass at the front of the building and saw his old Corvette glide up to the curb outside. "There's my ride." He walked toward it, trying not to walk so fast that it looked like he was running away.

10

Anne Bailey sat at the breakfast table in the apartment in Albany pretending to eat the eggs she had cooked, but really using her fork to make colorful swirls on her plate with the bright yellow yolk. She watched Jane at the other end of the room doing Tai Chi.

"Do you do that every morning?"

"If I can."

"Why?"

"It helps me stretch and stay flexible. It improves my balance. It works a wide variety of muscles, some of which people should use more than we do. It gives me a way to think without trying to or focusing my attention too much. It improves my mood."

"What else do you do?"

"I run," she said. "If you want to do any of these things with me, you can."

"I don't know if I could keep up with you."

"You couldn't, but I'd let you set the pace."

Jane's cell phone buzzed and she glanced at it, then went into the bedroom where she'd slept, closed the door, and said, "You've got me. Talk."

It was Elizabeth Howarth's voice. "Allison told me you needed a call."

Jane said, "Did you send someone to me?"

"Yes. She was a client who testified against —"

"I've heard the story. I just needed to know if it was real. You could have called."

"I was afraid to trust my phone. He had a really sleazy attorney and I wasn't sure he hadn't had it tapped during the trial. I got rid of my old phone. This one is a throwaway. Then I worried that I was being followed."

"Since you never called me, I don't know about the phone, but you could have been right. She was certainly followed when she drove to see me, because they showed up the day after she did. So your instincts were pretty good."

"I'm really sorry about this. I didn't know anything else to do for her."

"It's okay. We're pretty hard to find for now, and I plan for things to get better soon."

"I'm so relieved. I owe you five pro bono defenses."

"I hope I don't collect on any defenses. Just don't forget to throw away that throw-away phone when you hang up."

"I won't forget."

"I'll get rid of this one too. And do me a favor. For at least a few months make sure you watch your back. If they don't find her, there's still you. Don't forget it."

Jane hung up, but kept up the sounds. "Uh-huh. Uh-huh. No." She was silent as she walked to the door and flung it open to find Anne Bailey's face a foot away. "I guess you heard." She popped open the phone and removed the battery.

"I think I get the idea."

"Good. This way I don't have to repeat it." She grasped the circuitry of the phone and pulled it out.

"I'm sorry. I didn't mean to."

"Yes, you did. You're in danger. You should want to know everything there is to know. Your instinct is right. Just because somebody says she'll help you doesn't mean she won't trade you to the hunters for money. You barely know me. Eavesdrop. Spy on people. My only advice is to get better at it. If there was something going on, then being caught might get you killed."

Jane finished destroying the cell phone, put the pieces into the center of a paper towel, wrapped them in it and set the towel on the table. "We'll toss the pieces when we go out. When you get rid of a phone or most other devices, don't put them in your own trash."

"Why not? You took the battery out. They can't use the signal to find us, because there isn't any."

"They can't use the GPS. But if somebody notices the parts in your garbage, they might get curious. Why did you use a burner phone? Are you a drug dealer or a terrorist or a kidnapper or a blackmailer? A fugitive? From what?"

"Oh, yeah," Anne said. "I guess it makes sense. I keep forgetting I'm doing things that criminals just happen to do too."

"Right. It's never good to draw any kind of attention, because it can get somebody interested. The human brain is always looking for patterns. If it hears one note it listens for more of them so it can identify the tune. If it sees something the least bit unusual it starts forming theories and watching to see what appears next. Don't get anybody started."

"I've got to start remembering all these precautions."

"You can't remember everything," Jane said. "So what you do is remember an attitude and apply it. You don't want attention because it puts you at risk, so you turn away from places where it is and avoid arousing it. Each instance is new and separate."

"I think I'm getting depressed."

"You were depressed when you showed up. You don't have depression the mental illness. You have a life that's a mess, and you're engaged in fixing it. Do you have something you can wear to run in?"

Anne shrugged. "I guess so."

"Get dressed."

Ten minutes later she was back in the kitchen wearing shorts, sneakers, and a T-shirt. Jane pointed to the table, where there were a pair of sunglasses, a baseball cap, and a sweatshirt. "Bring those." Jane went out, got into the car, and started it.

Anne said, "If we're running, why are we taking the car?"

"If we run from the apartment into the neighborhood, anybody who notices us knows where we live. If we drive to another area in a car that's not conspicuous and park the car in a not very visible spot, anybody who sees us will assume we're from there. And if they get interested and try to follow, we have a chance of noticing. If we wear clothes that don't invite attention or give them a perfect view — sunglasses, sweatshirts, and baseball caps — we've improved our safety. Besides, this isn't California. It's cool out."

"All right." She pulled the sweatshirt on over her T-shirt.

Jane drove up Albany's Madison Avenue, an old street in Albany's downtown section, through the entrance to Washington Park, and drove around, exploring. It was a large public park with paved and gravel paths, big stands of old trees, green lawns, and patches of colorful tulips. There was even an artificial lake that looked like a water hazard on a golf course, and it had an arched footbridge across it. "This looks like too nice a place to torture ourselves running," Anne said.

Jane said, "We'll have to ignore the beauty and suffer. It said online that the park was built in the 1870s. That must be why it's not built for cars. There weren't any." Jane drove up the entrance road and then turned off on a broad gravel path and parked the car in a line of others.

"You're going to park here?"

"There isn't any parking lot, so everybody seems to park at the edge of a road. And I can see one, two, no, four people jogging without even turning my head. If you want to do something like running, do it where other people are, too. Places you pick won't always be like this, so let's enjoy it."

They got out of the car and stretched for a few seconds, and then Jane said, "Ready?"

"I guess so." Jane began to run along the margin of the grass beside the road toward the interior of the park, and Anne pushed off and followed. Jane ran easily and comfortably, her long legs taking natural, relaxed steps. Anne, who was three inches shorter, was expending greater effort to keep up.

Jane talked to her as they ran. "Keep your eyes open. What you're looking for, primarily, is anybody you've ever seen before in your life."

"Umm."

"Second in your mind should be anybody who shows more than the normal level of interest in you. If you see either of those sorts of people, say so right away."

"Yep."

The pace that Jane had set was strenuous enough, but the conversation made it hard for Anne to get enough air. Soon she was winded and breathing hard as she strained to keep up with Jane. "You promised you'd go at my speed."

"That's true," Jane said. She ran in place and watched Anne's legs for a few seconds, and then fell into step with her. "How's this?"

"Okay for now. If I collapse don't trample me."

They ran along the paths at a steady pace for about twenty minutes before Anne slowed to a walk. She walked for a minute with her hands on her hips, catching her breath. Jane walked with her. Anne turned to look at her and said, "All right. You beat me."

"You did great. We ran at least a couple of miles. Let's see if we can find a drinking fountain and relax a little before we start back. It's a beautiful park, isn't it?"

Anne's breaths were still short and shallow. She swept a lock of hair out of her eyes. "Uh-huh." She walked along for a minute. "Do you do this every day, too?"

"Most days."

"Why?"

"The short answer is that it makes me feel better than if I don't. Same as the Tai Chi."

"You live in a cold climate, don't you?"

"We like to call it temperate. Warm in the summer, cold in the winter."

"You run in the winter too?"

"Most winters include a fair number of

days when the pavement is clear or they clear it, and there are synthetic fabrics that you can run in, and waterproof sneakers. If you keep moving you don't freeze in place."

"You've got me intimidated."

"You can still live in a warm place. California has forty million people and has plenty of places to live quietly under a new name. There are other sunny places — Hawaii, Puerto Rico, and plenty of warm foreign countries. All you have to do is decide and we'll start working on it."

"I'm curious about something else. You knew there was no chance that I could be faster than you."

"Yes."

"How?"

"I've been out running nearly every day since I was about eight or nine. I couldn't run track in high school because they didn't have a girls' track team, but I ran on my college team. After that I never found a reason to quit, so I never got out of condition, except one year when I had an injury and had to stay off one leg to let it heal. I'm fine now."

"I could see that. What happened?"

"A long story, and the name of it is 'poor me.' We've heard that one."

A few years ago, Jane had been leading

enemies away from a man she was helping to escape from a courthouse, and the men who were trying to capture him had only her to take. When she tried to escape from their car at a stop one of them shot her through the thigh. She didn't bleed to death and she didn't die, but it hadn't been a sure thing.

They spotted a drinking fountain near the path, walked to it, and each took a drink and then another one. When Jane straightened, she said, "Have you ever seen that man down there along the path before?"

"The one with the blue windbreaker?"

"Yes. I noticed him when he walked close to that pair of women on the path a minute ago. Now he seems to be looking at us."

"I hadn't noticed him before, but I see him. He's nobody I know."

"He's probably just a guy who likes looking at women," Jane said. "There are plenty of those around, and it's probably nothing. But check out his jacket. It's sort of odd with a pair of dress pants. Maybe he came out and realized that it was cool out, and put that jacket on because it was all he had with him. But that's also the kind of thing a man might wear if he needed to hide something he was carrying. It wouldn't be a bad idea to keep him in mind when we start running again."

"You don't think he's, like, somebody working for Albert, do you?"

"I don't know what he is. Right now, he's just a guy. When you're trying to be invisible you pay attention to who's looking. Are we ready to run back to the car and go home for a shower?"

Anne took another surreptitious look under the brim of her cap and studied the man while she retied her running shoes. He looked forty or so, with short hair that was sort of bristly and blond. He was in good shape. The blue windbreaker, gray pants, and walking shoes made him seem older. "I'm ready."

"Then start."

Anne ran in a straight line across the nearest lawn, then turned slightly to plot a course along the circular path around a big round fountain. Its center was a large outcropping of rock with four bronze statues that appeared to have climbed up on it in an exultant mood, but it was impossible to guess why while running past.

Jane half turned to glance at the man she had noticed, and then turned forward. She was surprised, because he had stopped walking to watch her and Anne. Maybe he looked only because the human brain could never resist looking at anything that moved suddenly. She ran a few steps and looked again, but this time he seemed to have his cell phone up in front of his face. Was he talking or taking their photograph? Neither would be good news.

She said, "Go that way, through the willow trees along the lake."

"You lead," Anne said.

Jane drifted to the right and down the grassy incline toward the section of path. The slope brought them below the man's horizon, so he would lose sight of them unless he came closer. Ahead were several willow trees along the bank, their long vine-like branches drooping downward all the way to the path like a beaded curtain. She ducked her head and parted them as she ran beneath the first tree, and listened to Anne's footsteps to be sure she was keeping up. There were four big willows in a row, and Jane ran under them, trying to keep herself and Anne invisible for the moment. She could see that to her right and across the lake was a building, but she had no idea what its purpose was, or whether it was a place to lose a follower or a place to be trapped. She used the time in the shadowy bower of willows to change course to head away from the lake toward the next large stand of trees on the way to the place where she'd parked the car.

Jane kept looking around to see if there was any sign of the man who had been watching. She reminded herself that there was almost certainly no reason to worry about this man, but she didn't feel right about him, so she kept looking.

Jane kept up the run across the long open space leading to the wooded area. When they ran in under the big trees Anne said, "Wait. I need to catch my breath."

"Sure," Jane said. "Sit down, and enjoy the shade." She sat with her back to one of the large trunks and Anne did the same, breathing deeply to recover. Jane watched the cars moving along the road beside the grove, going in and out of Washington Park.

Then a car went by, moving slower than the others nearby. It was a new gray SUV that had the General Motors logo on the front of the hood. They could see the driver inside. Jane and Anne both moved around the trees where they had been sitting, trying to stay behind them. Anne said, "It's that man again."

"I know," Jane said. "I didn't expect to see him again. He's oddly persistent."

"What do you think he's doing?"

"He could be looking for us. He's seen

us, but he hasn't seen the car we came in yet, so all he can be doing is either forgetting us and leaving the park or waiting to see which car we go to."

"Good," Anne said. "So we can skip that, right? We can just abandon the car and get out of here. I don't want to be killed for a car, especially not for a car I paid five hundred bucks for."

Jane pointed at the rectangular object in Anne's pocket. "That's the phone I gave you, right?"

"Yes."

"Call for a car to pick you up at the other side of the park and have the driver take you to the apartment. I'll meet you there later."

"Why? What are you going to do?"

"I'm curious about this guy. If he had wanted to meet us and see if either of us was single and interesting, he would have. He had plenty of time to come and talk while we were resting. He didn't. He took his phone out. Why? Now he seems to be trying to find us. I'm just going to try to get a better look at him."

Anne said, "I don't see why you can't just come with me."

"Because if he only seems to be focusing on us, but isn't, it will mean we can forget him. If he's just a guy who's not good at meeting women, we can forget him. But if he actually is somebody helping Albert find you, then he's found you, and this may be our only warning and our only chance to find out anything about him. So do what I asked."

Jane didn't wait for Anne to answer. She just turned and ran toward the stretch of road where she had parked the car. She cut into the extension of the grove, staying far enough from the road so that the tree trunks lined up most of the time to block any view of her.

When she approached the road where the grove ended, she waited until there were no vehicles to be seen before she crossed the open space and disappeared into the low bushy area beyond. She made a broad circular path and scanned cars parked along the narrow roads searching for the SUV the man had been driving. He would be parked in a spot that would enable him to see the two women arrive on foot and go to their car. He would not want them to see him watching, and he would want to have a clear route to the park exit from the spot if he intended to follow.

Jane kept moving, careful to stay in the surrounding vegetation. She didn't want to be caught in front of the man's windshield or behind his car in the field of his mirrors. She wanted to stay on the right side because his own car would block the lower half of his view from the driver's seat

When she found his SUV she was surprised. He was parked only about fifty feet from Anne's car and facing away from it. He didn't have to wait for Anne and Jane to come up the road and show him their car by walking to it. He already knew which car was theirs. He was parked directly in line with it and facing away so that he could sit comfortably in his SUV and watch it in his mirrors.

Jane lay in the bushes and called the phone she had given to Anne. She answered, "Yeah?" followed by heavy breaths as she ran.

Jane said, "Have you called the car to pick you up yet?"

"No. I thought I'd get to the pickup point first."

"What's the pickup point?"

"Remember that big goofy fountain that looks like a rock with a bunch of people on it?"

"Yes, I do. Don't call for the car yet. Just get to the statue and wait for me. Don't call me, no matter what."

"All right."

Jane hung up. She moved as far as she could from the man's car to the other side of the thick grove while she went looking in the trash cans placed at intervals near the roads. The first one was wet garbage, as though somebody had an overflow at home and brought their garbage here to dump it. But she did find a large plastic bag and a beer bottle. The next can held an empty pint whiskey bottle and a quart vodka bottle. The third had a quart bottle that had held orange soda. She added it to her collection and moved on. There were sprinkler heads on the grass margin, and walking in line with them she passed an eight-inch length of board, painted grass-green. She could see the heads of four large screws in the wood, so she knelt and pulled on it.

The wood had rotted from being constantly wet, and so it came up easily. Jane could see that it was the cover of a box that shielded the place where the sprinkler pipe met the water supply. There was a lever like a knife switch for shutting the system off. She tried wiggling one of the screws, found it gave a little, and then unscrewed it and put it in her pocket. She took three more screws and pocketed them.

She moved off the path into the vegetation to reach the side of the line of cars that included the man's SUV and Anne's car. She tightened her grip on the plastic bag so her four bottles would not clink against each other, crouched, and made her way along the lower right sides of the line of cars. Then she reached the vehicle that was parked in the line behind the man's SUV. It was a van with a tall cargo compartment, and it was on oversize wheels like the SUV. She judged that it was too close to the SUV to allow the SUV's driver to back up. When the SUV left it would have to go forward. She crawled under the van and listened. She could hear a man's voice talking, but could make out none of it.

She crawled from the underside of the van to get under the SUV. The engine was not running, and now she could hear the man's voice more clearly. His window had to be open. She noted it and realized she'd just have to be quiet. She took two of her liquor bottles in hand and slithered to the front beneath the engine. She wedged the two bottles in front of the man's front tires. Then she took out one of the large wood screws and pushed the point into one of the grooves of the left front tire at about mid-point. She pushed on it and turned it with her hand, trying to make it bite into the rubber and screw in deeper. It was too hard. She took out the keys to Sara's car, and found she could fit one edge of the car key into the screw's groove and use it as a screwdriver. She repeated the process with the other front tire and slithered back to the rear tires. She wedged her remaining bottles ahead of the rear tires and inserted the two screws into the grooves of the treads and turned them with the car key until they bit in deep enough.

She moved closer to the left side at the moment when the man said something more loudly into his phone, and she recognized the language. It was Russian.

Jane left the plastic bag under the SUV and kept crawling. She crawled back under the tall van, and slithered to the far side of it. She kept moving to get out from under it, and then rose to a crouch and moved ahead until she could see Anne's car up the line.

She couldn't help studying it for a moment. The car was nondescript, its once-silver finish now tarnished to a dull light gray. The average person would not have noticed it, but here was their stalker, about four vehicles away.

The only way this stranger could have found Anne's car was if someone had sent a photograph of it to his telephone. And the only people who could have taken a picture of it were Albert McKeith or the friend of his Anne had recognized, Jason DeLong. Who else had seen the car?

Jane reached into her pocket for Anne's car keys and gripped them in her right hand, and walked toward the car. Behind her she heard a car's engine start, and she had already seen that there was only one car back there with a driver. She pushed off on the balls of her feet, running hard. It took seven steps for her to dash to Anne's car. On her third step she pushed the button on the key fob to unlock the driver's side door, and she ended the eighth step sliding behind the steering wheel while turning the key. She shifted into drive and hit the gas pedal so she was streaking to the intersection with the park road.

As she made the turn to get onto the wider, paved route that led deeper into the park she looked to the side and saw the man pulling out of his space fast. His SUV bumped up onto the four bottles and they broke at once, making his tires fall onto the shards of glass. By the time he stopped, the tires had rotated far enough so the screws must have been driven in. She couldn't see the fate of the screws or tell if the broken glass had done anything, but she saw the man jump out of the SUV to find out what he had run over.

In a moment Jane was taking her first shortcut. She drove across the lawn where she and Anne had run, and then she was on the same pedestrian path, straddling it at times to fit the car through the narrow spaces. Jane stayed on the route she and Anne had taken from the parking spot, past the first bright patches of spring flowers, across a lawn to the next path, along the winding course of it to the shade of the grove of trees, and then beside the lake. She passed the willows and turned up from the path past the big building and then joined the circular road that ran around the fountain. The young woman sitting on the rim of the fountain saw the car and sprinted to get into the passenger seat.

"What did you find out?" Anne asked.

"That we're in trouble. As soon as we get to the apartment, we have to grab whatever we want to take with us as fast as we can and bring it back to the car. Grab everything, because we can't afford to leave anything that might give them any information."

11

Albert McKeith and his friend Jason De-Long sat in the old red Corvette in front of the black glass cube. Albert got out of the car and started to walk around the rear toward the sidewalk.

"You forgot your keys," DeLong said.

"I know. We have to leave them."

The young man who had taken the Corvette on Albert's first visit came out of the dark-tinted front door and down the steps without speaking or looking at the two men, got behind the wheel, started the car, and drove off as he had done the first time. Albert met Jason's eye and said, "I know. He's just parking it."

"It gives me the creeps."

"I think it's supposed to," Albert said. "When you come you don't see any cars, so you don't know how many people are here. And if they kill you there's no car parked outside they'll have to explain."

"If they *kill* you?"

"I don't expect them to. But these people are organized crime, from a country that's run by organized crime. They have a reputation that they're more violent than anybody else. They must kill people once in a while just to keep up their image."

"Jesus," said Jason. "Shouldn't that tell you something?"

"I killed somebody."

"It's not the same. You got pissed off one time."

"I'm still pissed at Sara now."

"Okay, you're a Russian gangster. I'll walk home." Jason stood still in the center of the sidewalk as though his legs were paralyzed.

"Come on, Jason. You'll embarrass me. They said they wanted both of us."

"They shouldn't even know I exist. This is your thing. I just tried to help you get through the trial and find Sara. That was all."

"You're a good friend, Jason. So keep being a good friend for another half hour, until that guy brings my car back."

"You give me lots of reasons to watch out, but you're not watching out."

"I'm watching out," Albert said. "I am."

They walked up the concrete steps to the level slab on top and Albert reached for the darkened glass door, but the door was pulled open by the man who had come to his apartment to wake him up for his first visit. The man's expression was stony — neither hostile nor friendly, just noninvolved. He stepped back a pace to let them in.

"Thanks."

The man let go of the door and looked up over their heads. Albert looked in the same direction and saw what seemed to be the screen of a body-scanning machine from an airport. "It's a metal detector," Albert said to Jason. "I guess that's why there's always somebody hanging around the door. He was checking us for weapons."

"Shit," Jason said.

"Could be worse."

"How?"

"Not sure." Albert was already distracted because he could see that the tall, black-haired woman was waiting with Mr. Porchen. He whispered, "There. That's Magda, the one I told you about."

"I could have figured that out. Who's the old guy?"

"Mr. Porchen."

As usual, Magda was staring at Albert as though she could see through his skull if she looked hard enough. Mr. Porchen beckoned to Albert and turned to walk into his office.

When Albert and Jason came in, he was leaning back against his big desk with his arms folded. "Hello, Albert. And you're Jason, right?"

"Yes, sir," Jason said. "Pleased to meet you." He wasn't. He looked at Porchen's weathered face and saw a pair of gleaming predatory eyes like coffee beans and two rows of unnaturally bright white teeth clenched as though they were clamped on something. He guessed it must have been what Porchen had instead of a smile.

"Albert, I knew that there was something about you that was worth my time. I don't know how I always sense these things. You know what that means?"

"That you found out good things about me?"

"No, it means that you're lucky. You have luck falling out of the sky like rain and dripping off you. You're nobody. You were dumb enough to make your girlfriend watch you kill her lover."

"Well, he wasn't exactly that."

"Then that's worse. If he wasn't the one she picked to replace you, then it was all about nothing. But I don't want to talk about that. Nobody gives a crap about your girlfriend. She would be worth nothing, except that the woman she got to help her escape is worth a great deal. Do you know why?"

"Why?"

"Because she's so good at it. She's been doing this for about ten, fifteen years. By now she's taken in at least a hundred people that somebody was hunting for and made them all disappear. Some of the hunters have been looking for those people, and never found them. They've spent a lot of money and they're willing to spend a lot more to find them. But what they all want most of all is the woman who hid these people. She's the only one who knows where she put them and where they all are now and what they're calling themselves."

Albert said, "I don't want to mislead you. I don't know anything about her that I didn't tell you already."

"You've seen her. You both have."

"That's true," Albert said.

"And the woman she's hiding now was your girlfriend. Finding one of them is finding the other one too. You understand that?"

"Yes."

"Over the past few days, I talked to some friends in the part of the country where you lost the two women. One of their people saw them this morning."

"Where?" Albert asked.

"Albany, New York."

Albert half turned to his friend Jason. "We should get there as fast as we can. They must have kept driving east after we lost them instead of heading west like we thought." He looked at the older man. "Thank you, Mr. Porchen."

"Don't bother. You can't get there fast enough. They were in a park in Albany jogging at ten o'clock. That's seven in the morning here. The woman with your girlfriend knew right away what the man who saw them was. She fucked up his car while it was parked so she could get your girlfriend away and he couldn't follow them. They're in another state by now. If you get a six-hour flight to Albany they'll be two more states away and have a different car before you land."

"What should I do, then?"

"Not make mistakes. Everybody thinks that they've got to do something. Your girlfriend is cheating on you, so you have to rush right out and do something. You have to drag her out and have her watch you shoot the guy. You had ten million other options."

"Like what?"

"You could have realized that the guy wasn't the one cheating on you, so he wasn't the problem. If you had to do something, you could have shot your girlfriend instead of him. Then she wouldn't have been alive to turn you in and testify against you. And you wouldn't be chasing all over the country looking for her now."

Porchen seemed to feel neither malice nor even contempt, only to be weary of the mistakes of amateurs. "The best thing to do was nothing. You want to live to be thirty, you have to learn to think fast and act slow. Your luck won't keep you alive forever."

Porchen seemed to remember Jason as an afterthought. "Jason, give your phone to Magda."

Jason's mind stopped working. He didn't want to give anyone his phone, but he could think of no way to avoid it. He took the phone out of his pocket and handed it to her, and she went out the office door.

Porchen said, "I want you to go home and take Albert's Corvette with you. I think I'm going to want to talk to you again, so be sure you don't go anywhere without your phone."

"You don't want me to help Albert find them?"

"No. Albert is going to work with my

people on this. You'll stay in Los Angeles. You can wait for the car in the lobby out there." Jason looked at Albert. "You okay?"

"Yes, sure. Park the car under my building and put the top up." He was afraid but didn't want to draw attention to the fact that staying here was not voluntary.

"If you want to talk before he goes, you can walk him out."

"That's okay," Albert said. "See you, Jason." It occurred to Albert that this might be the last time he would ever see Jason De-Long or any of his friends. He wondered if Jason would tell the police what had happened to him, and knew he would not.

As Jason sat in the lobby, the tall, thin woman they called Magda returned from a room along the hall carrying his cell phone. She held it with her thumb and forefinger as though it were dirty and distasteful. She stood over the couch where he sat and dangled it in front of him so he could snatch it before she dropped it. "Thanks," he said.

"You're welcome." She turned away from him and kept walking, not looking back as though he had already vanished from her mind.

Jason saw Albert's Corvette arrive, so he got up and walked out the front door. Jason was confused. He was worried that Albert was stuck in this place full of terrifying people whose tolerance of him seemed conditional. Jason was also angry at Albert for getting him involved with such people. There were plenty of criminals in Los Angeles who were at least not so unremittingly threatening.

Magda was exactly as Albert had described her, with the tight clothes and the unnaturally black hair and the feral expressions. He was impatient to go where she wasn't, but he was also tantalized. She had big hazel eyes and a body like a fashion model, but the kind of model that looked icy and unfeeling rather than welcoming. Everything he noticed about her raised the probability that she was somebody's girlfriend, and that would bring the sort of possessiveness that left somebody dead. He took a last look at her over his shoulder, but made it brief so nobody would notice.

He went down the steps to the Corvette and turned the ignition key. He listened to the engine idling and then depressed the clutch and fiddled with the floor shifter to get a feel for it. He wasn't used to driving a standard transmission car, but at least he knew how. He considered it an affectation, but he made an exception for Albert because that was not something Albert had asked for. He pushed the shifter up to get the car into first gear, let the clutch out too fast and made the car jump and stall, then restarted it and overcorrected his pressure on the clutch to make it shimmy for the first few feet before he got it right. He drove the car conservatively for a few minutes before he entered the freeway, brought it up to fourth gear, and headed home.

Magda entered Mr. Porchen's office to find him still engaged in conference with Albert McKeith. She remained silent until he asked her in Russian if there was any reason why she didn't want to do this job. He seldom asked anybody what they wanted, so she thought it was a test and replied quickly that she was willing.

Porchen reverted to English. "All right, Albert. Tonight you'll be heading east to find these women. I want you to understand me perfectly about this. We're helping you find your ex-girlfriend, but the one I'm interested in is the other one, the woman who makes people disappear. Never forget for a minute that the most important thing you're doing is finding that woman, who just happens to be with your ex-girlfriend.

"That woman is a professional who already got away from you and your friend and then from an experienced *vor* in Albany.

But I'm sending you with Magda, and Magda is a professional. She'll be the boss. If she says something to you, no matter what it is, it's the same as me telling you. Do what she says and don't complain. If you do a good job, she'll let you kill your girlfriend. I may even give you some money if she thinks you deserve it. Now get going."

Magda opened the door and walked out, and Albert followed. They walked along the hallway for a distance and she went into a room and shut the door. He didn't know what to do, so he stood there waiting. After about a minute she emerged carrying an overnight bag with a shoulder strap. She walked back along the hall to the lobby.

She gave a short, sharp whistle, and the man who had gone with her to wake him up for his first visit to the cube came out of a room behind the counter. She said, "Yevgeny will drive us to your apartment."

Yevgeny looked down into a drawer and took out a set of keys, then went to a stairway and disappeared down the stairs.

"Oh," said Albert. "That's where you keep the cars. It's an underground garage."

She moved her eyes toward him without moving her head. "What did you think?"

"I didn't see a garage entrance. I thought — I don't know what I thought. Maybe that you had a lot around the back, because they always turned right when they took my car away."

"You should get up to stay awake in the daytime more. You could learn a lot about things."

Yevgeny appeared around the corner of the building in a gray SUV and pulled to the curb, staring straight ahead. Magda went to the rear door and sat in the back seat, but slid over to let Albert get in beside her. Albert had assumed she would sit in front beside Yevgeny.

When the two had invaded Albert's apartment, Albert had interpreted their movements and speech to indicate that Yevgeny was the senior partner and Magda was the junior, maybe an assistant or even a nonparticipant companion. Yevgeny had been all muscle and bluster, charging in already talking loudly. Now he could tell that Magda outranked Yevgeny. Today he was just her driver.

They had been to his apartment before, so Yevgeny drove there without directions or discussion, stopped the car outside, and waited for Magda to get out with her bag. Albert followed her.

Magda said something to Yevgeny in Russian that didn't sound especially friendly or even personal. Maybe it was "You can go."

Albert said, "Thanks for the ride," and Yevgeny didn't reply, just drove off.

Magda didn't wait for Albert to collect himself, just went to the door of his apartment, took a key out of her jeans pocket, unlocked it, and stepped inside.

"Why do you have a key to my apartment?"

"Because when you came to see the *Pakhan* you had an apartment key on the ring with your car key."

"Oh," Albert said. "Do you always make a key without asking?"

"Someone does, unless there's a reason not to."

"What does *Pakhan* mean?"

"It means boss."

"He said the man in Albany was a *vor.*"

"It means thief. It's a good thing. He's not a beginner, a victim. He's a full member of the *Bratva.* Brotherhood. I'm a *vor.* We don't have time for Russian lessons. Time to pack."

She walked into his room and sat on the bed. "Get a small suitcase and fill it."

He opened a cabinet above his closet, took out an overnight bag and opened it on the bed. He put in some underwear and socks from a dresser drawer and then opened the closet door.

"Wait," she said. "You have a clear memory of the clothes your girlfriend wore when she lived here, right?"

"Right."

"She has a clear memory of what you wore too. So think before you pick something out. If she's seen you wear it before, leave it. Even if it's straight from the store but it's a style that you wear all the time, leave it."

"I've been in jail, and then I was traveling to find her. Since I got home I haven't been shopping."

"Then leave some room for new things and we'll try to buy some when we get there. Did you ever wear a sport coat with her?"

"At my trial."

"Then you own one. Wear it on the trip." She waited while he found the jacket, then said, "Do you wear hats?"

"I have a knit cap and a couple of baseball caps."

"Why are they called caps instead of hats?"

"I . . . I don't know."

"I didn't think you would. Bring the darkest, dullest baseball one to hide your face, and the knit one, if it hides your hair. What shoes do you have?"

"Running, basketball, brown, black, flip-flops."

"We're chasing people who are running away, so bring only shoes you can run fast in. After you kill your girlfriend somebody might be chasing you, so you'll need them again."

He took two shoeboxes out of his closet and held up a pair of shoes, then another.

"They'll do. Now pants and shirts. Bring three shirts that button and have collars. All should be dark. One pair of gray pants and one black."

He found some and folded them into the bag.

"Get your supplies. Toothpaste and brush, deodorant, razor. Just what you need. Now sunglasses, keys, phone. Close the bag."

He did.

She looked at him closely. "Your girlfriend is being helped by someone who's good at this. Do you think she didn't do this with her? By now she's got her hair cut and colored, replaced her clothes, given her at least one new name and put it on all the cards she carries. But right now we have a plane to catch in two hours, so hurry."

"You got a plane to Albany that leaves in two hours?"

She looked displeased. "We're not going

there. It's the one place we can be sure she won't be. Somebody saw her there, but she saw him too. They have to be on the way to one of the big cities now."

"Do you know which one?"

"We're starting in the biggest, New York. Call for a ride to pick us up for the airport in fifteen minutes."

He took his phone off the bed and walked into the living room as he engaged the app for the car.

Magda opened her bag and took out a simple dark blue pullover dress. She took off her leather jacket, her T-shirt and jeans, slid the dress over her head, and tugged it down straight at the hem. Her eyes were on Albert's in the bedroom mirror. "Maybe you shouldn't kill your girlfriend. You need one."

"Sorry," he said. "I just —"

"You don't have to explain men to me. Take this time to clean out your refrigerator. You don't have pets, do you?"

"No." He went to work emptying his refrigerator into a large black trash bag and then taking the bag outside to the cans. When he returned she was standing at the door with their two bags.

He said, "Can I ask why you put on a dress?"

"So I don't look like what I am."

They both saw the rideshare car pull up in front of the building. She took her bag and went down the steps. He locked his front door, switched off the light, and then hurried to catch up.

12

Anne drove the car south along Route 8. "I've been thinking for hours about what you did this morning."

"What makes it worth all that thought?" Jane said.

"The first thing was, I saw that man. I saw he seemed kind of interested in us. You saw something more."

"When you're being hunted, you have to keep your eyes open and your mind working in the most basic way. We knew this man was paying unusual attention to us. There wasn't any chance that this attention was going to bring us any benefit. We weren't going to become interested in him. We weren't going to make an ally of him. The effect on the rest of the people in the park was to draw their attention to us too. 'What's he looking at? What did those two do?' We left, and he followed. That was a bad sign, but we didn't know how bad. I decided to find out."

"Aren't you ever afraid?"

"Yes, I feel fear. Fear isn't all bad. Sometimes it keeps a person out of a situation she might not live through. Fear reminds me to look again, to listen for a few seconds longer, and to ask myself more questions."

"You haven't told me where I'm driving to."

"Since we've been seen, we're going to drop out of sight again," Jane said. "We've based your new identity in New York State. The driver's license, the library card, the passport all say you live in New York, and the credit cards are tied to mailing addresses in New York, so it should be easier to be unremarkable in this state and keep it up for a longer time."

"We're heading south. Does that mean New York City?"

"For a day or two, yes. After that, probably not. New York is a big, overpopulated place. It's easy to show up and spend a short time living on the fifteenth floor of a hotel and not show your face much. You can stop running long enough to catch up on your sleep and eat nice food and lose your aches and pains."

"And then move on again?"

"Yes. Is that a problem?"

185

"I don't know. I came to you and you helped me, so I don't want to complain. But I'm tired. We've had to get up and move every day or two. What if we went to New York and just stopped?"

"It's possible, if that's what you want."

"But?"

"There are good things. It's one of the few places where you can get along fine without a car. We could get rid of this one and not replace it. We would need to find you a pretty good job, because it's an expensive place to live. But New York has more good jobs than most places."

"Wouldn't just the numbers keep me safer? I'd be one of a zillion people riding the subway, and live on an upper floor in a huge building."

"When I was with a runner there not too long ago I started reading about the city to explain some things to myself. The subways have sixty-five million riders a year. The busiest subway station is Times Square–42nd Street. It has two hundred thousand riders a weekday. Most of the other big stations — Union Square, Grand Central, and so on — have about one hundred thousand a day."

"They'd have to pick me out of two hundred thousand people a day? Great."

"But if the people helping Albert have a lot of manpower, it's not so great. Say Times Square–42nd is your work stop. That means you're not one of two hundred thousand, because you're there twice a day. You're one in a hundred thousand. You come and go only in the morning and the evening, at rush hours, so that makes it a little easier to spot you. And of course, you would also have a home stop twice a day where there are no more than half the riders. Your exposure is twenty subway stations a week if you don't have to transfer."

"It's starting to sound less inviting."

"It's just something to be aware of. Big cities are complicated, but they have a fairly small number of gateways that practically everybody of a certain industry or interest will pass through. There are districts devoted to certain activities, like investing on Wall Street or theater on Broadway. I'm not great at New York, but people who hunt there are."

"So you like smaller places."

"I like places that can't be narrowed down easily. Los Angeles is like that, because it's much bigger — about sixty by eighty miles in hundreds of separate communities. People live their whole lives without ever going downtown. It's even better if a hunter can't narrow things down at all. The less predictable you are, the harder you are to kill."

"Unpredictable sounds good to me."

"It is good, but it takes work and caution to get everything right. And there's one thing I haven't had time to explain to you yet, and now is a good time. When I was crawling around beneath that man's car, one reason he didn't hear me was that he was talking to somebody on his cell phone. He was speaking in Russian."

"So? Does that mean something?"

"It might. He didn't want to meet us or talk to us. So why was he stalking us? When I got to the place where we had parked the car, he was already there. He had recognized this car. That means somebody sent him a picture of it. He was alone, but not without connection to other people. And since he was on the phone speaking Russian, he might be part of a group working together, the way a gang does."

Anne whispered under her breath, "Oh my god."

"Don't forget to breathe and to remember that you're the one who's driving."

Anne took a couple of slow, deep breaths. "This doesn't feel real. I feel like I'm losing my mind. It does feel like all of a sudden a big part of my mind is missing. I heard what you said, and I've been told on good authority that the Russian mafia exists. They're into criminal businesses — drugs and trafficking and kidnapping and so on. But when I've heard about it on the TV news, it never had anything to do with me, and it never would, right?"

She drove for a few seconds in silence. "Of course, I never thought I would have a boyfriend who would commit a murder, or that he would drag me along to see him do it. I had been living the same life since I left the coffee shop with Albert. On the same night I realized that instead of serving coffee I could be Albert's girlfriend. It was comfortable and easy and sort of amusing. I meant it to take the place of working a cash register, which I saw as temporary, not to take the place of my whole future. Being with Albert was just for the moment, but it was a life in the sense that it brought in enough money to let over a thousand sunny days pile up on each other without a lot to worry about.

"I didn't attach a definite future to Albert, but I didn't reject one either. The traditional bond with Albert as the one man in my life was there, and it felt like a marriage sometimes. We sat beside each other in his old Corvette all day long making deals with people and went to a party at sundown. Late at night we opened a window, took off our clothes, and fucked on top of the bed sheet until we slept. I would wake up cold, pull the blanket up, and sleep until eleven.

"I didn't know how Albert was interpreting things, so I didn't pretend I did. I knew how men are. They'll sleep with your best friend and her sisters and her mother and then come home and kiss you sweetly and tell you they love you. I recognized that might happen, but I didn't think it had, so each day was okay."

"If that life had been okay, wouldn't you have been satisfied with it?"

"I've already told you what I did. I said yes to another man. Why that one and not any of the hundred who asked before him, I don't know. That afternoon was the start of the unreality. Doing it once made me unreal. I had been Albert's sincere girlfriend for years, and then suddenly I was only pretending to be the same person. I was wearing my own face like a mask. I pretended to be the Sara who had this loving, or at least honest, feeling for Albert, but I had fooled him and, because I could, I was on the lookout for the next person I might fool him with. Once the unreality took over, I let things that couldn't have happened at

190

first be perfectly possible. Of course, they started to happen, one after another."

Jane said, "Up ahead there's a place called Newburgh. Take the exit and pull over when you can. I'll drive from there."

"Are you going to take us into New York?"

"I think we'll stop and sleep somewhere first. We're tired, and New York isn't a good place to arrive tired."

Anne said, "I have to say one thing before the subject gets changed."

"What's that?"

"Albert has never had the kind of money it would take to hire gangsters to search for us."

"I didn't think so," Jane said.

"Would they just help him for nothing?"

Jane looked at her, almost amused. "Gangsters don't do anything for nothing."

13

Oleg Porchen sat in his office grumbling to himself. It was nearly eleven P.M. and he had hoped that the *Bratva* would have simply found and scooped up the two fugitive women by now. He knew that Magda and Albert would be arriving at JFK airport soon. He had hoped to have a thief waiting for them at the baggage claim to take them to see the two captives handcuffed and waiting in Brighton Beach.

Albert could have had the satisfaction of saying what he thought of this Sara's behavior and then put a borrowed gun to her head, or simply cut her and let her watch her blood flow out. Then Magda could have taken possession of the other woman, the one who made people disappear. She was worth money only if she was intact.

If Magda was the one to transport her, she would at least arrive in LA without being molested. Magda's first conviction in

Russia was for luring, drugging, and robbing men she met in bars. She was expert at keeping prisoners or kidnap victims sedated but still alive when she wanted to wake them up. But none of that was going to happen tonight. Nobody from the brotherhood in New York had called.

Porchen was frustrated. Could he possibly be the first one to hear that a woman like this existed? No. He'd heard of her years ago, and waited patiently to hear something more that would give him a name, a location, a description. Could he be the first to think that she would be worth money? He knew he wasn't. A smart man could make money from a million things. He just needed enough imagination to realize what each thing had about it that people wanted.

He picked up the remote-control unit for one of the five smart television sets mounted on the wall across from his desk. There were five screens on the wall and five remote controls in a special wooden case on his desk, but the other four had never worked right on the Wi-Fi. He liked to check his email on a big screen, and he wanted to check it now in case someone outside New York had sent him a message about the woman. It took the damned television set a minute to warm up, with a plain black screen slowly displaying white symbols. Why did they have to warm up, when the television sets he saw when he first came to this country thirty years ago hadn't? He hit the right keys on the remote control and then a small arrow appeared, curled around itself and began to rotate in a clockwise motion. Then the words came. "Unable to connect with the Internet. Check Internet service connections or try again later."

He turned it off and tried again, but found the disappointing notice appeared again, but even then it took just as long as it had the first time. The television system was a machine for telling him to go fuck himself. He forced himself to set the remote-control unit in the wooden case with the others. He had found it was expensive to hurl the unit at the screen, so he didn't.

The television system was like everything in this stupid black cube he had ordered built. He had hired the most expensive architectural firm in Santa Monica. They had said that the building would be sleek and technical, but seamless, like the headquarters of the villain in a James Bond movie. It had cost him millions, and he had wasted two years of construction, sometimes driving down here and walking on bare concrete surfaces to look at metal framing and electrical conduits he was supposed to approve. He spent time with subcontractors to look at lighting fixtures, water faucets and sinks, toilets and shower heads, elevator systems, alarm systems, firefighting systems. Three months later he would be looking at other lighting fixtures, water faucets and sinks, toilets and showerheads in showrooms because the ones they had ordered were no longer available and new and more expensive ones were about to be introduced.

And all the electronic systems they installed were shit. He had moved his people into this black cube of a building two years ago, and to this day if you wanted to go down to get your car from the underground garage you had to take the stairs because the elevators didn't work right. A couple of his people had been caught between floors like animals in a trap. He could only use the Wi-Fi system about half the time, and the air conditioning was designed by the devil. When the temperature got hot it turned on and blew hotter air from a series of ducts placed just under the roof, where it was superheated by the Southern California sun. This would make the thermostat force the air conditioner to work harder and harder until it blew some internal circuit breaker and stopped.

He'd had the subcontractor who had installed the garage doors dragged down to the garage and given a chance to make them work. Then he had been driven up into the mountains in his truck, and the truck had been pushed off a cliff. None of the replacement contractors had fixed them either, but Porchen had needed to refrain from killing them before the police recognized the pattern.

Porchen waited for the phone call to tell him Magda and Albert had landed in New York. He had confidence in Magda. She was a true thief, a person who deserved respect. But she was a person of a different generation from him. And no matter how much he liked her he had never been able to feel any sexual interest.

Oleg Porchen was an expert in the human appetites. He understood greed, lust, addiction, and the other urges, and had made a steady income from them for all of his business life. Many young men looked at Magda and loved her tall, thin body, her long legs, and cold, predatory eyes. Magda was having her day, and he was happy for her because she had not been given many advantages. But, before she was born, Oleg Porchen had learned that women who looked like that did not make him happy.

They felt hard to the touch, like skeletons.

The women he liked to be with were the ones who weren't ashamed to have women's bodies. Most women were still like that because they couldn't help it, and most men preferred these women anyway, just as Porchen did. Early in life he had been a purveyor of rooms to adulterous couples on an hourly basis. In the Soviet Union at that time rooms for affairs were scarce. Even engaged couples spent most of their time walking and talking because it was all they could do. But Porchen would pay families to vacate their apartments for an evening so he could rent their beds to couples by the hour. A tiny fee and a bit of intimidation were enough to ensure their participation. And he had a supply of high-quality imported condoms and later even added a special service in introductions. He observed that both men and women cheated with partners who most clearly and vividly represented the opposite sex. Big muscles, hairy chests, and aggressiveness still mattered in the calculus, just as rounded breasts and bottoms and flirtatiousness did.

Porchen's businesses had never been limited to one type. He watched the world around him and found opportunities. When he had the chance to smuggle things into

Russia for the black market, he might sell them to friendly distributors. When he learned something that gave him a chance to rob the same distributors, he did. He imported drugs and sold them and, if the going price was higher in another country, he sold them there.

During the years when the Soviet Union fell apart and Russians discovered that their economy was actually about the size of Mexico's, he had taken advantage of the general desperation. He returned to one of his old strengths and offered pretty girls from Russia and its former dependent states a chance to go to America. The price of the passage was that they agree in advance to work for him in the sex trade for a year. Magda had been one of those girls. He'd had little hope for such an odd girl, but she was confident and smart and had been to prison, so she had to be tough. He took a chance on her.

He noticed that she never tried to cheat on their bargain or even complain. She had been pleasant and enthusiastic to the customers, paid her debt, and got through it. He had then expected her to disappear into the new country as most did, but instead of leaving, she had asked him if she could work for the *Bratva.*

Nobody in the *Bratva* respected anybody for how easy he'd had it. The ones who had tattoos had gotten them during stays in Russian prisons, where artists had taken lavish amounts of time to incise traditional symbols and images that were actually coded messages of identity and experience. Magda's were hidden most of the time by her clothes. The fact that she was a woman and engaged in various kinds of thievery in which her unblemished skin made her money bought her the same respect as a male's history of strong-arm robbery. People used what they had. Porchen had taken her on and she had found things she could do.

The phone in his pocket buzzed and he pressed "accept" hoping it was one of the thieves from Brighton Beach or Long Island calling, but it was Magda. "We're at Kennedy Airport."

He said, "They haven't called to tell me anything yet."

"Then we'll get some hunting time in before we sleep. I'll call you if we catch anything. And you have my number."

"Of course."

"Goodbye for now," she said. She ended the call and set her phone in her purse and started walking. She didn't look to see if Albert was following because she knew he would be. He had no choice, but he said, "What are we doing?"

She said, "We're here, so we'll use the time. We'll start with the airport parking lot. Before we go to the parking lot, spend a minute looking at the pictures in your phone of the car they're driving."

He took out the phone, but as he thumbed from one picture to the next he said, "This is a big place. There must be ten or twelve lots in the airport, and at least that many private ones around it."

She smiled. "We're at the terminal, we have our used boarding passes from our flight here, and so nobody will have any questions we can't answer. You even look like you sat through a long flight. There are many places to park a car, but we're going to look at the most likely one. Their car has been seen a couple of times, and they know it. If they left it at JFK and took another flight it will be in Lot 9, the long-term lot inside the airport. That will give them the most time before people start asking questions about the car and why nobody has picked it up."

Albert compared the pictures that he and Jason DeLong had taken in Buffalo and the nameless Russian had taken in Albany. The Russian's were better and closer, and they showed the rear license plate from Utah. He memorized the number.

"Are you ready?" she asked.

He nodded, so she stood up, hung her bag on her shoulder, and led him to the Air Train. She knew this airport in his country much better than he did, and he had begun to resent her for all of the little superiorities she was demonstrating.

They got off the train at Lot 9. They had only brought light carry-on bags. Since the people who got off the train with them had all parked in the long-term lot, most of them had been away on long trips. Many had multiple large suitcases that they had to drag behind them, bumping along noisily as they searched for their cars.

As Magda and Albert walked with the crowd of travelers, the others found their cars, got in, and drove off, until Magda and Albert were alone, walking along the aisle. Ahead of them were what Albert estimated as a half mile of rows of cars. They trudged along in silence for a few hundred feet, and then Albert heard a car engine behind them that stayed there instead of passing. He turned his head, shielding his eyes from the glare of the headlights. The car pulled up beside them, where Albert could see the words "Port Authority" on the door and a man in a dark uniform driving. Albert thought "Cop." The driver rolled down his window. "Having trouble finding your car?"

Magda transformed herself, hurrying up to the driver's side and bending her knees to look into his eyes. As she crouched, she assumed a cringing pose to squeeze her shoulders upward a little so she looked smaller and more delicate, and as she leaned forward the neck of her dress hung forward slightly and provided a teasing view of her chest. Albert noticed her voice had risen to a sweet, whispery sound that was a feat of theater. Her accent became thicker and she was now a young, inexperienced traveler in a strange country who just needed some patience. "I've looked and looked, but I haven't seen it yet. My cousin here hasn't seen it yet. I came to pick him up."

The driver, whose mind must have been running through the many reasons she had presented to help her, said, "Get in the back seat. I'll go up and down slowly, so you can see all of the cars. Watch for it, and if you think one might be yours, we can stop and look."

Magda and Albert watched for the car, staring hard in the yellowish light of the overhead lamps to find it. It occurred to Albert that there must be thousands of small, old, dull-finished gray cars in this lot. The most distinctive feature was the out-of-state license plate, and if the pro Sara had hired was so smart, she had probably stolen a new plate in New York.

It took another fifteen minutes before they had driven past every car in Lot 9. The driver said gently, "Could you have left your car in another lot?"

Magda became even smaller and more vulnerable. "I must have. I'm so very sorry to have wasted your time and your kindness like this. We'll take a taxi and start looking in other lots in the morning, when the sun is up and we can see better."

At the terminal they took a cab to an upscale hotel along Central Park and checked in. She handled the transaction while he watched the two bags and then carried them. They didn't speak again until they were inside their room. He said, "Is there any chance that they traded the car in and bought a new one?"

"Of course. Or abandoned it on a street with the key in it, or took it to a paint shop to have it painted black, or put it in neutral and rolled it into a river."

"You don't seem disappointed," he said.

"I'm not easily disappointed. We checked off one big possibility, but there are others, and we're not the only ones looking tonight. Take the first shower. Morning comes three hours early in New York." She dialed a number on her phone and said something in Russian, then ended the call.

14

Jane drove the car into a lot in Newark, New Jersey, where Pamela Cashman, a philanthropic but imaginary young woman, donated the car to the veterans' organization that ran the lot. In return she received a receipt that entitled her to claim a $200 deduction on her federal income taxes, if imaginary women paid taxes.

The veteran who ran the lot told her and her friend that the car probably would be either fixed up for resale or stripped for parts and then junked, but even if it was junked it would contribute to the cause. Given the high price of parts, it might be more valuable disassembled.

The two women departed in a rideshare car headed for Manhattan. Donating to a charity was a way Jane had discovered for making cars disappear some years ago. It often took weeks or months before a refurbished car reappeared, and, even then, it had new license plates and often a new paint job. If it was cannibalized it was reduced to nothing.

While Pamela Cashman finished filling out the forms with her false address, Jane used her phone to make an online reservation at the Hilton in Manhattan. She liked big hotels that hosted lots of conferences and conventions. Within an hour they were at the hotel checking in. As they stood in the hotel lobby, Jane checked the electronic display for the events scheduled for the next couple of days. A group of electricians' union representatives was holding its annual meetings in one row of meeting rooms. There were a couple of large corporations that had meetings and training sessions set up in other meeting rooms. Some organizations were not as easily identifiable as others. She had to be careful not to choose a group that was impractical to impersonate, like doctors or police officers. She tentatively chose the annual meeting of a group of librarians, and then walked past a few and saw that they had badges that said only their names and cities, and that they were overwhelmingly female and between Anne's age and her own. On the way up to their room in the elevator Jane noticed that a group of librarians got off on the fourth floor.

After they put their suitcases in their room, they took the elevator down to the fourth floor and then got into a line leading to a table with a sign that said "Registration." When Jane reached the front she said, "I'm Andrea Kibel and this is Beck Rieger. We need to register late. We're from Tarsus, Florida." She paid the double registration fee with her Andrea Kibel credit card. In return they received two canvas bags containing convention schedules and directories and a couple of complimentary books.

When they were back in their room Anne said, "Was that necessary?"

"No," Jane said. "It was just a bit of opportunism. If Albert is getting help from gangsters, they will probably be visiting places Albert thinks you might be. I'm hoping he's convinced that you got on a plane to Europe. But if they're searching in New York, this kind of thing will help us. If somebody sees us in the hotel wearing our library convention badges, we're just two of five hundred or so. If we want to eat dinner, a safe way to do it is to go to the big meeting room where they're doing their welcoming dinner at seven tonight. If we want breakfast, there's a convocation and opening session at seven in the morning. We just paid in advance, and the only people there are going to be our fellow librarians."

"You're always about a mile ahead of me. I don't think I'll ever learn to think that way."

"You're learning things every hour, practically," Jane said. "But the specifics aren't the point. It's the alertness that matters. You have to look. Being part of the librarians' group makes us part of a crowd of women. If a criminal is looking for you, most of the time what he's going to see is a lot of closed doors. He'll see a sign on the door that says 'Cataloging Workshop' or 'Community Outreach Programs' and he'll move on to another floor, maybe to another hotel. You've just made your chance of being caught that day a bit smaller."

"That's what my life will be? Finding ways to make the chance smaller?"

"If you can."

"Does it go on forever?"

"The danger? Sometimes it does. There are feuds in Europe that have lasted since the fourteenth century that people still kill each other over. But most of the time, when it's not heated up by religion or politics, the hatred loses its urgency. The fact that you cheated on your boyfriend and then said, truthfully, that he killed somebody over it might be the other kind of hatred."

"What's the other kind?"

"How old is Albert?"

"Thirty."

"His ego is injured but his body isn't, and he's not in trouble with the police anymore, right?"

"Yes to all of that."

"And I take it that catching you won't give him sole possession of a treasure you two buried together in the desert?"

"No treasure."

"So it's purely a case of revenge by a person who hasn't really lost anything that can't be replaced. At some point he's likely to see another girl and realize there's a better reason to pursue her than you."

"You mean you think that he might give up?"

"Searching for somebody is boring, time-consuming, and expensive. There are a lot of people who get angry enough to kill somebody who betrayed them or testified against them. A high percentage will go through with it if they can get it done within a week or a month. As time goes by, the percentage who keep trying goes down. It's one thing to spend fifteen minutes killing someone you hate. It's another to spend your whole thirty-first year hunting for her. The benefit isn't worth the cost."

"You think Albert is going to say, 'This is too exhausting, so I might as well forgive her'?"

"No. Most people are not smart enough to realize that if they haven't really suffered that much harm, revenge isn't a wise idea. But they are monumentally selfish, and most of them are lazy. As time goes by, more of them move on — in Albert's case, probably to the next girl."

"What are you trying to persuade me to do?"

"To outlast the people who are trying to find you. Often it only takes wanting to live more than they want you to die."

An hour later they went to sleep. Jane sank into a deep, unconscious sleep for a long time before her mind began to work again. She felt drawn upward. She sat up and looked straight ahead and realized she was in the hotel room, but not awake.

In her dream she swung her legs off the bed, walked into the bathroom, and closed the door, and then went to the smoked glass window and slid it open. She climbed up on the sill, put her legs out over the sill, and sat, dangling her bare feet out over the street far below.

"Come down."

His voice had reached her from two floors

below her. She leaned farther out to see down there and realized that his voice had come from a balcony. This one was large and stuck out from the side of the building a few feet, and had a set of French doors that led into a room that seemed huge, like a ballroom. It was a public place, but the lights she could see through the French doors were dim and yellowish, like candlelight.

Harry was standing on the stone railing of the balcony looking up at her. She knew that, by the logic of dreams, she couldn't say no, that she was afraid of heights and wasn't going to climb down. Her father Henry Whitefield had been an ironworker. On his final day he was standing on a girder being lifted into place above a bridge across a river gorge in the state of Washington when the cable snapped. All Jane could do was what she did when she was awake, which was to risk her body and breath for whatever had to be done. In the dream she could see the street below her so far down it looked like a thin black ribbon. By the odd rules of dreams she knew that if she woke up while she was still outside the building the fall would become real.

She eased herself off the windowsill and clung to the indentations in the mortar between bricks, straining with her fingers and toes as she lowered herself, trying to keep a grip. She clutched the bricks and kept moving until she felt the rough concrete railing of the balcony under her foot. She turned, bent her knees, and dropped to the surface of the balcony.

"What do you want this time?" she asked.

Harry raised his bony shoulders in a shrug and held both hands palms upward. "I don't drop by to see you because I'm lonely. Dead people don't lack company."

"I can't help this, Harry. People in my family's religion get messages in their dreams. I don't know why a murdered gambler gets picked so often to deliver mine."

"You don't? I do."

"I do know, Harry. You're my mistake."

"Yes. The one who didn't get away."

"I'm sorry."

"That's the truth," Harry said. "You are always, eternally, sorry. Your sorrow only reminds me of how worthless I was when I was alive. But you asked me what I want. I always want the same thing. I want the universe to be in balance and healthy — 'Sken:nen' in Onondawaono. The right-handed twin Hawenneyu and the left-handed twin Hanegoategeh never rest, one always creating and the other destroying. I hope for them to be in dynamic equilibrium."

"What's up tonight?"

"They seem to be looking in your direction again. Have you felt their eyes?"

"Are you warning me that they're using me in their fighting, or that evil is rising?"

"They use everything, and you know that they're not the same as good and evil, any more than day is better than night. This new girl is a problem."

"She's just a young woman who made some choices that she shouldn't have when she was barely eighteen."

"If it weren't for young women agreeing to do things they shouldn't have, there wouldn't be any people born after the last batch grew up."

"That's right. From now on she might live a valuable life, have children, and make them and their children happy. That would be a nice string of good things."

"Did you not hear her when she told you how she slept with a man she wasn't even attracted to just to see what he would do for her in return? She got him killed."

"When people confess, they don't always make their own best advocates. I think she's probably being harder on herself than she needs to be."

"Some people feel guilty because they are guilty."

"Sometimes it's a matter of degree. Having sex with somebody who got killed for it isn't the same as killing him. People all do things they wouldn't want televised, but hardly anybody deserves to die for them. And keeping somebody from being killed almost always makes sense. So I'm going to try."

Harry made a lazy swatting gesture, as though dismissing it. "That isn't what I came about anyway. Things are heating up now, getting bigger and more complicated."

"Yes. The Russian-speaking criminals. Why would serious gangsters bother to look for a little former barista whose crime was cheating on her boyfriend?"

"Who said they were looking for her?"

15

When Anne Preston Bailey woke up in the hotel in the early morning, she saw Jane was fully dressed and sitting at the desk near the window looking at one of the phones she had bought before they'd gone to Stewart's house.

Anne blinked and sat up. "What are you looking at?"

"Maps. It's another GPS app."

"Where are we going?"

"Massachusetts, I think, but I'm willing to hear your wish list."

"I'll think about it."

"While you're thinking, get showered, dressed, and packed so we can have some breakfast with the other librarians before we go."

Anne rubbed her eyes with the palms of her hands and then walked to the bathroom and shut the door.

In fifteen minutes, she was out and ready

and Jane had read the day's convention schedule. Anne followed Jane to the ballroom and soon they were part of the crowd, sidestepping in a buffet line along a series of silver-covered servers. Jane's eyes occasionally rose and moved from one exit to another to reassure herself that the people coming in were still librarians. She had already decided that if a problem developed, she would take Anne through the door where the food was coming from because a big hotel kitchen always had loading docks for bringing in supplies and a door for taking out the trash.

When they had filled their plates Jane and Anne went to join some women from a library in Rapid City, South Dakota, who seemed cheerful. Jane kept the conversation directed at the women — what they were enjoying about New York, what meetings and events they planned to attend today, and which hours might be better spent exploring the city.

The breakfast was beginning to wind down when an older woman at the head table stepped to a microphone to announce that the morning events would begin in just under ten minutes with a few opening remarks and a convocation. Jane nudged Anne and said to her tablemates that they would be back, but it was accompanied by a wink to the woman beside her, to whom she had hinted that she was going to sneak out to Fifth Avenue and 42nd Street to visit the New York Public Library this morning. They stepped to the row of meeting room doors and went out into the hall.

Jane hurried Anne to the nearest bank of elevators, hit the button, and surveyed the other people in the area. Most of them were from the librarians' group, and in the distance across the lobby she could see that there was a group wearing a set of turquoise name tags. She had seen tags that color near the front desk the night before and she suspected these people were a subcommittee gathering itself for a day of "Welcoming" or "Registration" or something for the chiropractors coming in later. But one person didn't seem right — a man who was facing to the side where there was nothing to look at and speaking into his cell phone, holding it vertically as though it were a microphone. If she kept her eyes on him she would see what he was looking at. A second later she saw him turn his body and look in her direction. She heard the elevator and spun to join Anne inside. She saw that as the door rolled shut the man began to walk quickly toward the bank of elevators.

Jane hurried from the elevator to the room she shared with Anne. "Wipe any surface you can see with a towel or washcloth," she said. As Anne went to work, Jane used the house phone and spoke to one of the doormen downstairs. "This is Miss Sireno in room fifteen nineteen. Can you please get me a taxi right away and ask them to drive around to the back of the building near the loading area? Thank you. What's your name?"

She hung up, snatched her overnight bag and stepped toward the door. Anne took her own bag and followed. "Are we headed for the airport or are you going to surprise me?"

"We have to talk but we don't have time now. When we're in the hallway keep your head down and stay close to me. I'm pretty sure we got spotted downstairs. He's a man about thirty-five with a dark gray suit and a green tie."

She looked out the peephole in the door. An elevator door opened and a few women got out, but after them came the man with the green tie. He looked past the women who had been in the elevator with him, and walked up and down the corridors. When he heard the next elevator open, he hurried to get into it.

As soon as he was gone Jane opened the hotel room door and walked to the row of elevators and pressed the button. In a moment it arrived and Jane and Anne got in with three other women who wore badges from the librarians' convention. The elevator descended two floors and stopped. When the door opened, a fourth middle-aged woman stepped inside. She had no convention badge, but held a cell phone in her hand. She was about the same age and physical type as this group of librarians, but Jane had a different feeling about her. The others were affable, talkative, and relaxed. This woman was none of those things.

Jane faced straight ahead toward the closed elevator doors and glanced downward. The woman's cell phone was lit up. Jane looked harder and recognized the screen held a picture of Jane's own shoes. The camera was on. The woman's body shifted slightly and Jane saw that the image on the screen was changing. The lens was moving up Jane's body.

Jane clutched her overnight bag in her arms and turned slightly so she could keep the bag between the phone and her face. As the elevator descended the woman surreptitiously turned the telephone and moved it to one side. Jane blocked it with the overnight bag. When the woman moved her phone to the other side, Jane moved her bag to keep it blocked. The phone's screen had now held only a picture of the bottom of Jane's leather bag for at least two minutes. The elevator was too crowded to permit the woman to move. Then Jane heard the chirping signal to let the woman know she was getting a text message.

The woman had to twist her wrist to face the screen upward so she could read it, and as she turned the phone up Jane could see the display for a second. The text message was in the Cyrillic alphabet.

Jane's eyes moved away from the woman to the row of numbers above the elevator's door while her hand snaked downward beside her leather bag to the elevator's controls. The woman seemed very anxious and preoccupied now that her phone had startled the group. She hunched over and tapped her thumbs rapidly on the keyboard to send a reply, her eyes only on the screen.

Jane saw the number seven light up, and she pressed the button for floor six. In little more than a second the elevator stopped, and the door rolled open.

Instantly Jane stepped forward with her arms clasped around the woman in a bear hug, lifting and pushing the woman out in front of her. The woman gasped, but she had no way to resist. Jane didn't slow down, just hustled her away from the front of the elevator as the doors closed. Anne stood with her back to the closing door, blocking the other women from seeing what was going on.

Jane hooked her left forearm around the woman's neck under her chin and squeezed to choke her unconscious. She sat her in a plush chair in the elevator alcove, picked up her telephone and ran for the stairwell. Jane removed the battery from the phone and dropped the telephone over the nearest railing so it would fall six stories to the concrete floor of the stairwell.

Anne went down the first few steps in the stairwell as quickly as she could, but Jane said, "Don't go down, go up." They ran up the first two flights taking steps two at a time, and then burst through the door into the hall and ran around two corners to the second set of elevators. She hit the number B-1, and they began to descend.

Anne said, "What's B-1?"

"I'm not sure. B-anything is usually a basement."

The door rolled open, and they could see that they were in a parking garage. There was a man in his forties giving orders to a couple of younger men in maroon vests and black pants who were retrieving cars for hotel guests.

Jane and Anne went around the nearest corner, which brought them to a level where there was daylight visible in two directions. What they could see out one side looked as though it could be at the back of the building, so they moved quickly in that direction, and came out a cavernous entrance. Jane could see the cab she had ordered waiting about fifty feet from the loading dock at the rear of the building. Jane ran toward it and Anne followed.

The driver seemed to notice them, pulled forward, and swooped in to pick them up. He stopped and got out to open the back door. "Where to, ladies?"

Jane said, "White Plains."

"What's the address?"

"Just head there while I look up the address on my phone. I'll have it in a second."

"All right."

"Near the art museum." She had no idea whether there was one in White Plains, but probably there was, or somewhere nearby.

"Okay." As he drove away, he was punching something into his phone, and then he put it back in the dashboard phone holder where he could see it. She sat far back in her seat to keep her head from being visible to anyone on the street, and Anne did the same.

As the taxi took them toward White Plains, Jane looked at her phone. On Google she found "Best Ten Car Dealers," "All Used Car Dealers in White Plains, NY," and a dozen similar entries. She picked out a couple of them, but then went on to the method she usually preferred: "Used Cars Westchester County for Sale by Owner."

She saw pictures of cars that were cheap enough and had reasonably low mileage, made notes, and then called the owner of the most promising and asked if she could see the car right away. Within an hour and a half Anne Bailey had arrived and paid cash for a clean six-year-old Toyota and was driving it northeast into Connecticut.

She held the car on the highway and waited for Jane to start the conversation, but finally felt she had to say, "You told me this morning that we had to talk. When would you like to do that?"

Jane said, "I was just listening to the car, but I think we did okay. I guess this is a good time. Things seem to have changed. We're not running the race I thought we were."

"Yeah," Anne said. "I've been wanting to

ask you about it. I just can't imagine all these people in New York even knowing Albert. Why would they be willing to help him kill me?"

Jane said, "The thing I realized last night was that they haven't been doing that, exactly. Albert has been looking for you. We know that because we saw him and his friend DeLong. So I still have to believe your lawyer Elizabeth that he really does want to kill you. The big part that doesn't fit is the Russians."

"Have you figured out what they're after?"

"They're after me."

They drove in the steady traffic into Stamford, Connecticut. Jane said, "By the way, this is Stamford, with an *M*. It's a nice town, but at the moment it's too close to where they last saw us, and it's too expensive to fit your age and any of the believable covers for you. But keep it in mind. In a year or two it might be a better fit."

Anne said, "This is maddening. You're maddening. You can see I'm terrified and suddenly you're talking like a real estate agent. I need to know what we're going to do."

"For a while we're going to have to do different things."

"What does that mean?"

"When you first came to me, I told you the things I thought you ought to know. One of them was that being with me might be the most dangerous thing you could do. I've taken a lot of people out of the world over the past fifteen years and that makes me seem valuable to certain people."

"You mean the Russians?"

"Yes, but not especially them. To a lot of people who make their fortunes by stealing and exploiting other people. This isn't the first time people have seen an opportunity to turn me into money. I apologize that it seems to be happening again while you need my help. But we've made some progress and we'll make more before I have to split."

"Don't apologize," Anne said. "This has to be Albert bringing them in, and that makes it partly my fault. It's just too much of a coincidence that you kept him from killing me, and then a few days later a bunch of Russians show up."

"When you were with him, did he know them, or have any business with them?"

"Not that I ever knew about, and I was with him day and night. All the money he made came from the parties, ones that had some show business connection. In four years of those parties, I never heard a Russian accent."

Jane sighed. "Well, we've got an infestation now."

"What do we do?"

"Starting tomorrow we get to work finding you a nice, safe, comfortable apartment in Massachusetts and get you settled."

"The thought of it makes me scared. I've never pictured myself living in New England. I've spent my whole life in California."

"That's one of the biggest reasons to be in New England, at least for now. The best and most practical places for the moment are in and around Boston."

"Have you turned runners loose in Boston before?"

"A few," Jane said. "It's a good place for a person who is young and healthy and employable. There are usually jobs, and there are always young people. During the school year there are a quarter of a million college students, not counting grad students and ones in medical, dental, and legal schools, who are too busy to be visible anyway. That brings with it a lot of places where people about your age like to eat, shop, etcetera. We'll look around a bit before I cut you loose."

"Boston is a big place, right?"

"In the good sense, yes. I'm thinking East

Cambridge or Quincy are about right for now. From Quincy you can take the Red Line subway into downtown, and East Boston to Downtown on the Blue Line is about fifteen minutes. Find a place where people look like friends of yours. Just don't forget that they aren't until you know them, and you'll do fine."

16

Magda and Albert took a cab to the Millennium Downtown Hilton hotel in New York. A half block ahead of the entrance Magda told the driver he should pull up to the last car in the cab line and let them out.

Albert got out and started toward the hotel, but Magda said, "We're not going in." She began to walk away from the hotel, and Albert hurried to catch up. "Why not?"

"You and I live far away, and we come and go. Our friends who are helping have to live here forever. The people who run things like this big, shiny hotel aren't here to sleep. When ten or fifteen Russians show up at once they notice, and wonder what's going on. We don't want them to start trying to find out."

"I'm not a Russian. Maybe I should —"

"No. You shouldn't. And that's just one reason."

Magda saw two men standing with their

backs to the front of a building two hundred feet down, and walked along the street toward them. When she reached them she spoke to them in Russian. They turned and greeted her, and she hugged one of them and gave the other a pat on the cheek that was too hard to be anything but a joke, and they laughed and spoke for a moment in a way that could only be banter. Then she stood beside them and launched into a question and answer session during which all three shared the same serious expression.

Albert stood about twenty feet away and looked at the hotel. As he watched, an ambulance appeared from somewhere on the other side of the building and drove off without a siren or warning lights. He felt a moment of hope that maybe one of the Russians he hadn't seen had killed Sara, because there clearly was no rush to get the victim to the hospital. But immediately it occurred to him that there wouldn't still be Russians standing around, and there would be police instead.

Magda came back to join Albert, not slowing down as she passed him. He turned on his heel to walk with her. He said, "You aren't going to introduce me?"

"They know who you are. They all had

your picture already."

"They have my picture? Why?"

"So if they saw the women and you were there they wouldn't kill you. Mr. Porchen didn't want to lose you that way."

"They know me, but I don't know them."

"You don't want to know them. Those two would steal your bones from your arms and legs if they could. I just had to make sure they knew we had searched the airport for the women's car and I wanted to find out what went on here."

"What was the ambulance for?"

"Your girlfriend's professional spotted the woman who was following them, pushed her out of the elevator, and choked her unconscious. The ambulance was driven by a *vor* sent to get her out before anybody asked her questions."

"Do your friends know where Sara and her professional are now?"

"Not yet. But this is good. They're angry at her now, so they'll put more people on it."

"What about us? Where do we look now?"

"The *Bratva* already have people watching the train stations and airports and now they'll have people searching the streets. But the two women are probably not here anymore. Once a fugitive has been spotted, that place is used up for them because they don't know how we spotted them."

"Then what now?"

"We go back to our hotel and wait for word on where they go next. It could take time." They walked along in silence for a few paces. "Do you think I'm pretty?"

He was shocked. It seemed to be a concern that would never occur to her. "I think you're beautiful."

"Good. Then we'll be able to find a way to pass the time." She looked at him and her eyes narrowed. "But afterward, don't think you can touch me whenever you want. That would be a mistake."

17

Jane and Anne checked in at the Sheraton Commander hotel in Cambridge, Massachusetts. They used the next set of cell phones to look at the listings for apartments, then took virtual tours. They picked out a few places and drove to the best ones the next day. On the way to the first one Jane gave Anne the rules for apartments.

"A woman should never take a room on the first floor, because they're too easy to break into. The locks should be expensive and well-made, but not too new, because it means the neighborhood is dangerous and they've had to be replaced. It should be easy to see the grounds outside, but not easy for people outside to see in. Even if there is a fire escape, have a rope ladder rolled up near a window and securely attached to the bed or a radiator. It should be easy to see your car and get to the car safely. You should keep its gas tank full and have driven at least three escape routes out of the city for practice. It would be better to try some more because some of the streets are so old that they're narrow, and the tunnel across town is a mean joke the city played on itself."

They found Anne Bailey a small but bright apartment on the second floor of a building in Quincy with heavy doors that had electronic locks. The mailboxes were indoors and the unit had air conditioning, soundproofing, and assigned parking spaces.

As soon as Anne had moved in, Jane said, "Now that you have an address we can search for jobs. First you figure out what you would like to do. If you want to become a violin maker, you have to find out what gets you into that field. Is it a school? An apprenticeship? Does anybody pay you to do it? We can work, and then get you into the entry level."

"How do we do that?"

"The main thing is that it's what you want and that you're willing to work hard. You're young and pretty and you're quick, and those all help. Not every runner is any of those things. They help you get in the door, but that's all. What I do helps you get from the door through the interview."

"What do you do?"

"Lots of lying. I supply the job descriptions and recommendations from your imaginary last job, your grades from your imaginary school, your licenses or degrees as long as they don't say you can do something you don't know how to."

"Isn't that a lot of work for you?"

"I've done it so many times I can spot people who got their jobs the same way. The idea is to get you hired and started, and then for time to pass so your real record begins to gradually replace the one I made up. Eventually my company's records get to be too old to check, but until then I respond to inquiries."

"Still more work."

"We're trying to design a life for you, one that you will feel is pleasant and worthwhile and provides some security. Then you'll be happy."

"Why do you care if I'm happy?"

"Simple practicality. If you're not scared, you won't look scared. If you smile, you'll get along with people. People who are content with their lives don't do anything stupid to make themselves happy. That's the theory, anyway. They do, but less stupid and less often."

"Fine. How do I start?"

"Write a résumé on the laptop. We'll revise

it, so don't waste much time on formatting and things. The main issue is what you want to do and be. After you know, we'll start looking. Don't ignore internships, trainee jobs, and so on. I can keep you supplied with money for a while."

It took a week to get the applications ready and email the first barrage out. Jane didn't like using headhunter companies, because she had no way of knowing who had access to the information they collected, but she had her own, the McSchaller Company, which she was holding back for the moment. Companies like that worked best for older people who had worked in businesses for years. She did use her invention, the Furnace Corporation, as Anne's former employer.

Anne said, "What if somebody wants to check on me?"

"There's a live response. A woman I know offers the service of keeping companies responsive that don't actually have any offices or employees. She has a few options for any inquiry that arrives about you. I already wrote some out and sent them to her and she plugs in the appropriate one. If nothing fits she'll say the manager is at a sales conference and will have to get back to her."

Anne said, "Her job sounds like a good one for me. Maybe I could start managing imaginary businesses."

"I don't recommend it. It's best to deal with honest people. Her clients are so crooked they try to cheat even her. If they can, they put off paying their first monthly fee until the end of the month, and then claim their check is for the next month, not the last. The next month they can't be reached, and then they start answering their phone a month after that. If they can, they claim they were available all along but couldn't reach her, so they should get a refund. The next month they say they're the new owners who just bought the business. So by now they've got five months free and claim to be somebody else."

Each night, Jane would slip out the back window and close it, then spend an hour or more sitting in the darkest spot outside the apartment at that random hour and watching for enemies. She saw no signs of them in the first week.

Every day since she had left Amherst Jane had spent hours missing her husband, Carey. The nights were the worst, because she would wake up and think about him, wondering what sort of day he'd had. On the eighth night in Boston, she called Carey.

"Hello?" he said.

"Hi. It's me. I'm sorry I couldn't call sooner. It took me a while to figure out what her problem was, and how to make her scarce."

"Does that mean you've finally got her in a safe place?"

"I think so, but I'm giving it a little time before I say the transplant is a success."

"I was hoping you were calling to say you were coming home tonight."

"I think I'm calling to say that I love you. I know that I've done that a lot of times over the past few years. Now when I hear myself say it, I sound to myself like a crooked politician making campaign promises to her own husband. But it's always been true that I love you, even before I was so brazen as to admit it. I'm sorry I had to do this again. Just once it would be a thrill not to have to say anything to explain why I had to disappoint you."

"You have your good moments."

"Believe me, I will again. I want to be with you. All the rest of this stuff isn't about our life. It's just about salvaging other people's mistakes so they can still breathe and giving them another shot at things. At first it always seems simple. But it's been pretty clear for a while that I've done this too many times. After this I'm going to be very hard to recruit for any good causes."

"It's that bad but not bad enough to come home?"

"There are some puzzling aspects to her problems, and that's what's taking time. I'm trying to get home as soon as I can."

"Is there anything that I can do to help? I know that you feel you have to do the work alone, but something minor and anonymous, like picking you up or sending money or anything?"

"Not a chance. I would only be putting you in danger for some kind of convenience. It's a crappy offer."

"I'm kind of at the end of my patience, and you don't seem to leave me anything I can do about it. But if you need me to, then I'll wait."

"Please do. I'll be out of touch for a while again, but I'll be back before you know it. Bye." She hung up and went inside.

Three days later Anne came home from an interview, dropped her purse by the door, and did a little dance.

Jane raised her eyes for a moment, closed the laptop, and said, "Congratulations. Tell me about your job."

The job was to be a team member in a business that produced advertising art and copy for a number of larger advertising companies in and around Boston, and also for a growing group of smaller freestanding businesses like restaurants, coffee shops, boutique clothing stores, antique shops, decorators, and hair stylists. She said, "I mostly owe it to your frauds, but I actually am good at this. And while they were giving me a tryout I did a pitch and brought in a customer, a guy who makes over buildings to be green and self-sustaining."

The next night when Anne came home Jane had the table set for a celebration dinner taken out from a Boston restaurant. After that she watched the neighborhood, the apartment, the car, and listened carefully to Anne's descriptions of her day to be sure that she was continuing to do well at work. And she began to pack some of the belongings she had brought with her from the cache in her old house or purchases from their trip.

A week later Anne returned at the end of a workday and found Jane sitting in the living room wearing an olive drab shirt, a pair of gray pants, and hiking boots. There was a backpack on the floor near the door.

"What's going on?" Anne asked.

"It depends," Jane said. "You just finished another week of work and another week of living in this apartment. How do you feel?"

"It's been great," Anne said. "I like it." She reached into her purse, took out a slip of paper and handed it to Jane.

"Your first paycheck!" Jane said. "Wonderful." She handed it back.

"I already deposited it electronically." She frowned. "But I suppose that means we're done, doesn't it?"

Jane shrugged. "I've done my best to look around here for trouble, and I haven't found any. Everything I've seen says you'll be fine in Boston. But if things change, get out. Do not hang around thinking things will go away or get better. Get into your car and go. Call me from the road while you're driving at the speed limit."

"Thank you."

"I've left you some things in your room. One is the pistol I showed you at Stewart's that night. It's loaded. I've taped it on the inside of your closet above the opening so nobody will see it, but you can reach up, take it down, and use it if you need to. Another present is ten thousand dollars, split between the inner zipper pocket of your jacket and the zipped compartment of your purse. As a rule, you should use your Anne Bailey credit cards. But if you have to travel anonymously, use cash. I also left you one more burner phone so if you have to ditch yours you can still call me or the police."

"Thank you, Jane. You saved me several times and kept me from needing to be saved a dozen more. My whole chance amounted to making it to you."

"I have one favor to ask of you. Drop me off at a car rental place, and then I'll be gone."

"All right. When?"

"No time like now."

They got into Anne's car and Jane Googled for a rental place ten miles away. Then she conveyed the phone's directions to Anne, who drove her to a place in Chelsea, not too far from Logan Airport, and let her off, then drove down the street to watch from a distance while Jane rented a car. After a few minutes Anne saw Jane drive out of the lot and down the street.

Anne drove off in the opposite direction from Jane, returned by a roundabout route to Quincy, and climbed the stairs to her apartment. It occurred to Anne as she sat in her apartment alone that she had spent most of her time for the past month thinking about Jane and about what Jane knew that she would need to know. But now the lessons were over. If there was something else she had desperately needed to know how to do, she hadn't learned it. The parts of her training that she was fairly certain she had acquired were the quiet, time-related parts — patience, the willingness to forego the attention of strangers, the ability to look at herself without illusion and, if necessary, change her appearance, habits, and habitat.

She had been too busy being scared to spend too much time thinking about the part that Albert had contributed to her life. She had spent four years thinking she was in love with him and then realizing that she couldn't possibly be. Maybe she just wasn't capable of loving another person and it had nothing to do with him. She was certainly selfish enough to cheat on him.

For a few weeks Jane had supplied all of her need for human companionship. She was, in a way, like a parent — very reliable and in charge, but not really willing to open up about what being her was like, what she felt in her guts. Most of the time she had talked about Anne. Who in the world didn't love being the one who was talked about? But because they were trying to design, build, and train this new person together, much of the conversation about her was theoretical. And now Anne was real and alone.

That, at least for now, was Anne Preston Bailey. She was a young woman who was always going to be alone. She would be going to sleep in a few hours in an apartment alone. Tomorrow morning she would be waking up for the first time completely alone. There would be no friendly chat, no tips about how to live wisely, no observations, just the sound of her own heartbeat and her own breathing. She imagined she would probably become one of those women who show up at work in the morning early every day because there is nobody at home.

It occurred to her that she didn't really know very much about Jane. The lessons weren't about Jane, whatever her life was. They were about self-preservation. Anne decided that might be enough to have learned in one burst. She spent the next three hours working on a project for an Ethiopian restaurant. She had taken some pictures of the interior of the dining room during the day, and they had brightly colored tables that made her want to be there. She was able to be captured completely by the details of the job and push out of her mind the fear and the lonely feelings. When she finished the parts of the project she could do that night she sent the files to her computer at work and went to bed, already falling asleep.

18

Jane got on Route 90, intending to take the Massachusetts Turnpike west to the Hudson River at Albany. It occurred to her that in the old days some of her Haudenosaunee grandfathers must have followed the same route to get home from scouting missions to the coast. The Haudenosaunee followed the policy of keeping track of what was happening as far north as James Bay in northern Canada and as far south as the countries of the Cherokees, Catawbas, and others at the southeastern end of the Appalachian Mountains, and as far west as the Hurons and Ojibways in the western Great Lakes. Groups of three or four men would travel hundreds of miles by canoe and on foot, remain invisible, and watch the people who lived in those distant places. Some of them were perennial enemies in the endless wars of the forests, and others were people who might be either enemies or potential allies.

The best way to know was to watch and wait. Sometimes the warriors watched and waited alone outside foreign villages for a year or two before their role was determined. They might become unexpected emissaries or unexpected attackers.

The things that Jane had spent her adult years doing had seemed to her to be simply logical responses to the situations she encountered. She would learn that someone was being hunted by people who were a credible threat to murder him. The obvious response for a person like Jane, who had figured out how to hide people, was to do it. This involved taking him from a place where he was in danger to a new place where nobody knew him, manipulation or replacement of the governmental and commercial records that existed about him to make him hard to find, teaching him how to be a new person, and turning him loose.

What she hadn't realized at the time was that the idea for what she did must have been composed from pieces of the information that had passed from generation to generation from her remotest ancestors to her. For hundreds of years Seneca and other Haudenosaunee nations were engaged in the wars of the forests. The fighting was terrible and caused huge and constant casualties. The five — later six — nations were all engaged in replenishing their numbers by taking in and adopting refugees from distant wars, fugitives, captives, even at times whole bands who had come to them for safety, and even runaways from the English, Dutch, and French colonies. The way this was done was to give the new person the place of a deceased Seneca. He would inherit that person's family, friends, and clan members, and gradually take on his responsibilities. He would, to the extent that he could, live his namesake's life and be absorbed into the people. Jane realized now that what she'd been doing was performing almost exactly the transformation her tenth great-grandmother had probably done — taking the endangered person out of existence and making him into a new person with a second chance at life.

The longhouse-shaped tract of land from the Niagara to the Hudson, with the Senecas at the western door and the Mohawks at the eastern, the Onondagas in the center tending the council fire, and the Oneidas and Cayugas to the east and west of them, had become New York State, and Jane had been raised in a modern town to be a modern woman. She had gone to Cornell University and later married a man she met there who had become a doctor. There was much about the world that had not changed. Jane was on her way home, hoping to get there before her husband left for his surgeries at the hospital in the morning, but home was situated at a place where the Senecas out on missions had been returning to forever.

She saw a lighted supermarket and pulled her rental car into the lot to buy a few supplies — some bottled water, nuts, and fruit to eat while she was on the long solitary drive. But as she pulled in she saw another set of headlights appear behind her, make an abrupt turn to get across the right lane she had just left and swing awkwardly into the lot. She kept going around the building and parked, then stepped to the corner of the market where there was a long line of shopping carts. She took one and headed for the entrance, but held the new car in her view.

There were four men in the car. They ranged in age from about forty to about twenty. They were all white — very white. Two were blond, one had brown hair, and the other the sort of black hair that looked dyed against his pale skin. They were wearing clothes that made them look as though they had been out at a bar. They had sport coats, jeans of blue or black, and dress shirts with one too many buttons unbuttoned at the neck. She looked up as she pushed her cart. When she could she held them in the reflection in the big dark front and side windows, and at other times she would check the big mirrors that were up above the corners to keep forklift operators from hitting customers.

Jane studied the store. There were about ten reasonably attractive women in the place at the moment — three women in their thirties, two in their early forties, and about five younger ones who seemed to be all together in a pack. There was no reason why Jane would be the only person the four men would stare at, but they had an unhealthy interest in her and only her. Jane noticed one of the men carrying a red plastic hand basket that he filled with sugary snacks and two bottles of clear liquor. When his nearest friend started to overload it with more items, Jane was close enough at the time to hear him protest in what sounded like Russian. She kept walking, went to the express aisle to check out with a credit card, and hurried toward the door.

In the corner of her eye she caught a quick movement and saw two of the men stride to the automatic door marked "IN" and slip past an old man hobbling in. Jane moved around the outside of the building, snatched her bag of snacks out of her cart, got into her car, and started the engine.

The two men appeared on both sides of her car and tugged the door handles in the hope that she had left one of them unlocked. She shifted and drifted forward, but the two men pounded on her windows with alarmed looks on their faces as though there had been an accident and she needed to stop to talk to them. She tapped the gas pedal and turned her steering wheel to swing the front wheels toward the man on her left. He dived to the pavement to avoid her car, then tried to get up in time to move in front of her, but she veered away from him. The other man pushed an empty shopping cart toward her to stop or at least damage the car, but its wheels spun sideways and it toppled without hitting anything.

In a few seconds she was out of the lot and heading for the entrance to Route 90. She had no idea what they knew about her, but she certainly wasn't going to lead them in the direction of her home and her husband. When she reached Route 90, she accelerated onto it, drove west at a high speed, and then took the interchange where it met I-95 and headed north.

Jane could see no sign of the car she had seen them drive into the lot, a dark blue Lincoln Navigator. The men could not possibly have finished checking out and made it to their SUV in time to see which way she had been headed on I-95, or in fact to see her at all on Route 90. She was, if things were as they appeared, entirely free of them.

As Jane drove north, she thought about the four men in the Lincoln. They had somehow found her after she had rented this car. The gang could have guessed in advance that a person on the run was going to need things — a place to sleep, food, a fresh car. But even if they had, they wouldn't have known or been able to predict where she was going to get them. To rent a car, Jane had simply pulled up dots on the map of the Boston area and picked out one of them. She had deliberately chosen one that wasn't especially close or convenient to Anne's apartment, but was not far from the airport, a common area for rental cars.

As Jane went over the past few days, she could find no moment when she had slipped up, no time when she had not been aware of the people around her, the cars and trucks that might have been hiding a watcher, all the mistakes she might have made. There were none.

The four men had not followed her from the car rental lot, either. She had been extremely careful from the beginning of her trip until she had stopped at the market.

She knew what must have happened. The Russian organization that was after her must have sent copies of the pictures the man in Albany had taken of her and Anne to all of their colleagues, friends, and affiliates in the Boston area.

Some Boston friend of theirs in the car rental business must have recognized Jane from her picture. Rental car lots had systems for tracking their fleets of cars based on the old LoJack systems, and they had turned this one on. Those systems weren't like the cheap portable transmitters she had removed from Sara's old car. She had learned the way to kill one. It began with disconnecting the negative cable from the car's battery, removing a fuse, and then finding and cutting as many as ten wires that the installer had hidden in the car's regular wiring. That part took hours.

She probably didn't have a lot of time before the four men caught up with her again. She would have to do something. She got off I-95 onto Route 1, and then glided into Newburyport. She parked the car on the main street in front of the police station, put the water and nuts in her daypack, locked the car, took the keys, and set the alarm. She walked a few blocks at a brisk pace and put her arm out to hitchhike.

The streetlamps were bright, so drivers had a good look at her before they stopped. Her appearance was in her favor. She was female, slim and uninjured, was wearing clothes that were clean and in style, and smiled as she signaled for a ride, but not too enthusiastically. After a few minutes a car pulled over and she trotted up to the right side. The car was a Cadillac CT5, and it looked new. Jane leaned down when the window began to slide open.

The driver was a woman about forty with long reddish-brown hair. She said to Jane, "You're not a robber or a sexual predator, are you?"

Jane laughed convincingly. "No, if you're hoping to collect a reward, I'm not wanted. I just had my rental car break down."

"Was it back there a ways on the street? The black Lexus?"

"Yes. I left it by the police station so the tow truck could find it."

"Can I take you somewhere?"

"I'm trying to get as far north as I can. I was supposed to meet somebody in Bar Harbor, Maine, for a little vacation. If I can get far enough, maybe she'll be able to meet me and we'll drive up there together."

"I live in Portsmouth, New Hampshire. I can take you that far if you'll help me stay awake."

"That would be wonderful," Jane said. "Should I get in the front?"

The lock button on the door popped up and Jane got in and sat in the passenger seat. She set her backpack on the floor and settled in with her feet over it. She had no idea what might happen tonight, and the pistol was in the backpack, so she didn't dare put it in the back where she wouldn't be able to reach it. The woman checked the mirror before she pulled out, and then headed for the I-95 entrance. "My name is Clarice Endicott," the woman said.

"Janet Fortin," Jane said. They made a show of shaking each other's hands, really just a grasp and single shake and release. Jane hadn't been Janet Fortin in a long time, but the name felt like who she was going to be tonight. She mentally located Janet's license and American Express card in her wallet, made a few advance decisions about Janet, and enjoyed the feeling of accelerating into the night again.

After a few minutes she was persuaded that Clarice was a competent, experienced driver, and not insane or criminal. Jane said, "If you get tired I'll be delighted to drive. I'm really good at it, and it relaxes me. I also would love to pay for a tank of gas."

"That's very polite, but not necessary," Clarice said. "This is my regular commute. I'm a lawyer, and I have to make the trip into Boston a couple of times a month, so I'm used to it."

"Well, you're doing me a big favor. I was sure I was going to have to waste hours outside that tiny local police station with that injured car while the mechanics from the rental place drove a replacement car up here for me. This way I'll at least get as far as Portsmouth before I have to give up and find a hotel for the night."

"I'm glad I can help."

"Thank you," Jane said. "This is such a beautiful part of the country that I like to get here at least once every year just to have my memory banks renewed. I was in Boston for a week or so, but now it's time to go turn myself over to nature for a while. The sea along the Maine coast should clear the cobwebs out of my brain."

"It's a good idea. My husband and I live up above the sea outside Portsmouth and so I get to walk the beach a lot. But I do envy your vacation. You know what I'd like to do sometime?"

"What?"

"Every year, when early spring comes, I start getting the urge to hike the Appalachian Trail."

Jane said, "I think you're a lot more adventurous than I am. It's two thousand miles. Mountains, forests, crossing ice-cold rivers and streams."

"More than two thousand."

"It could be dangerous," Jane said. "You could die from a twisted ankle on top of some deserted mountain."

"You could die from faulty wiring in your kitchen."

"But at least I'd have a nice warm send-off."

Clarice laughed. "I can see I'm going to have to keep picking up more hitchhikers and asking them before I find my hiking buddy. My husband turns me down every year, but it's not because he's timid. He's done the whole trail. It was when he was young, and he just doesn't want to do it again. A couple of years ago he did a cost breakdown to show me how many days of work we would lose, what each of us had made per day in the previous year, what we would spend per day, what it would cost to board our dogs and have a caretaker watch the house, and so on."

"That didn't work, did it?"

"No. He thought because I'm a practical person I'd care that the trip wasn't practical, but his arguments just made the whole idea more real and specific, and made me want to keep on with the planning. I told him we could start on this end and just do the northern part. You can get right on the trail by stepping between two buildings off Main Street in Hanover, New Hampshire, a block from Dartmouth College."

"What did he say?"

"That the northern end is the worst. The strongest wind ever recorded on the planet was on a mountain in New Hampshire. And then in Maine you have to get through the Hundred-Mile Wilderness."

"What's that?"

"Pretty much what it sounds like. The last hundred miles, from Monson to Mount Katahdin, is still wild, with no civilization, no services, no food. And I guess for him it would include his wife the lawyer talking his ear off the whole way."

There had been steady, unchanging traffic on I-95 since Jane had gotten her ride, but she had not forgotten that the four men might not have stopped where she had abandoned the rental car. She had expected that they would spend some time driving around in the town of Newburyport searching quiet streets and public buildings for a glimpse of her. They would not find any sign of her, and at that point they would have to make a decision. Either they could go back to Boston or drive their Lincoln back onto the I-95 and try to learn what had become of Jane.

She felt the answer in her body, first the irritation of a flash of white light as the high-beam headlamps of a vehicle coming up behind poured glare into Clarice's car. "That's awful," Jane said, and leaned back so her head was below the level of the headrest on her seat. The source of the light was coming up fast, and Jane could hear the growl of an engine.

Clarice reached up to flip the switch that made the mirror darken so the glare in her eyes was dimmed. "I just hate people like that. It's so rude."

Jane leaned slightly to the right so she could see the side mirror and recognized the Lincoln. Crouching lower enabled her to slip her right arm down beside her leg and wrap her hand around the grips of the pistol she had hidden in the pocket of her backpack. She prepared herself for the next thing she would have to do, which was to touch the automatic window switch with her left hand to lower her window into the door so she could shoot the Lincoln's driver.

She held the gun, flexed her legs to prepare, and waited for the car to move forward far enough so she couldn't miss.

The car that was just to the right of theirs and moving ahead was the Lincoln. Jane could see the driver, and she was sure he was the older man from the supermarket. The two younger ones who had come out of the store after her were in the back. Once the driver was dead they wouldn't matter.

The sedate Clarice exploded. She leaned on the horn, pounded the window switch so the window came down and turned a face of rage toward the driver of the car beside her. "You moron!" she shouted. "Turn off those brights!" Her flame-red hair flared wildly in the wind and her teeth were bared in a feral snarl. Jane raised her left eye just above the door as she held the pistol ready, hidden at her side, but Clarice's blaring horn had startled the Lincoln's driver so badly that he veered away from Clarice's car two lanes to the right.

There was a moment when the two cars were running parallel, but then the Russian accelerated rapidly to pull ahead. Jane was fairly certain that the driver had looked at

Clarice and realized she wasn't Jane, and that was all he'd wanted to know. But as he moved ahead, Clarice changed lanes after him and turned on her high-beam headlights.

"Wow," Jane said quietly. "That was fun." She hoped the fun was over.

Clarice switched off her bright lights and resumed her lane, and then laughed. "Sorry. It's a pet peeve. Sometimes these people will get on the interstate behind you and keep blinding you for fifty miles. Somebody has to say something."

Jane slid the pistol back into the pocket of her backpack and looked ahead for the Lincoln to reappear. She hoped that they would speed ahead as quickly as they could and search for her. She formed a tentative plan to stop at Portsmouth with Clarice, discard the gun and wait in the airport for the first plane to anywhere. By then the four men would probably be backtracking, but she could go through the airport security checkpoint and stay in a ladies' room during the wait.

She was aware that as they drove north along the seashore, they were moving into areas that were less crowded in early spring and where the police were not used to opponents like Russian gangs. But at least until Portsmouth her best strategy was to stay with Clarice.

For the next fifty miles Jane searched the northbound lanes of I-95 for the blue Lincoln, but never spotted it. As the traffic thinned with the late hour she searched harder, looking at any parallel road, any parking lot she could see from the interstate, and cars coming south on the left lanes, when she could see beyond the flare of headlights. She kept Clarice talking, asking her about life in Portsmouth and New England in general.

"You ventured out of Boston at a good time," Clarice said. "From the minute the snow melts until Labor Day we're up to our asses in tourists. Around Labor Day Boston gets even worse, because of all the students. But we're almost at spring break, when they go learn things that aren't in the syllabus. Your little trip should be nice."

"I'm glad to hear that," Jane said. "There's nothing worse than going somewhere you know you'd love and having all the rooms occupied."

They chatted steadily for the next hour and then Jane saw the sign for the first Portsmouth exit. "It looks as though we've about reached our destination," she said.

"I'm happy to drop you off anywhere,"

Clarice said. "In fact, I have an idea. Why not stop at my house for an early breakfast? While we're doing that, we can call a rental place to bring you a fresh car."

"That's a terrific idea," Jane said. "But I think I'll opt for the airport and fly out. And breakfast is a lot to ask of you before dawn."

"Oh, that's okay. I'm not tired." She took the exit, and as they coasted down the off-ramp, she said, "It'll be fun. Bart's away in San Francisco, so we won't wake him up and cause him to doubt my sanity. Again."

She drove into town along a series of roads that took them through the harbor and then up a hill above the ocean to a pretty white house with a view of the town. "This is it," she said. She parked and got out, opened the trunk, and took out a suitcase and a huge lawyer's briefcase. "You may as well leave your pack. I'll drop you at the airport afterward." She closed the trunk and walked to the back door. She let Jane into the kitchen and took her own luggage to another part of the house. She came back a few seconds later and said, "The nearest rest-room is through there and to the left."

Jane followed the directions to the bathroom. She decided it was a good time to refresh her makeup. The dashboard lights of a car were flattering or at least forgiving, but daylight was coming soon, and she would be out and traveling again. As she finished, she heard noises coming from the part of the house she had left, and couldn't make sense of them. One sounded like a man's voice, but muffled and low. Had Clarice's husband stayed home after all? Clarice's voice joined in, and then the outer door slammed. Things seemed wrong. The bathroom window was translucent, textured glass, so she couldn't see anything.

She stepped into the hall and saw the master bedroom doorway. Clarice's overnight bag and her legal case were on the floor, and her keys were on her dresser. Jane stepped to the window. She could see the blue Lincoln parked in the yard near Clarice's Cadillac. Jane stepped to the dresser, slipped Clarice's keys into her pocket, and crouched below the level of the windows as she moved down the hallway toward the kitchen. She listened as she went, trying to figure out what was happening. Had the four men waited in Portsmouth to ambush Jane because it was the first good-sized city in that direction? Had they simply spotted Clarice's Cadillac and wanted to punish her for honking her horn and shouting at them? Had they seen Jane's head when she'd ducked down in the other window? Or was it the purest bad luck, four criminals choosing this house as a place to stop for the morning because it was the only one with lights on?

Jane reached a point where she could see into the next room and learned that none of her questions mattered. Clarice Endicott was lying on her back on the floor, her open, unmoving, and unseeing eyes staring up at the stainless steel hood above the island cook top. What had sounded like a door slamming had not been that. Jane retreated down the hall, looking for a way out.

The master bedroom window was too close to the blue Lincoln parked in the yard. Jane kept going a few steps down the hall into another bedroom. She closed the door and went to the window that didn't face the Lincoln or the driveway, but the neighbor's house. She reached above the lower curtain, slid the latch open, and very slowly and carefully raised the window. There was a metal screen that was held in place by a hook and eye. She opened it, pushed her legs out the window and lowered herself to the ground. Then she lowered the window again and pushed the screen shut. She inserted one of Clarice's keys under the frame of the screen and used it to push the hook back into the eye, and then went down on her hands and knees beside the house.

Jane heard male voices talking indistinctly, and then some thumping feet as the men spread out inside the house. Jane looked in the direction of the sounds, and saw the curtain in the master bedroom tugged aside, then released. She heard heavy footsteps inside the house, so she pushed her body against the side of the house and remained still.

She heard the thudding steps come to the other side of the wall and stop, then heard a scrape as the curtain inside the window was jerked aside. There was a two second pause, and then the footsteps moved off.

Jane crouched, then made her way around the house to the driveway. Clarice's Cadillac was still sitting there while the men ranged through her house, probably looking for plunder of some sort. Jane stayed low and as close to the side of the house as she could without touching it and making some subtle noise. She made her way to the driver's side of the Cadillac, got her thumb and forefinger on the ignition key and clutched the rest of the keys to keep them from swinging, and used her free hand to push the car's door handle.

The fact that the door was unlocked excited her. She had a chance. She wouldn't have to push the button on the key fob and make a beeping noise to unlock it. She shifted her body to the edge of the door, swung it open, and got inside. She inserted the key and pulled the door almost shut, started the engine, and looked behind her.

She saw two men coming out of the house as she backed out of the driveway. The men began to run toward her and she slammed the door beside her, then swung out to take the car out the way Clarice had driven to bring her here. As she accelerated away from the house, she heard the sound of pistol rounds being fired in her direction, but they stopped after a couple of shots, as though one of the men had batted the gun out of the other's hand. They certainly didn't want police coming to investigate shots.

Jane headed north, driving as fast as she dared. The road was still sparsely traveled, so she kept pushing her speed until the sun was up and more cars trickled onto the highway. When she reached the exit for Portland, she switched to Interstate 495 and headed north away from I-95. As she reached Lewiston, she made up her mind about her destination. It almost seemed as though Clarice Endicott had given her the answer. Her decision meant she had to stop in a big sporting goods store, so she began to look for one on her phone. She found a mall with a couple of them. It was after ten A.M., and so the first store was open. She parked Clarice Endicott's car beside a dumpster, hurried into the store, and took a shopping cart.

Her shopping had to be done efficiently, because it wasn't out of the question that the men in the Lincoln would guess correctly that she had gotten off the interstate. Her important choices came quickly. She needed a good, large waterproof backpack, an ultra-light freestanding tent, and a 30-degree-rated sleeping bag. She found a good pair of waterproof hiking boots, a first-aid kit, soap, DEET mosquito repellent, a compass, waterproof matches, a lighter, a hunting knife, a hatchet, a cooking pot, monofilament fishing line. They had hundred-pound test line, presumably because they weren't far from the ocean, so she chose that. She added two one-liter bottles that incorporated water filters, a supply of water-purifying pills, biodegradable toilet paper, and toilet bags. She went to the women's clothing area and picked up hiking pants that could be converted to shorts with a zipper, wool socks, underwear, synthetic fabric tops and a hooded jacket, a cashmere watch cap, and a hat with a wide brim. She knew she had to save room in her pack for food, but she was pleased to see they had three items all experienced woods travelers knew about — mosquito netting, gloves, and a pair of Crocs shoes. When Jane reached that point, she studied her purchases and then went to find waterproof sleeves and bags for every item. She added a rainproof poncho, a thick plastic tarp, fifty feet of climbing rope, and a self-inflating sleeping pad. At the end of the trip through, she picked up a roll of duct tape, a pack of six steel arrowheads, a bag of assorted fish-hooks, and a tube of quick-setting epoxy cement.

When she got into the car she took the time to pack everything into and onto her large backpack. She put the small daypack containing the things she had brought with her — sunscreen, lip balm, eye drops, and the bottle of distillate she'd made from the juice of *Cicuta maculata,* water hemlock — into the big pack. The liquid looked like perfume, but a tablespoon of it would kill her in minutes. She had always felt that promising one of her runners that she would die rather than give them up would be a lie unless she carried the means to accomplish it.

When she was ready she drove again. She went north on Route 4 to Farmington, which was a pleasant-looking small town with a college. She switched to Route 2 as far as Skowhegan, slept in the car on a deserted lot, and then switched again onto Route 150 and drove the rest of the morning on Route 6 to Millinocket. There she found other outfitters' stores that offered maps of the Appalachian trail. She made another stop at a food market.

The trailhead she was here to enter was the most difficult part of the Appalachian Trail, the Hundred-Mile Wilderness. The terrain ranged from mountains to swamp. She knew the sort of food she needed — a modern simulation of the food the old people had taken. It needed to be compact, high protein and moderate carbohydrate, and it was essential that it be light. She selected things like tuna or meat in packets instead of cans, protein bars, soup in envelopes, powdered eggs. As she worked at her shopping she didn't just guess, she counted meals. A hundred miles could easily take ten days, which was thirty meals. But a happy ten-day trip included ten snacks.

She drove to the start of the trail at the Athol Bridge near Baxter State Park. She parked Clarice Endicott's car with the few others already there, stepped into the trail station, bought a permit, signed the name Karen Sireno, provided identification, and listened to the volunteer's tactful questions. Was she a very experienced hiker, in good health and physical condition? He didn't recommend hiking alone anywhere, least of all here. It was April, so the bulk of the trekkers hadn't arrived yet, and it was still a month or two before the first large groups of northbound hikers would get this far from Georgia. Jane listened politely, thanked him, and left.

When she stepped onto the trail, the first sign was a large wooden one painted the reddish color of a barn, giving hikers fair warning. "It is 100 miles south to the nearest town at Monson. There are no places to obtain supplies or help until Monson. Do not attempt this section unless you have a minimum of 10 days supplies and are fully equipped. This is the longest wilderness section of the entire AT and its difficulty should not be underestimated."

Jane removed the battery from her cell phone and sealed both into one of her waterproof bags and stowed it. Then she began to walk. The northern stretch of the two-thousand-mile trail began in the shadow of Mount Katahdin, a giant rock covered with smaller rocks. Katahdin meant "the highest mountain" in the Penobscot language. She smiled to herself. One of the things about Indian names for places that others didn't all remember was that most of them were coined for giving people directions, not attracting tourists.

While it was the highest mountain in Maine, it wasn't the altitude that mattered to Jane. It was the angle of ascent. The difference between the foot and the peak was over four thousand feet. The other sign that mattered to Jane was that although it was April, there was still some snow visible near the top. If there was still snow up there, then the spring melt was not over. Some of the streams could be torrents fed by melting snow, and the wet places could be swamps swelled into lakes.

Jane began by following the first stretch of trail into the forest. She reminded herself that the decision to disappear into the woods was her own. Even though Clarice had given her the idea, Clarice had known nothing about her that was true. Clarice had thought Jane was, like her, a prosperous woman in early middle age, thinking about Clarice's invitation to take a strenuous wilderness walk. Jane was those things, but she was also an athlete in superb physical condition.

Three or four years ago Jane had engineered the escape of an innocent man named James Shelby from the Clara Shortridge Foltz Criminal Courthouse in Los Angeles. Things had gone smoothly while she disguised him in street clothes and got him to the ground floor as the courts adjourned for lunch so he could get out in the lunchtime crowds. But enemies had recognized him and Jane had needed to buy him enough time to get to the car she had parked for him. She'd had to stop in the sunken patio entrance, turn back, and fight to delay three men to keep them from catching up with him. She had been successful because she had made male bystanders think the three had attacked her. But after a few minutes men impersonating cops had pretended she was under arrest, and a few minutes later one of them shot her.

Over the next few days Jane had learned what a group of criminals would do to get her to betray the runners she had saved. Even after she had been shot, she had been drugged, beaten, burned, cut, and clubbed. When it was over she'd had to spend years healing her body and relearning to walk normally and then run again, and then building herself back up to the level of strength, speed, and endurance she'd had before.

Right now she was carrying a pack that was almost fifty pounds. She knew she could do it as long as she had to, and she also knew that as the days went on she would use up many of the things in the pack and maybe find that others weren't useful enough to continue to carry.

Jane followed the trail upward because the peaks were the best vantage points for seeing the approach of enemies. The earliest Paleo-Indian village sites were in the high places, so the hunters could see the movement of the migrating caribou herds.

Jane had come here to follow a different strategy. Jane was confident she had succeeded in saving Sara, resettling her, and giving her a good chance to become Anne. But along the way Jane had attracted a new, and far more formidable, set of enemies, and she was the one they wanted. The network of gang members had found her in Albany, traced her to New York City, tracked her rental car from Boston, and found her again in Portsmouth. Jane had no doubt they would find out where Jane had left Clarice's car. They might not find the car, but soon the police would be looking, too, and if the Russians didn't succeed, the

273

police would. She hoped that by the time the gangsters learned where Jane had left the car they would think Jane was too far ahead to catch.

But if they were determined to come after her away from the settled places and the pavements and into the wilderness, they would be following her into a different world, a place where the advantages were no longer all on their side.

19

As Albert McKeith drove the Chevrolet Tahoe onto Route 95 North near White Plains,
he was relieved to be in a car and feeling
useful again. Much of his life in California
had been spent behind a steering wheel. The
stay in the hotel in New York with Magda
had been an experience that he would
remember until he died.

Right now, a week after it had occurred,
he could easily see the moment when she
had stripped off her clothes for the first
time, and then his. Her body was incredibly
beautiful, even defaced with the weird Russian prison tattoos she said showed she was
a thief. She was wild and playful to the point
of being rough and aggressive, but she could
also be gentle, and even submissive. She
told him later that she had learned to be
everything for a man when she had come to
America. She had worked as an escort for a
while to cover her travel expenses. There

275

was a pride in her skill, but maybe a hint of resentment, too, and the two feelings seemed to compete.

Magda moved back to the second set of seats and lay down across them. "This is comfortable," she said. "When we have her, we're going to have to drive her across the country back to California. This wouldn't be a bad car to use." She rolled over the second set of seats to the third row, knelt in the center and looked over into the back. "This I don't like."

"What?"

"This place in the back, where the trunk would be. It will only hold three suitcases. It says so on the rental receipt. Why would you want a car that seats seven if there's only room for three suitcases?"

"We only have a couple of overnight bags. It's enough."

"It wouldn't be."

"Probably it's rare to have seven people in the seats. You could put some bags on seats, or even fold some of the seats down and stack the bags."

"Ooh, you're so smart, Alberto. You look so dumb, like an old rich lady's handsome boyfriend. You're always thinking, but people don't know it. That could make you powerful some day."

"Thank you," he said.

"Why?"

"Because you're thinking about me."

"You're always thinking about me, so why not?"

"How do you know that?"

"Because when I crawled over the seats you couldn't take your eyes off my ass. Is that why they call it a rearview mirror?"

Magda's telephone buzzed. She took it out of her pocket and said, "Magda." A male voice spoke to her in Russian. She listened and answered every few seconds "Da. . . . Da. . . . Da." Then the call ended.

"Find out anything?" Albert said.

"Maybe a setback for you. The professional is alone now, the dark woman. She rented a car in Boston, and your girlfriend wasn't with her."

He glanced at Magda in the rearview mirror, and her eyes were on his. She said, "Are you sad now, Alberto? Are you starting to miss her?"

"No," he said. "I'm just going to kill her because she deserves it. I'd rather be with you."

"You don't get to choose between us, Alberto. I'm warning you again not to treat me like I'm your new girlfriend. It will only end in sorrow for you."

Albert drove on for two more hours while Magda slept, and then Magda's telephone rang again. She woke instantly and said into it, "Yes, Mr. Porchen. This is Magda," and she began to speak in Russian. The conversation went on for what seemed to be a long time to Albert. He wondered if Magda had a sexual relationship with Porchen. He was too old for her, but it seemed to Albert that every really rich and powerful man in the world kept at least a couple of much younger women around. Now that he knew her a little, he was sure Magda would not have been scandalized or even reluctant, and she certainly would not have resisted the idea if Porchen mentioned it.

Just before she had taken her nap, she had warned Albert again that she was not having a romantic relationship with him. If he thought about it, he had to admit that her attitude wasn't even very friendly. What she had actually said — that pushing their relationship would end in sorrow — was particularly chilling coming from her. He didn't know what her idea of sorrow was, but he was positive that it was much worse than his.

In spite of his understanding of the situation, he couldn't help feeling a twinge of jealousy when he listened to her talk. Her voice was softer and more respectful when she spoke to Porchen, even if she seemed to be making some remark that was intended to be witty or humorous. Whatever the relationship was, the intimacy of it bothered Albert now.

He drove at the speed limit and not faster. During this trip he had decided that he would have to take care of his own intentions and his own safety, because those things were not terribly important to the *Bratva*. They were in a position to make a lot of money if they devoted all of their attention to capturing the professional who had been helping Sara, so that was what they were doing.

The last conversation he'd had with Magda had brought him very bad news, and he'd spent the next two hours thinking about it. If the professional had settled Sara somewhere with a new identity and a place to live, then two things had changed. One was that the Russians would have no reason to search for Sara anymore. She and the professional had split up. The other was that because the Russians had lost the need to find Sara, Albert was no longer an essential asset to them. His only contribution had been that he knew Sara well. Now his contribution was driving and keeping

Magda occupied during slow times. What was that likely to get him from the brotherhood? And what if his spending time with Magda brought out a case of jealousy in one of the gangsters? If he was no longer a person who might be the key to serious money, he might get killed.

Magda fell silent and Albert didn't hear Porchen's voice coming from her phone speaker. He waited for her to speak, but she didn't. Maybe she was searching her phone for another number, and she would call somebody else in a minute to pass on orders or questions. The longer she stayed quiet the less likely that seemed.

She sat up in the seat behind him. "That was Mr. Porchen. He said to say he was sorry that we don't have time right now to find your girlfriend. We need to get the other one, and it's urgent that we go in the direction where she is before she does what those people do."

"What do they do?" he asked.

"They make themselves disappear. We had sent her picture and your girlfriend's to the boss in Boston, a man named Tcherinsky. He had sent it to the people who worked for him or owed him or paid him for protection, or whatever. Some work in businesses — parking lots, gas stations, fast-food places, motels, or car rentals. When the guy at the car rental counter saw her, he knew who she was. As soon as he had rented her a car, he turned on the GPS tracking system they have installed in case somebody steals one of their cars. He called his boss and told him. The boss sent four really good thieves to follow the signal. They followed her for a while, and eventually they caught up at a supermarket in Massachusetts and tried to corner her, but she got away. They found the car parked in a little town in Massachusetts. Somehow she got into another car with another woman driving it."

"What other woman?"

"Not your girlfriend. An older woman. Maybe she was somebody who worked for the professional, or a friend or relative. I don't know. You really are attached to that girl, aren't you?"

"I just wondered who else was getting involved in this."

"They followed that one all the way to Portsmouth, along the ocean. She had parked at a house and gone inside. They went in and killed her, and then they searched the house for the professional. Somehow, she got away in the woman's car. It's a metallic-color Cadillac CT5, this year's model."

"How did she get away from these four 'really good thieves'?"

"That's not something I'd ask a man. You're all so wrapped up in how big and tough and smart you are that you'll fall apart inside like babies, and then get even with the person who asked. But these four really are good thieves, so if there was anything that would help catch her they would have told us."

"Okay," he said. "How can I help now?"

"Keep driving. When she left Portsmouth, she was heading north into Maine."

Oleg Porchen was at his desk in Los Angeles watching a movie that was about some future time in which the world had degenerated into chaos. The place appeared to be populated by people in their twenties who wore jumpsuits made of synthetic stretchy fabrics. They were engaged in throwing off some oppressors who seemed a bit older. The fighting took place mostly in corridors and the wreckage of buildings. The weapons were futuristic and threw off sparks and caused explosions, but they never seemed to kill anybody. Nobody spoke, only yelled. Nobody walked, just ran in a perpetual emergency. When the phone in his pocket rang, his mind simply fitted the sound into the ambient noise of the battle at first, so he almost missed the call. He snatched it out and looked at the screen.

"This is Porchen."

"Hello, Oleg. This is Tcherinsky. My guys know where the woman's car is."

"How?"

"They took some time looking around in that woman's house in Portsmouth, taking a few papers, a few bills, some cash, and tax returns."

"They took time to steal that crap?"

"There was nobody alive in the house by then, and you know those things can be valuable. They're thieves. We all are. What do you expect?"

"That told them something about the car?"

"The car was a Cadillac. General Motors cars have all had an OnStar system from the factory for at least twenty years. They had picked up a car payment receipt with the names of the owners, the vehicle identification number and all that. One of them — Gregor — you know Gregor?"

"Yes."

"He called the OnStar office, pretended to be the husband, and asked the phone advisor if they'd gotten a signal on the system that the car had been in an accident or broken into or anything. He said his wife was supposed to be home hours ago, but hadn't called or anything. The advisor checked and told him that the car seemed to be okay. It was parked in Maine at the start of the Appalachian Trail."

"How do we get there?"

"I've got a better idea. This crew — Gregor and the others — are on their way there now. That trail is a really wild place, with mountains and swamps and forests, and no roads. It's pretty clear this woman is trying to lose us by going on foot. It would take your guys a day to fly to Maine, a day to get ready, and a day to get onto the trail. My guys are an hour from there."

"You're willing to send your guys to catch her in a hundred miles of woods?"

"This is a special group. They're all outdoorsmen. They hunt and fish together all over New England and across the border in Canada. At home, they run, swim, and lift weights together. They're the perfect ones to go after her. They're tall, long-legged, and tireless. Imagine a pack of wolfhounds."

"What do you want for that kind of help?"

"We don't have time to negotiate if you want them to catch her and bring her back. I just want you to live up to what you already promised — that I'll share in your good fortune if I bring it about."

"You already have my word."

The sun had gone down, but Jane had not stopped walking. She had walked for about eight hours from the trailhead, and had seen only half a dozen hikers, all of them north-bound trekkers. In order to reach this stretch of the Appalachian Trail going north, a person would have had to walk from somewhere farther south. They didn't look as though the experience was bringing them joy. The six were exhausted, walking with a monotonous zombie-like trudge, and their faces telegraphed misery.

None of them seemed to have come pre-pared with netting, so they had visible mosquito bites and kept slapping their arms, necks, and faces, waving to keep the mosquitoes out of their ears. Because Jane had expected the mosquitoes, she had bought a blanket-sized piece of netting and draped it over her hat and down to cover her to her ankles, which she wrapped with tape to seal it. Her gear kept the net away from her body, and the mosquitoes with it.

She had read that she could expect a shelter of some sort about every ten miles. She had determined that, unless the weather became impossible, she would avoid any place where hikers might congregate. It had rained for about three hours during her first day of hiking, but she was able to use her waterproof poncho to keep herself and her gear relatively dry. The rain, the poncho, and the netting together defeated the mosquitoes.

When night was about to fall, Jane moved off the trail and onto a plateau elevated about eight feet from the forest floor that was under an overarching stand of leafy trees and screened by a thicket of saplings. She spread out her tarp and untied her tent to let it spring open and then put it in the center. Then she gathered a bundle of leafy branches, spread her poncho open on top of the tent in the hope that it would dry overnight, and leaned her branches on the tent to improve its camouflage. She watched the trail for a while before she lit her first can of Sterno to heat up her dinner of powdered eggs, dried beef, and soup in her small pot. When she had cooked, eaten, and urinated, she returned to the tent and zipped the door shut. She let her mattress inflate, hung her socks and boots where they might dry, and went to sleep. Her sleep was dreamless and lasted more than eight hours.

Jane woke when the birdcalls began. She put on her Crocs and silently walked toward the trail until she could see that it was clear of people. She started to heat some more powdered eggs and pork and beans, and then took her empty water bottle and went to explore. She found some spots where boots would have left prints if anyone had already passed on the trail, and then found a small clear stream that looked to her eye as though it were spring fed. Since she had not stopped at a regular campsite and there were no signs that anyone had camped nearby, she walked upstream a distance, filled her filtered bottle, added purification tablets, and hung it on her belt to walk back.

Her breakfast made her feel stronger. She went back up the stream and used the water for a sponge bath, and then returned to her tent. She dressed in fresh clothes, re-arranged the items she had brought to keep some things ready to her hand when she expected to need them and others bagged and packed to stay dry. This morning she took the time she needed to roll everything tightly and make sure she was as well prepared as she could be. She draped the mosquito netting over her again, sprayed herself with mosquito repellent, and started off.

She was a whole day's hike south on the trail, and she intended to do at least as well today. The best plan she could follow was to keep moving steadily, to keep from having accidents that might cause injury, and to be observant. Her plan was to get as far as she could on the trail each day. If, after seven to ten days, she reached the end of the Hundred-Mile Wilderness healthy and uninjured and her pursuers had never realized she was on the trail, or had simply never caught up with her, that would be a victory. She could go home and stay out of sight for a few months and probably never have to think about Russian gangsters from California again. People who hated someone might never give up. People who were chasing them for money reached the point at which the sum didn't seem big enough.

That afternoon, she went down a slight incline that began to worry her because the trail didn't seem to rise right away. After a few more minutes she began to hear something. She hoped the sound was a wind in the tall trees, but she knew it wasn't. As she walked, her heart began to beat harder. She was hearing the rush of water running over rock.

A few minutes later she reached the source of the sound. There was a narrow stream with rocky banks that ran across the trail. She knew by looking at the stream that if she had come through this spot in August the bed would probably be six inches to a foot deep and she would be able to see the rocks at the bottom, and probably walk over them barefoot to keep her socks and boots dry. But this wasn't August. It was early April and just below the mountains. The water was icy snowmelt, and it looked as though it was rushing down a toboggan run. But the stream was less than fifteen feet wide, and on the far side were some substantial trees back a couple of feet from the rocks.

Jane sat down on the rocky shore and stared across the water. After a few minutes she tried an experiment. She picked up a nearby branch, crawled close to the bank, and stuck the branch in. The current jerked it horizontal and nearly out of her hands. She crawled upstream a few steps and stuck it in at a slight upstream angle, then pulled it out. The water was at least to her shoulders and, if she were fighting that current, she would never be able to stand. She walked a hundred feet downstream to see if there was a wider, shallow ford, but when she got to the next curve, she could see that the water must have been gouging out this narrow, deep channel in the rock every thaw for thousands of years. She tried going upstream, but that seemed even worse, because a bit higher up the vertical drop made the stream into rocky rapids.

She went back into the forest she had come from, and found a stand of young trees that were about as thick as her wrist near the roots, but narrowed over their height. They were about twenty feet tall. She searched the area until she found one that had been undermined by water, and rocked it back and forth until it was loose enough to cut out with her hatchet.

She took the pole to the stream and set it down on the rock surface, then lifted it and tried to extend it across the streambed to the trees on the opposite bank. It reached. She took out the climber's rope she had bought in the sports store, tied a noose in one end, and draped it over the fork at the end of her pole. She tied the other end to her backpack and set the pack on the rock. Next, she extended the pole over the water and pushed the noose over a thick branch. She pulled the rope to tighten it, and tugged hard to test its strength. She unrolled her mattress and blew it up, and then strapped her pack to it.

She studied what she had done, took a few breaths, and then decided. She climbed up on a higher part of the rocky bank, jumped and swung above the stream. She made it nearly to the opposite bank before she scraped the surface of the water, then let go and sprawled on the opposite rocky shore. She caught her breath and then carefully pulled the mattress with the backpack on it until it slid into the stream. The mattress was swept down the torrent while Jane pulled the rope hand over hand to keep the mattress and pack moving toward her. As soon as the mattress was in reach she wrapped the rope around her leg to hold it, and gingerly pulled it and the pack out of the water. When she had repacked her backpack she kept the mattress strapped to it so it would dry while she walked. For the rest of the day, she did not have to cross another rushing stream, so the mattress was ready to sleep on that night. She slept better that night because she was confident that the next people to come along could not cross that stream in the dark.

Jane's decision to make a quick, but not careless, hundred-mile hike had another advantage. If she did meet the four Russians down the trail, they would find her as healthy, well-fed, and rested as she was at Katahdin. If the four men who came after her were ill-equipped or too impatient to maintain a sensible pace or unable to keep up a steady one, then she might find them exhausted, hungry and thirsty, sick, or injured.

Most of the men who became professional criminals she had met were not woodsmen. They were city boys who hadn't been able to find a way to make a living without taking it from somebody else. She didn't know much about this group, but she hadn't seen anything about them that was different. There was no question what they would do if they caught her.

She consciously increased the tempo of her steps. The farther she carried herself and her fifty-pound pack before an enemy got to her, the stronger she was likely to be and the weaker they were likely to be. The ground was rough and rocky and rose and fell, and the foliage narrowed the trail. The mosquitoes were voracious and swarmed in clouds above her as she walked. The conditions worsened while Jane hiked that morning, and the time was past one when she saw the first of that day's northbound travelers, a couple in late middle age. Their faces looked weathered, with deep wrinkles that reminded Jane of the antique photographs of Plains Indians who had spent lifetimes being sunburned.

They were friendly and called themselves Melody and Jack. Jane said she was Dana Solomon, from New York City. When they shook hands and moved past each other to press on, Jane saw that Jack's pack had been neatly stenciled with "Brian Combs, Clearwater, Florida." Jane had read a post online before she'd left that said many people used false names to avoid being stalked or having their homes robbed while they were away, so she wasn't surprised. She decided that she liked the trail name Melody and considered using it the next time she met someone. About three hours later she did. In a couple of days, it might help create confusion, because there would be long-haulers who could report having met Melody, and there would be trail books for the whole length of the trail signed "Melody." That afternoon she found several striped wing feathers from a bird that might have been an owl or a wild turkey. They could hardly have been lighter, so she picked them up and put them in a plastic bag and then in her pack.

She kept walking until it was almost fully

dark before she selected a place, so she made about fourteen hours. This time the elevated and level space she found off the trail was in a pine woods, which verified for her the felt impression that the trail had been climbing. She spread her tarp and pitched her tent among the pines, draped her camouflaged poncho over it again, and used pine boughs to make it look less like a tent. This time she ate tuna from a pouch with her soup, took off her shoes and socks to let them air out and dry, laid out her inflatable bed and sleeping bag, and fell asleep quickly.

In the middle of the night she passed out of the silent and pitch-dark part of her slumber and into a dream. In the dream she opened her eyes and looked out the door of her tent. The door was a woven synthetic fabric she could see through with a zipper down the center so it could be closed. What she saw was an Onondawaono man. He had the usual scalp lock down the center of his head, the hair on either side plucked rather than shaven.

He wore deerskin leggings and shirt and moccasins decorated with porcupine quills, which were used in the times before the glass beads Europeans brought for trade became plentiful.

He said, "Sken:nen," which meant both peace and health.

"Sken:nen," Jane answered.

"Thank you for wishing me health," he said, "but I'm not in danger of dying by war or disease anymore, Onyo:ah."

"Why do you call me that?"

"Because it's the name that means most to you."

That was the secret nickname her father had called her when she was a child. It was the term for a possible score of a throw in the peach-pit game. It meant that all the pits had landed with their burned side up except one. Onyo:ah meant "one white," and it scored one point for the thrower. He said the nickname was to tell her that she was a valuable score, a prize, a treasure.

"My father called me that. But you're not my father."

"No. I'm your father's ancestor, and yours. I died a long time ago, not imagining that there would ever be a woman like you."

"Why are you here in my dream?"

"It's because I'm who your thalamus, medial prefrontal cortex, and posterior cingulate cortex felt they needed when dream time came tonight."

"I thought you would say that one of Sky Woman's grandsons, the twin brothers Hawenneyu and Hanegoategeh, sent you to me."

"That's just another way to say the same thing. You could be working for the left-handed twin or the right-handed, or both. You can desire to help the Creator, but if you don't know everything, you don't know what act of yours will create, and which will destroy."

"You admit one of the twins is using me."

"That's what we're made for, and only the brothers know what purpose we serve to help them keep the universe in balance."

"Are the four killers coming onto the trail after me?"

"I'm an electrochemical reaction in your brain. I don't know things you don't know, but you can use me in another way. You wanted me because I'm a man of the old days."

"A warrior. You fought the wars of the forests."

"I was a son, a brother, a singer, a dancer, a storyteller, a player of games, a lover, a husband, a father, a friend. But tonight you need the warrior."

"How can I use you?"

"Remember what you know about me."

"I know that when enemies were chasing you, then you would make them chase you to a place where you'd be stronger. You would set a pace that made the enemy tire themselves out getting to you. You would come for them with weapons that were silent. You spent the early decades of your life practicing with stronger and stronger bows. Or you could throw a tomahawk or an ironwood war club two hundred feet and hit an enemy's head every time."

"What's in your hand are only tools. The weapons are the ears, eyes, mind. Nobody ever won by thinking his enemy wouldn't catch up with him." He stood up, turned away from her tent, and faded into the forest.

Jane woke before dawn to the birds again, put on her Crocs and netting and went out to find water. The first days of her trek had reminded her of the huge importance of eating, drinking, and being comfortable. After she refilled the filtered bottles and put in the purifier pills, she washed and went back to her camp to cook her food.

As she took care of her practical chores, she thought about the dream of her ancestor and then forced herself to pay attention to her pack, taking an inventory of the ways she had of defending herself if the four men caught up with her. She decided that even if she were to forget the Glock pistol and ammunition magazines in their plastic pouch, she was better equipped than her ancestor would have been. But she decided that there were things she could do to prepare herself.

During the day Jane studied the trees she passed and collected two things. One was two-and-a-half-foot hardwood saplings. She took only the ones that had grown in the open where they grew straight. Before she put them in her pack, she would use her pocketknife to strip the bark, then roll the sapling between her palms to be sure it was perfect. The other things she looked for were branches with the right shape. These were longer and much thicker, and they each had a slight curvature. She carved each one to shape it in a particular way and stowed those too. By the end of the day she had found, inspected, and worked three of each.

The fourth day she stopped at her usual time, when the sun was already down and the light getting dim. She took her usual care to camp far from the trail where her tent would not be visible. She heated her food with a can of Sterno in a shallow hole she had dug on the side of the tent away from the trail.

Her task for camp was to finish working the curved branches she had been collecting into bows and string them with hundred-pound test fishing line, then unstring them again. Next, she began to rework her three arrows. She rubbed them smooth and straight as she could, put a notch at one end of each one so she could nock the strings, then scraped a groove on three sides of each shaft into which she could use epoxy to glue the feathers she had saved. Her last task was to glue the three arrowheads in place.

When she woke the next morning, she also decided that this was the day she was going to start checking the trail behind her. She supposed that this thought, this concern, was what had made her subconscious mind arrange the dream conversation with her ancestor. He was a way of reminding herself. Today would be a reconnaissance day. She devoted the usual care to her packing and her preparations. She had glimpsed a set of ridges off to the west of the trail and, when she reached a spot that gave her a clear view of them, she turned up a game trail and began to climb.

The climbing made Jane more aware of the weight of her pack. As she climbed she thought about each item she had selected and put into the pack. It occurred to her that people in the modern world didn't have a true relationship with the world of objects anymore. Each item stood between her and some problem. She pictured each of them. Without the filtered water bottles and the purifying pills, she could have gotten some illness like dysentery, cholera, or typhoid. The mosquito net and repellent had saved her from being a feast for insects. The tent and poncho had kept her warm and dry, the mattress and sleeping bag let her rest. The food, pot, and spoon kept her from starving. Those were the basic things. Just a bit less important were the soap and sunscreen.

The other objects she had included were light and took up little spaces between big things — fishhooks and line, the knives, arrowheads, Crocs, gloves, and extra clothes were either luxuries or brought for contingencies. If she concentrated on each item in her pack, she could feel the weight and position of it.

She shifted the pack now and then or adjusted the straps to keep it from rubbing her or tilting. She liked the sunshine and the moving air as she reached a higher altitude. Whenever she reached a spot where she could look back and down at a section of the trail, she would lie on a rock shelf or place herself behind some foliage and spend a few minutes scanning for the four men.

Late in the morning she saw four people, but when they were closer she saw that two of them were women. They were moving at a measured pace toward the south, not burning up the trail, but making progress. And then she realized that one of the women and one of the men were using pairs of bright orange walking sticks, and as they moved closer she realized she'd met them earlier. They had been heading from the south. They must have finished the short stretch they had intended, and were heading south again. She waited long enough to see the other pair's walking sticks collapsed and stored in their backpacks.

She started moving again, and went a few yards down the far side of the high ridge so she couldn't be seen from the trail and then headed south to parallel the trail. After two more hours she climbed back up the ridge so she could see the trail again. This time she saw nobody, and went back to moving along the far side of the ridge.

As she thought about what she was doing she remembered reading the complaints that the colonial-era governors had sent to the New York governor around 1700 because Seneca war parties used the upper ridges of the Appalachians as a highway to attack their enemies in the Southeast. The colonists didn't like having parties of heavily armed men trotting along above their settlements. Jane knew the reasons why the Senecas chose the high route.

She kept it up for the day. She had seen a few trekkers, including the four heading south. When the sun went down she found a flat place just on the other side of a jagged ridge that gave no view of her tent from the trail below. She lay under the domed surface of her tent and thought about the things she had seen and then about what she needed to do now. And she thought again about her dream of two nights earlier.

She was now about forty-five to fifty miles down the Appalachian trail, almost the middle of the Hundred-Mile Wilderness. She was healthy, rested, and well-fed. Maybe she was perfectly safe, but she had remembered something the old warrior had said. Nobody ever survived by assuming his enemies had given up.

21

That night Jane camped in the heights again. She slept well, but something woke her in the dark. She listened for the birds, assuming at first that they must have awakened her. She couldn't hear them, but she heard something rhythmic, like a human movement. She crawled out of the tent, climbed to the best vantage point along the crest of the mountain, and saw four lights on the trail below.

They were coming along the trail in a way she had not seen anyone doing since she had begun the trek. They were four men trotting like soldiers in double time. They were wearing caps with headlamps strapped on above the visor. When a man's headlamp shone briefly on the man ahead of him, she could see they wore dark-green or olive-drab shirts and gray pants. They had boots that came to mid-calf with the pants tucked into the boots, which she assumed helped keep the mosquitoes out. After she had watched them come closer for a full minute she saw that the men were wearing netting over their clothes and gloves on their hands. As she watched, the man in front raised both hands, stopped, and turned back to talk to the others, and she was sure. He was the man in his forties with short blond hair, the one who had seemed to be the leader of the four Russians.

Jane kept herself from ducking down reflexively, because nothing caught the human eye like motion, and if she caused one of them to turn in her direction, his headlamp might illuminate her. Instead, she very slowly crawled backward down the rocky incline to her tent and began repacking her backpack. She had become adept at it over four days of repetition and experimentation, so the work went quickly. She had also been preparing herself for the moment she was in right now, when she would need to travel light. As she packed, she set aside the items that would slow her down.

Within about fifteen minutes Jane had packed her large backpack and placed the things she thought she would need in the much smaller daypack she kept in a pocket of the big one. Then she went to a hole she had found that might have once been the den of an animal, pushed the large pack inside, and covered the opening with rocks, then dirt, and last pine needles. Then she began to move. Her pack was much lighter and smaller now, and she was rested. The route she chose was along the crest of the steep hills that she had been following the previous day.

She began to walk fast and then to trot as soon as she had a sense of the terrain ahead of her, using the moonlight to pick out the even, flat parts of the rocky heights. She had to be sure not to turn an ankle. She kept looking down and ahead to try to spot the four headlamps moving along the trail below. She had used only ten or fifteen minutes to pack and hide her gear, so she was sure she was going to catch up with them, or at least spot their lights before long. She began to concentrate on picking up her speed. The four men had been trotting when she'd first seen them, but maybe their distance had made them look as though they were inching along when they were much faster.

She kept looking for ways to speed up her pace without turning on her own head lamp. She couldn't take the chance. Even if she was on the far side of the crest, her beam might illuminate a portion of the foggy air above her and create a glow. She followed a smooth, hard stretch for a hundred yards and saw them below her.

Jane adjusted her course and her pace so she stayed far above them and behind. They and she trotted another hour and a half. She stayed back where they would not see or hear her. And then, as the sun prepared to come up and the shapes of objects could be discerned again, the four men turned off their headlamps and stopped.

They collapsed, shrugged off their packs, and sat for a few minutes and talked. After only a short rest two of the men built a small fire and took out food that looked from a distance like the things she had brought — packets rather than boxes or cans, dried strips that looked like jerky or fruit, and water. They fiddled with the ingredients, mixing them into two pots and a pan, and cooked them.

The other two men selected a tall pine tree with a few thick branches about fifty feet from the camp. One of them took out a coil of climbing rope like Jane's. He already had a small weight like a fisherman's sinker tied to a spool of fishing line, which he tied to the climbing rope. He swung the sinker on the line and threw it upward to go over a branch and watched it come back down to the ground.

Meanwhile, the fourth man was busy running the rope through the straps of two backpacks. Then he repeated the process at another tree with another length of rope. The men ate their dinners, wiped the plates and pots and pan, let their freestanding tents pop open, set them up facing away from each other on a high spot, took their sleeping bags and water bottles, and went into their tents. The last two men pulled the climbing ropes up so the four backpacks, which all contained food, would rise to just under the two branches and hang there, out of reach of bears or other animals.

Jane realized this was probably a good way for criminals to travel. They were on the move and visible only at night, so nobody saw them. They made a camp away from the trail and slept during the day, so if anybody came past their camp, they would be invisible.

Jane could not help worrying. These men were not what she had assumed they were. They weren't street thugs. They were experienced in the outdoors. Everything about the way they behaved indicated to her that they had military training, she assumed in the Russian army. They were accustomed to moving in double-time for distances. They divided tasks so everyone's needs could be met at once. They had the right gear in the right quantities for the wilderness, and everything they did was done in unison so they could work quickly.

They were very scary people. They had come after her, and they had not stopped coming. They had guessed correctly about her choices, which showed that they had some experience chasing the kind of people who might fight back. And they were experienced murderers. They had been very comfortable killing Clarice in her house, either because she was a possible witness to their intended kidnapping of Jane or because she was in their way. Jane had to do something to harm them. She knew that the time to act was when they were asleep. After today, fighting them would be harder, maybe impossible.

She rearranged some items in her daypack and waited fifteen minutes before she began to move down the hillside toward their camp. They had been moving faster and longer than she had last night, so she had a hope that they would be asleep already. She paused behind the shrubs and rocks that she could find coming down the hillside, and listened. When she moved she tried to keep her steps utterly silent.

Coming down from the heights in silence was extremely difficult. It required intense attention, an exertion of most of the muscles of the body to keep her arms and legs holding her torso above the ground. Sometimes she crawled from rock to rock to keep from sliding. Jane took another fifteen minutes to bring herself down the hill, and then another to make it to the first tree, where a pair of backpacks were hanging.

Jane used her left hand to hang on the rope that held the backpacks and create some slack. She studied the knot that was holding the rope, and then untied it with her right hand. As soon as it was loose, she very slowly lowered the backpacks to the ground.

She opened the first one and carefully removed five packets of food — three meat, two soup. She took three things out of her pack — a drinking straw, her bottle of the distilled juice of the water hemlock, and the tube of epoxy glue. She inverted the five food packets and leaned them against the backpack to make the food and juices sink to one end. Then she poked a small hole in each packet. She dipped the straw into the poison bottle and capped it with her finger like a pipette, then stuck it through the hole and emptied a straw-full of the poison into the packet and leaned it against the pack again while she refilled the straw and emptied it.

When she had poisoned five packets of food, she inserted the tip of the glue tube into the same hole and held it closed tightly for a count of fifteen. When she had closed all five she examined them. There was no leakage on any of them, and no change in the appearance of the packets. She returned them to the pack exactly as she had found them.

Jane repeated the same process with the other pack. Because her work had gone so smoothly, this time she poisoned ten food packets. As she was putting them away in the pack, she found something else — a pint bottle of vodka. She looked at it closely. It had been opened, and a couple of ounces were missing. She held her left thumb at the current level, removed the cap and poured some of the vodka into her own water bottle so there would be no alcohol smell left behind. Then she poured in some of the water hemlock until it reached its original level exactly, capped the vodka and put it back in the pack.

She grasped the rope and hauled the two backpacks back up to the level just below the branch, retied the knot exactly as she had studied it, and looked over at the second tree, where the packs of the other two men were hung. That tree was a bit closer to the four tents, and so she had to consider carefully whether she had enough poison left to make the risk worth taking.

As Jane sat by the tree, she considered other options. When she had divested herself of the big, heavy pack she had retained the gun and ammunition, the hunting knife, her pocketknife, and the hatchet. Right now might be a good time to sneak up on the tents and try to discern whether there was a chance to stick one of the men with the hunting knife and then get up to the heights before the other men realized what had happened. A few days ago, she might have tried a tactic like that, but now she wasn't so sure that she would be able to outrun these four. She knew she could just try to fire rounds into the backs of the four tents hoping to hit at least a couple of the occupants. They had murdered Clarice and intended to do to Jane whatever would make her give up the people she had saved.

She rose to her feet and reached into her daypack to find her pistol and pull it out of the waterproof bag. She would have to do her best to kill these men now, while they were still unaware that she had found them.

She heard someone moving, and pressed her body against the tree, her heart beating hard in her chest. As she strained to keep her whole body behind the tree, she was trying to search the daypack without bending her elbows and widening her silhouette. She listened intently. She heard the door of one of the tents unzip, and she froze. Motion was what people saw first. If a person's eye caught motion he couldn't prevent himself from looking. The reflex had probably saved the lives of monkey-like human ancestors thousands of times. But she had to see. With as little movement as possible, taken as slowly as she could, she looked.

One of the men was crawling out of his tent. He had a pistol in his hand, and he stuck it in the back of his belt as he walked into the woods a few yards away. She concentrated on staying on the side of the tree hidden from that man. She heard him urinating. It seemed to take a very long time. Then she heard him walking back toward the tents. She still hadn't freed her pistol from her daypack. She touched the familiar hard shape of the pistol through the plastic and then found the side with the seal that kept it closed. She risked showing some part of her body to tug the seal open, but she knew it was taking too long. Then she had her fingers around it, slid it out, and stepped out to fire.

He was gone. His tent was still, and the door had been zipped shut again. He had gotten past her but had not seen her. She prohibited her body from moving and thought. If she fired her weapon, there was already at least one man who was awake with a gun in his hand, or near it. She had already executed one strategy. It was time to go.

Jane left her hiding place behind the tree, but she kept her pistol in hand. She began slowly climbing upward. As she got farther away, she climbed more quickly, always careful to keep something between her and the tents. It took her a few minutes to make it back up to the ridge and then she kept going to place herself on the far side.

She spent a few minutes rearranging her gear, but this time the pistol was in the pocket outside her daypack, and the extra magazines with it. She shouldered the pack, adjusted her shoes and socks, and set off above the trail. She was going to get ahead of them.

22

It was about eight in the morning when Jane set off from the Russians' camp. She had been a runner for most of her life, and had trained herself for endurance. The way she explained it to people who wanted an explanation was that for her the difference between running and walking didn't feel as big as it seemed to for some other people.

Today she was up along the crest line of a mountain range in bright sunlight carrying only a daypack. She'd felt strong and sure at the beginning, and now she had been running on and off for about four hours, making good time. She had stopped at regular intervals to drink water and eat protein bars, but started again as soon as she could.

This kind of running helped her clarify her thoughts. She thought about the four men and what their training and capabilities would lead them to do in various situations. When she believed she had a sense of their probable tactics, she decided which of the plans she had been considering would work. After that, as she moved southward above the trail, she looked for the perfect formation of trail, hillside, and forest to fit her plan.

It was around five when she found it. Jane was in a wooded area about halfway up that was just to the side of the upper trail and had both old growth and young trees in the same area, with some bushes to complicate the place.

Jane went three hundred yards away to select three eight-foot lengths of sapling. She cut them and stripped them of all branches except the ones near the upper ends, so she had three forked poles. She carved them so she could fit and fix her three bows firmly to their ends, draw the hundred-pound lines she was using as bowstrings, and keep them drawn by snagging them in notches she cut on the poles, so they were like crude crossbows.

She chose the locations for the three bows with extreme care. One she drove into the soil so it was anchored at the base of a large boulder and aimed it at the center of the path four feet from the ground. The other two she placed above eye level in the trees, aimed down on the path. She spent time tying and running the trip lines across the stand of trees so each of the three bows would launch its arrow at the perfect angle at the perfect time.

When she was sure her installation was flawless, she drew the strings on the three bows, set the three arrows with their steel arrowheads in place, and then went to her lookout spot. She exchanged her shorts for long pants and her T-shirt for a black synthetic long-sleeved pullover, placed her hunting knife's sheath on her belt and her loaded pistol in the zipper pocket on her right thigh, and went to sleep on her poncho.

Jane slept more deeply than she had intended. She had not moved for hours, and when she woke, her left hip and shoulder felt stiff. She sat up and looked down at the trail, but it was too dark to see anything. She felt relief for a few seconds, but then it occurred to her that since she had been so deeply asleep, the four men could have already passed her on the trail.

She had run hard, but only for about half a day before she had stopped to build her snares. She thought about her dream from two days ago. The only way to be the one to come home from the wars of the forest was to use her weapons — ears, eyes, mind.

She moved down the slope toward the main path of the Appalachian Trail. If they had passed already, maybe she could wait until daylight and then dismantle her snares and take them with her when she moved ahead. In case they had not come past this point yet, she should be ready. She had to be very careful on the way down, because if she strayed out of position in the dark she could set one of them off herself.

And then she thought she heard footsteps. She crouched and waited. She guessed the hour must be at least three A.M. but she didn't want to move or light the display of her watch right then. She looked down along the trail and saw lights coming. It was the headlamps the men had been wearing when she had first seen them. The men seemed to be moving faster than they had the night before. She didn't dare think too hard about the possible meaning of that, but then she realized that there were only three lights, and she knew.

One of them must have eaten a big enough helping of the food she had poisoned with the water hemlock concentrate and died. One reason they were moving faster tonight was that if one of them had died, the others could not be certain what had poisoned him. If someone — Jane — had sneaked into their camp and poisoned some of the food, why wouldn't she have poisoned all of it? If they had just been unlucky enough to have bought spoiled or adulterated food, then it was unlikely only one batch was ruined. They must have gone through their backpacks, taken out all the food, and thrown it away. Maybe they'd poured out their water, too. There were sources of water every few miles — streams, springs, rainwater caught in rock depressions.

Jane knew that there was one other reason these men were moving fast. They wanted to catch the person they'd come to capture. If they suspected her of killing their companion, then they wanted her much more than before. They must hate her. Now was the time to take advantage of that hatred.

Jane stood up and began to move away from the lights, and made her way up the slope in the dark. She lit the light of her watch. She had been right — 3:23. Behind her she heard their footsteps, then she heard one of them dislodge a stone, and heard it roll downhill, hit a ledge, and launch itself a few feet to hit another stone. She glanced back and down, and saw the men had turned off their headlamps. But in the moonlight, against the light-colored emptiness of the wide path into the woods, she saw all three were scrambling up the hill fast.

Jane reached the trees, then the first path, ran into it for only one step before she cut over into the second path, and kept running. She kept going hard, her feet pounding the ground as she ran. A pistol shot shattered the silence and made her duck her head, but no bullet had hit anywhere near her. A man shouted, "Stop, or I'll kill you." She supposed that might have made some people stop sometimes in situations like this, but not Jane. There were more footsteps, and branch-scraping-cloth noises as the men ran in the dark and brushed the plants in the thickets.

There was the sound of a man hitting the ground, immediately followed by a sound Jane remembered from her work in the afternoon. It was like the plucking of a string, a hum and a thud as one of her snares triggered and let loose an arrow. Instantly a man's voice grunted "Uh!" and a second later came the "Aaah! Aaaaah!"

There were heavy footsteps as the man's two companions dashed ahead to join him. Jane was far enough ahead of the men now so that she could cut back to the first trail, the one she had booby-trapped. She didn't try to move silently, just ran hard. If the men heard her and ran forward toward the noise even a few steps, they would set off the next snares.

Jane never paused, never looked back or stopped to listen. She concentrated only on gaining ground. She sprinted for as long as she could keep up that pace, and then followed a gradual course to achieve the top of the next hill. When she reached it she kept going, trying to maintain a fast, even pace that would put her far ahead and keep her there.

The extra sleep she had gotten while the men must have been burying the man she had poisoned, investigating the cause of his death, and destroying their food was helping her now. She forced herself to keep up her speed. She knew these men were fast, maybe even as fast as she was, now that they had, as she had, lightened their burdens. But now they would be delayed for a while patching up their injured friend or burying him.

She was determined to keep running until the sun came up, even if it meant that she ended the night moving at an exhausted trot. She remembered that when she had lit her watch to attract the killers, the watch had said 3:23 A.M. She looked again now.

She had been running for two hours and ten minutes, and she could almost read the watch in the light from the sky.

Much of this section of the Appalachian Mountains had the look of big piles of gray and moss-green boulders. It was good to be able to trek on this part during the time when she could see. If the three men decided to take the same route to catch her, as she suspected they might, they would be wiser not to try to do it before full daylight. She wondered if they were wise. No, she decided, they didn't seem to be. Their profession argued against it. But then, so did hers, and just as strongly. She was out here in the same wilderness where they were, and they still had her outnumbered. At six, Jane took her first break. She had missed a meal at some point in the past twenty-four hours, but gave herself only five minutes. She let her breathing and heartbeat slow down, drank water, ate a packet of tuna, and then mixed some powdered soup and drank it cold as she walked.

When she was finished, she kept walking until her stomach felt settled, and then gradually worked her way back up to a run. She knew that her survival depended on her staying healthy and uninjured and ahead of her enemies at nightfall, so she concentrated on that single goal. She would run for two hours, drink water and eat something while she walked, and then speed up again. Each time she ate, she would think about how difficult this trek must be for her hungry pursuers.

She kept traveling as fast as she could until six P.M., when she found a place on a rise that gave her clear views in several directions. She could see the high trail she had just covered for at least a mile and she could climb one level up to a rocky plateau that felt like a fortress. South of her the main trail went through a forested area that looked thick and forbidding. The shadow of her hill had already darkened it and the foliage overhung the trail. Up on the plateau she had chosen, she could feel a growing force in the wind.

Jane changed into long pants, put on dry socks, a dry pullover top, and the olive-drab jacket. She walked around the perimeter of the plateau and found there were three paths up to where she was planning to sleep. It occurred to her that for about half of her life she had never gone anywhere without immediately looking for the escape routes — "If someone comes in that door and recognizes me, is there another door I can get to? If I reach the hallway, will it lead me

323

to a way to the rear exit of the building?" This time she looked for the ways up to this little plateau and down from it, but it was the same.

She studied the wind direction and found a big boulder, then picked out the leeward side. There she made herself the best meal of her day, sheltering by the big boulder and cooking powdered eggs and a packet of ham over the Sterno flame in the metal cup she had kept when she'd jettisoned her big pack. She made soup and drank lots of water. As the time passed she felt better and better. She used medium sized rocks to convert her tarp into a lean-to by arranging some along the bottom edge and the others along a level shelf on her boulder.

Jane strung a length of her monofilament fishing line across each of the three places where the paths reached the plateau, so that a person ascending the path was likely to trip on them and make noise. She looked more carefully than she had before at the paths, the area around the plateau, and the land to the south and made sure she had a very clear mental image of where everything was and how it looked before night fell.

Jane took her pistol and an extra magazine from her pack and put them in the same zippered pants pocket as the night before, and made sure her hunting knife was secure in her belt.

She used her daypack as a pillow and, long before the sun went down, she was ready to sleep. The lair she had built kept her from feeling the wind, and the strain and exertion of her day's work weighed her down into sleep.

Late at night the wind caught the tarp, filled it like a sail and tugged it out from under the rocks Jane had used to hold it down. Now it was flapping like a flag, making a slapping noise that punctuated the shriek of the moving air. She flung her arms around the tarp, gathered it in and folded it tightly. The wind had dislodged a couple of the rocks on the upper tier of the boulder and they had rolled off, but neither of them had hit her, so she was unhurt, but she was wide awake from being startled. She piled the rocks on the folded tarp to keep it down, and then got up. She walked around the big boulder to the edge of the plateau and looked out at the length of trail she had traveled during the day, but saw no moving shapes except some swaying pine trees lower down the slope.

She continued to walk around the perimeter looking for any indication that her enemies or anyone else was nearby. There was nobody that she could see on any side. She went back to the boulder and felt the wind again, and moved to the south side of the boulder. She looked at her watch and saw that it was now nearly four A.M. She unfolded the tarp, wrapped herself up in it like a caterpillar in a cocoon, and pulled the hood of her poncho up over her head to shield it from the wind.

It took her only a few minutes of being wrapped in the layers of plastic and fabric to get warm enough to doze off again. When she woke she had a sense that it was only a short time later. She unrolled herself from the tarp and crawled to the southern edge of the plateau, and then looked down. She saw nothing, so she looked north, the way she had come.

There were two headlamps bobbing along the trail below. She lay still and watched them. Could her snares have killed one of them? It was possible, but she couldn't quite accept the idea as a fact. The delay caused by trying to take care of him and then bury him might have caused them to reach this spot on the trail this late at night. It had been over twelve hours since she had heard the arrow fly in the dark and the man scream.

Jane waited, but there were still only two headlamps down there. She backed away from the edge, rolled her tarp tightly, and stowed it in her pack. She moved the tarp down a bit deeper so that some of the hard things would be padded and held off her back. The pot and the cup were metal, and the hatchet had a steel head with a sharp edge on one side and thick right angles on the other. She made sure to position that near the top, away from her body.

She returned to the edge of the plateau, and now could see the two men's lights shining ahead of them on the trail as they walked. One man had an arm in a sling and a large cloth bandage wrapped tightly over one shoulder across his chest. His companion was keeping him upright by holding the wounded man's free arm over his shoulder and half-carrying him.

She wondered about what she was seeing. It looked as though the man really had triggered one of her snares and gotten hit in the upper chest, possibly through a lung or in the muscle just in from the shoulder. He wasn't dead, but he was having trouble walking, and he was at least fifty miles from civilization and exhausting the friend who was helping him. Two days ago she had induced them to throw away most of their food. But there was something that disturbed her.

She had heard this man being hurt. She had not heard a second snare being triggered or a shout from a second man. Below her were only two men. She had built and armed three snares. The second had been aimed at the same place where the first one was aimed, because she had intended the first arrow to hit someone, and then his companions would assume that the only snare had gone off, and run to their wounded friend and set off the second. The third trip line had been farther along the trail so anyone chasing Jane could step into it and set it off.

It seemed too good, too easy to assume that one of the snares she hadn't seen triggered could have killed the missing man. She reminded herself that the wars of the forest were won by cunning, not by accepting appearances.

She sat with her pack beside her, reopened the top and took out one water bottle, opened it, and tipped back her head to drink. She took two gulps before she saw the third man. He was not dead, and he didn't even look injured. With her head back she was looking straight at him. He had climbed the nearest of the two short trails up to her plateau, and he was approaching. She closed the bottle and stuck it back into the pack, moving her arms under the poncho, where he couldn't see them. She used her right hand to reach for her pocket to unzip it and reach the gun. While her right hand was occupied there was a gust of wind that lasted a few seconds, and she felt the poncho rippling.

She could tell when he saw her. She hadn't moved, but the wind that had pressed the poncho against her body must have made her shape identifiable as human for a second. Rocks didn't have surfaces that moved. The man bent his knees suddenly as he brought up both arms to aim his pistol in her direction. She leapt to the side and broke her landing with her open backpack just as the man fired his pistol and sparks sprayed in front of him.

Jane's hand was in the top of the backpack, on the hatchet, and her fingers tightened on the handle. She jerked it out and back, then threw it hard at the place where the muzzle flash had been. She heard a thud coming from that direction. As she scrambled behind a low boulder she felt his next shot punch through her poncho without hitting her. She dragged her pistol out of her zippered pocket and crouched to look around from behind the big rock.

The hatchet had hit him somewhere on the upper body. He was on his back with his arms out to his sides, but the gun was still in his right hand. She dashed toward him. Just as she was a step from reaching him, he opened his eyes and raised the pistol. It was clear he'd been trying to lure her out so he didn't have to hunt her in the dark.

As Jane fired her pistol into his forehead, his dead hand tightened in a reflex that fired his pistol into the air before it fell limp on the ground. His blood had spattered her poncho. She took his gun and ran to snatch up her backpack and slip it on, and then stepped down the path that had led him up here. She moved to the trail where she had seen the other two men making their way before the third had attacked her. Jane climbed the hill as quietly and cautiously as she could, and then took a new position where she could see a long stretch of empty hillside, and waited.

She held her wrist under her poncho and looked at her watch. It was nearly five in the morning, and soon the sun would be up.

23

It was daylight. Jane found the dead man's pack, which he had set aside on the way up to the plateau. After that she moved away from the plateau and walked a circular course about a hundred yards from it, searching for the two surviving men. When she didn't find them, she returned to the plateau and dragged the dead man to the edge of the plateau away from the trail and pushed him over onto a slope that looked as though it had once been the site of an avalanche. In the dead man's pack she found a small military entrenching tool and she used it to bring down enough of the loose dirt above him to cover him with a few inches of it.

She searched his backpack to see what she could learn. He had three sets of identification cards, about four thousand dollars in cash, and a marine fighting knife with a blood gutter in the center of the blade.

There were three pages of notes written in small, neat Russian handwriting. She kept all of those things as well as his pistol and two loaded magazines, reloaded the one he had partially emptied, and put everything else back in the pack. She didn't trust his food or water, so they went in, too. She used the entrenching tool to cover the pack, and then covered the entrenching tool by hand.

Next Jane went into the forest at the base of the hill and walked far from the trail until she found a cold, rushing stream. She set aside her pack, walked into a calm inlet in the water up to her waist, bathed and washed her clothes there, then came out and dried in the sun for a few minutes before she put on her last dry clothes. She hung the others in the sun, put her hat, mosquito net, socks, and boots on, covered herself in the tarp and crawled into a thicket, and slept.

When she woke she heard the calls of chickadees and the distinctive sound of the gray catbird. The birds made her feel safer, because they tended to stop singing when humans arrived. She found that her hanging clothes had dried in the morning sun. She repacked, and began to walk again. It was after midday, and she knew she had to change her plan once more. The two men had been given a long time to move ahead of her while she slept. She was acutely aware that one of them was not only uninjured, but physically exceptional to be able to half-carry his friend this far. The other was going to be much weaker by now, so they would not have gotten too many miles ahead, but she knew she shouldn't make the mental mistake of thinking of them both as weak. They would almost certainly be looking for a good place to ambush her.

So far they had avoided chance encounters with other hikers by traveling at night and camping during the day and as far as they could comfortably be from the trail. If they still wanted to kidnap her they would have to try to keep doing that. She figured that by now their plan had probably shifted entirely to killing her, but that didn't change things much. She was sure that whenever the two men stopped they would set themselves up in a place where they could watch for her and shoot her.

It was the first and most obvious strategy. They couldn't outrun her with one of them injured. They couldn't walk longer than she could or significantly outmaneuver her on a marked trail that thousands of people hiked each year. All they could reasonably expect to do was kill her. By now they would probably be getting very hungry, and they might kill her just to get the safe food in her pack.

She decided she would use the hours from one P.M. until sundown making an attempt to overtake and pass them before the sun went down.

She was sure that if she caught up with them, it would be at a spot they had chosen for an ambush. She would just have to see it before she was in it.

As Jane walked she kept raising her eyes to see as far ahead as she could and then lowering them to see down onto the main trail. She wasn't sure exactly what style trap the two Russians would try. A tiger trap worked well in wet, heavily forested places where the ground was soft, a large, deep hole was easy to dig, and the sharpened stakes could be driven in far enough to hold. She had to stay aware of the possibility, but it wasn't the most likely. They seemed to be too physically compromised to dig a tiger trap, but the able-bodied one might find a ready-made depression and do the work to arm and cover it.

She believed that the most likely kind of ambush these two men might make would be something like a deer stand or a duck blind. Concealing themselves until she was in their sights would be efficient, and afterward they could just scatter the branches or use them to hide her grave.

As she worked her way up to a run she kept scanning and searching the landscape ahead for any configuration of plants and earth that might have been placed there to hide a man. As she ran, her mind was always looking for patterns, repetitions, right angles, hints of organization. As the day went on she tried to see anything that might relate to the two men. She reached the point after a couple of hours of running when she felt fairly sure that the two men couldn't have come farther than she had. She must have outrun them.

Then she saw the body. It was lying in the brush just off the main trail, where there were woods on both sides. She could see that it was the wounded Russian, because he was wearing the clothes she had seen him wearing on her last sighting. He was face-down and there was a pool of blood under his upper chest. Instantly a range of possibilities rushed into her mind. The man could have been slowly bleeding and weakening from the arrow wound all day, then collapsed and finished bleeding to death on the path. Or his companion might have decided that he couldn't afford to be held back by an injured man, but dared not to simply leave him. The left-for-dead had a way of reappearing in people's lives later and he wouldn't want that. The other possibility that Jane had to consider was the only one that mattered. This could be a trick. A body was the perfect thing to use as bait for an enemy. Corpses often carried things like identification and credit cards that could be essential information. They were such good bait that in wars bodies had sometimes been rigged with explosives. In fact, she couldn't even assume he was really dead.

This man could simply have been waiting for her to come along and lay down when he and his companion heard her coming. She approached slowly and with caution, going around the body about forty feet away with her pistol in her hand.

Jane paused several times to study the foliage on all sides, to look for elevated places where the other man could be hiding. Finally she reached a spot beside a four-foot-high boulder, crouched there, and stared at the body. It hadn't moved while she'd let her eyes stray from it to search the area. She bent down and picked up a stone that was one of a pile that seemed to have been smoothed in a stream. She took one more intensive look in every direction, then popped up behind the boulder and threw the rock at the body.

Her aim was good, and the rock hit the body hard. It bounced off the left leg, but the body didn't move. It was dead. Her eyes instantly swept across every angle she could see, but there was no sign of anyone ready to fire. The corpse was alone.

Jane took three steps, keeping her head down and her pistol in front of her, ready to fire. She paused and looked some more, and then moved cautiously to the body, knelt, and touched it with the muzzle of her pistol. Then she touched the back of the neck with her hand to see how cold it was. As she did, she dislodged the hat. The hair was curly and a couple of inches long. This wasn't one of the Russians. They all had short hair. She pushed the body onto its side. He had been young, probably not much more than twenty. He'd had his throat cut.

Jane rose and backed away from the body, going deeper into the woods between the thick bushes, and then kept going. She had thought of the possibility that they might attack a hiker, but hadn't really expected it. They had undoubtedly killed him for his supplies. The man she'd struck with an arrow had put his own clothes on the man to fool her and probably put on some of the clothes in the victim's backpack. Why hadn't they stayed to kill her when she came to investigate?

Jane heard a sound behind her, whirled, and saw movement. Twenty feet away and about six feet up behind a blind made of branches leaning and intertwined and propped among the living limbs of a tree, a hand gripping something black had already risen a few inches and was just completing its motion. Jane could see the man was not going to fire over the top of the blind, but through one of the spaces between the branches. She dropped to one knee and fired four times into the blind, then popped up and ran. There was no return fire, so he was probably dead. One left. Where was he?

She knew that the intention must have been to get her from two sides, but she knew something else that made a big difference. She had just been to a place where she knew the surviving man wasn't — by the body of the innocent boy they'd killed. If he had been there when she'd arrived he would have shot her.

Jane came to the boulder where she had been before, moved around it to be sure the man was not on the opposite side of it or on top, and then put her back to it, replaced the magazine in her pistol with a full one, then took a few rounds from the box and reloaded the magazine to its capacity, doing everything by feel rather than sight, scanning the foliage around her and listening intently for any sound.

She knew that the remaining man would have waited for five or ten seconds for his companion to call out in Russian "I got her," or something like it. The silence meant his friend, not Jane, was dead. Then he would have made some sort of attempt to see if Jane had left herself vulnerable near the ambush site — maybe going to the man she'd just shot and searching him or making sure he was dead. When he'd verified that she hadn't, he would be on to his next plan.

Jane waited. The man still had reason to try to move at night. There were four dead people along the first sixty miles of the trail. He had certainly redistributed the contents of his pack, his companion's, and the murdered hiker's. He'd had little to eat for three days, but now he had stolen food that he dared eat. What he had probably done was find a place where he could have a meal before the sun set, so he could leave when it got dark.

Jane waited another half hour, using the time to rest and think. Then she got up and turned south. She decided that the place the man would not want to have his meal was along the main trail. He might climb up into the heights as she had been doing, or prefer the shelter of the forests below, but not on the trail. She started along the trail heading south.

She moved very cautiously for the first mile or two, trying desperately not to break a twig or dislodge a stone, and stopping whenever she reached a sheltered place or one of concealment to listen for the sounds of running footsteps behind her or any sound ahead of her.

Jane thought about the past few days in the Hundred-Mile Wilderness. If she had known the four men coming after her would follow her there, she would have tried another route, another place, another strategy. She had simply done what prey do, which was to assume they were better at running than the chasers, and picked a rough and forbidding place to run. So far, she seemed to have been better at running, but not by much, and even that wasn't certain while the last man was out there. The four men had assumed the opposite — that not only were they much stronger and faster and more ruthless than the mere woman that they were chasing, but she was taking them to a place so remote that they could do as they pleased and never get caught. By now she was sure that they had admitted to themselves a few times that they too had made a mistake in coming here.

The one strategy that she was sure was to her advantage would be to get out of this wild country ahead of the surviving man. She couldn't be positive that he was out of her way somewhere to one side of the trail instead of straight ahead, waiting for her. Thinking about the situation made her want to run faster, and she gave in to the urge. She kept going through a number of opportunities to stop and listen, because after the first hour of running she didn't think there was much chance that he had skipped the opportunity to eat in order to run hard and get ahead of her. If he had chosen that strategy, Jane would already have reached his position. He would eat, then let it get dark, and then begin to move.

24

Magda got off the telephone, tossed it on the bed beside her, and looked up at Albert. "It's time for us to do some talking, Alberto. I have new information."

Albert leaned back in the chair with his fingers laced behind his head and looked at her. "What's the new information?"

"That Mr. Porchen will be here tomorrow morning."

"That's interesting," he said. "Did he say why?"

"He said it in a couple of different ways," she said. "The four men who followed her onto the trail that started at Mount Katahdin have had some trouble chasing and capturing her. The part of the trail they're on is called the Hundred-Mile Wilderness. Their phones didn't work there, so they couldn't tell anybody right away, but now one's close enough to the end to get reception. He said she outsmarted them a couple of times and killed three of them. There is only one left, and he just called his boss Tcherinsky for help, and Tcherinsky called Mr. Porchen. Mr. Porchen is on his way with a few men."

Albert sat up straight while he thought through the implications. "What do you think I should do?"

"When he arrives he's going to be thinking about his own business only. He is more determined than before to catch this woman and squeeze her brain to make her give up the people she's hidden. He's also disappointed and angry about the way things have gone. I have to stay here and help him get her. You don't. In fact, I think that if you're here in the motel room with me when he gets here he's going to be annoyed at both you and me."

"So you think I should go?"

"Yes."

"Where?"

She shrugged. "We know that the black-haired woman was in Boston, and that she rented a car to leave there. And we know that your girlfriend wasn't with her when she left."

"You think I should go to Boston now and look for her alone?"

She looked at him with a kind of amusement. "Albert. I'm not going to kill your girlfriend for you. I know that you and I had fun in bed, but I'm not going to be the one who kills her, and I'm not going to take her place as your new girlfriend. Whatever you think you have to do, go do it. I have work to do. If Mr. Porchen thinks you're in the way, it will be a problem for you."

"Are you breaking up with me?" he said.

"No. There's nothing to break up, as I told you when we left Los Angeles, and again at every city where we've been, and again here, which won't be a city until the rest of the world gets too hot to live in."

"What about later, when this stuff is done?"

"If we both survive and stay out of jail, you know where to find me in LA. You can talk to me then, but not about being your girlfriend."

"How do I get where I need to go?"

"There are buses. There is hitchhiking. There is walking. Or buy a bike."

"When do I have to go?"

"Why are you still here?"

He went to the closet, took his small suitcase out and opened it on the floor, and then folded his clothes into the empty space. He took the money and put some in his wallet, some into the inner pocket of his jacket, and hid the rest in his shoes in the suitcase. He took the gun that Magda had gotten from her gangster friends in New York to lend him and hid it in his belt under his shirt.

Then he went to the bed where Magda was, and she lifted her face to accept his kiss. "Goodbye," he said.

She held up her right hand and made a very small wave with her fingers, like a little girl.

He put his room key card on the dresser, went to the door, and stepped outside. As the door swung shut behind him, it was as though the other side of the door were now five thousand miles away. He walked. He headed toward the motel office and thought about the possible danger of drawing the clerk's attention to himself. There was no telling what might happen here tomorrow if Porchen was going to show up with a few of his thieves, and maybe Albert shouldn't make himself memorable by talking to the motel staff.

He almost walked past the door to the office, but then it occurred to him that what he wanted to ask them was where and when he could get on a bus. Having people know that he was not here tomorrow might be worth something later. Albert went inside and stepped up to the counter. The older woman who was minding the office said, "Can I help you?"

Albert said, "I understand there are buses that take people from the trail entrance to bigger cities. Is that true?"

"It sure is," she said. "But the season doesn't really get going for a few weeks. Most of the hikers start in Georgia where it's warm and don't reach this end of the trail until June at the earliest. You might have to get a bus in Bangor."

"How far is that?"

"East Millinocket to Bangor is about sixty miles."

"How can I find out about the bus to Bangor?"

"Not to Bangor. *From* Bangor. The easiest way to get there is probably to hire somebody to drive you."

"Do you know anybody who would do that?"

"Well, yeah. But it's kind of expensive. Anybody from here has to come back, so it's a one-hundred-twenty-mile drive. The going rate is a couple bucks a mile, so the price would start around two hundred fifty."

"I'd be happy to pay that if I could get going right away."

"I'd take you, but I can't get away until

around five. I could see if my son Bobby would do it. Do you have cash?"

"Yes."

She lifted the motel phone and dialed a number, turned away and talked quietly for a minute, and then turned to Albert. "Are you all ready to go now?"

He lifted his suitcase and nodded. "Yes."

She turned away again. He heard her say, "See you soon." She hung up and leaned on the counter. "He's right up the street. He'll be down to get you in a minute. You can have a seat over there if you want."

Ten minutes later, he was sitting in the passenger seat of an SUV that smelled like wet dog and had a layer of black hairs on it, while Bobby drove along a narrow, winding road that he referred to as "the short way." Bobby's brain was clearly not of a size to cause much of a strain on his neck, but he seemed even-tempered and not devious. Albert was feeling better every second. He was out of the motel, he was on his way out of the mosquito-cursed woods, and he was beginning to see the benefits of being away from Magda during the next few days of her life.

25

Jane ran at her best pace while it was still light. She could see where she was placing her feet and she could see the trail ahead and her body was on a daylight schedule. She got hungry and thirsty when she was supposed to and felt alert and energetic. She was getting near to the end of the trail now. She was thinking of her progress as the Eighty-Mile Wilderness today, because her estimate was that she had gone that far by now. What had taken her by surprise was the effect of being alone all the time for so many days. At the beginning she had not even considered it. She had been, in a very important sense, alone since the death of her mother the year she graduated from college.

She'd often spent months at a time away from home, observing either a person who needed to be taken away from his or her current surroundings or the people who were keeping that from happening. All that time Jane had pretended to be somebody else, or a succession of imaginary people. Then, when she was ready to make that person vanish, she had spent more time teaching him how to be a new and different person.

Since then, Jane had reunited with her college friend Carey McKinnon and become his wife. She had not been alone. But here she was, utterly alone again. It wasn't just that she was in disguise, living as a different person and only having honest communication with herself. She wasn't using any identity, because she wasn't letting other people be aware that she existed. She wasn't a person, but a forest being, like a heavily hunted animal that needed to avoid people to keep breathing.

As the sun went lower and the shadows lengthened, Jane began to assign more and more of her attention to the landscape and its potential for stealth and safety. This afternoon's theory was that her remaining pursuer was still asleep or just getting up to begin making his evening meal. She pictured him somewhere back off the trail, pouring, heating, and stirring the ingredients he had stolen from the boy he had murdered. While he was doing that he wouldn't be thinking about the boy, he would be thinking about her.

She reached a spot that reminded her of a place she had been once, years ago. It was in the Adirondack Mountains in upstate New York. She had been up there after the man she had known under the false name John Felker. It was where she had traced him after he had killed Harry Kemple. Since she had gone up into the mountains, he had been trying to kill her too. She had been in a canoe on Tupper Lake when he had taken his first rifle shot at her and wrecked the canoe but missed her body. Nearly all of her gear had spilled from the capsized canoe and sunk into the icy lake. They had hunted each other over a considerable expanse of forest before it ended.

The place she was remembering looked like this — maybe more thickly forested, but the rock was this way, with trees and bushes thick on both sides of a trail that ran along in a stone depression, so if a person looked at it in the right light it looked like a tubular cave with its roof lifted off. She stepped into the trail and looked ahead, and then reached the first turn and sighted along it. The trail was right at this point, just like the other one where she had fought years ago. Each straight stretch was at least thirty feet long, but then it turned, then turned again at the next place, so the trail seemed fairly straight, but a person couldn't see past any of the turns. The trail was like a channel, with the lower part worn over time to the bedrock in some places. It was a stretch of trail that was easy to enter but strenuous to leave before the end, because leaving meant climbing out of it and crawling through the brush beside and above it.

Jane felt a strong memory of the feelings of that day. She had been half-mad with desperation and anger as she fought to keep Felker from completing the task of killing her. As she remembered what she had done she stopped walking, knelt, and swung her daypack off her shoulder to the ground. She had been careful and sensible about the things she had included in her pack before she'd started this trek. She'd picked out all of the things that she had used or wished she'd had on other trips in the wild. She had also added a few things that she'd simply seen in the sporting goods store that were versatile and could be useful, but which were small and light. One of them was on her mind right now.

When she had abandoned her big fifty-pound pack so she could travel faster, she had put a number of things in her small daypack. There was one item that she could not remember making a conscious decision about in her rush to pack and be off, and she had not looked for it since. She began to lay out things that were in her daypack. There was food, there was the hunting knife, there were the water bottles, the tarp, the poncho, the hatchet. There were the guns and ammunition. She had used all of those things, so they were all near the top. As she set them aside she began to feel desperate for a couple of the other things. There was the reel of hundred-pound test monofilament fishing line. And there, almost at the bottom, was the little plastic box of fishhooks. She picked it up, carefully wrapped her hand around it, and closed her eyes in relief. She had not left them behind.

Jane stowed the things she didn't need and went to work on the trail. To the extent that she could, she reproduced all of the things that she had done that day in that lonely place in the Adirondacks years ago. She found a spot where the trail was very narrow and the sides were high. Just at the end of that stretch was an eight-inch-deep depression in the trail. She gathered some sticks and wove them together to make a grid, then placed it over the dip in the trail and covered it with leaves and thin branches so the spot looked as though it was a trap.

She cut and tied a length of monofilament fishing line to stretch across the trail at a height of about eight feet with eighteen- to thirty-inch lines that ended in fishhooks. Then she went farther along the trail a hundred feet and made her camp twenty feet from the trail.

Jane made the rest of her preparations. She made a mixture of dark makeup and streaked her face with it. She pulled the knit cap down on her head, partly because it helped keep her hair out of her eyes and face, and partly because it cushioned her head while she was lying down. She chose the clothing that would best camouflage her at night — the olive-drab shirt, the dark-gray pants, the black T-shirt, the gloves, and the netting. She took out the semiautomatic pistol from the man she had killed on the plateau and loaded its magazine and a spare with the gloves on so there would be no prints or DNA on the bullets, magazines, or gun. She kept her own pistol in the pocket of the daypack, loaded. Then she went to the spot she had selected, ate her cold dinner, and watched the sky turn black and the stars come out.

She knew that the last man would now be some miles to the north getting his gear packed, retying his shoes, and probably putting a fresh battery in his headlamp. Now he was standing up. And now he began to move south along the trail toward her.

Jane spent some time remembering exactly what had happened when she had made these preparations for John Felker. Why call him that? It was a fake name he had concocted for her. His real name was James Martin. It was because John Felker was the name he was using while he was charming her, fooling her, seducing her to get her to lead him to Harry Kemple, the sad, threadbare little gambler, so he could cut his throat. To her James Martin had only ever been John Felker. He would be until she died and forgot him. She fought off her mind's attempts to bring back the memory of his face, and then fell asleep.

She slept for hours in the silent, solitary place. The wind was not nearly as strong in these valley stretches as it had been for the nights she had spent up on the ridges. When she woke to urinate, the air seemed completely silent. She went off into a clearing fifty feet from her sleeping site, and then started to return. She was groggy from sleep, and wanting to curl up again and resume it.

The silent air changed. There were two

sounds. One was the *chuff, chuff, chuff* of boots trotting along this stretch of trail. A man was running along at a good pace, coming toward her. She stood still and listened. It was definitely coming this way, but something was wrong.

She heard the sound of leaves, dry leaves being crushed. He shouldn't be making that noise. He should be on the trail, which was a hard surface, just an inch or two of dirt on bedrock. She moved closer to the trail, and saw the glow of his headlamp. It was bouncing up and down as he ran.

He was off course. She reached to her belt for the Russian's pistol, but it was still at her bed. She had left it when she'd gotten up. Her own pistol was in her daypack. She moved quickly toward the spot to pick it up, but the sounds were getting closer too quickly. She had to get him back on track. She ran to her left so the diagonal would put her far ahead of him on the trail. As she reached it she pounded her feet on the hard surface, lifting her knees to run and make noise.

She heard him crunching through the forest to the other side of the trail, and then heard him jump into the trough that formed the path. She heard his feet now, listened to the cadence, and it was faster than she had expected. She made a turn, ran a few yards, and saw the beam of the headlamp sweep around the turn and saw her own shadow appear in front of her. She ran hard, but he did too. She had to get around the next turn before he could draw his pistol and shoot her in the back. She made the turn, running up onto the side of the trail to do it, and then saw the trap she had made in the trail.

Jane ran hard for it to coax him to gain on her, then ducked her head to jump over the sticks and leaves she had used to cover it the way a track runner jumped a low hurdle. She landed and ran on. As soon as she was out of the headlamp's beam she veered to the right to clamber up out of the trail into the woods above.

She caught sight of the man as he approached the trap, took some shorter steps, as she had, and leapt up and over the branches and leaves. The beam of his headlamp had not revealed the monofilament fishing line strung across the trail above that spot. As his body cleared the trap, he was caught on several of the fishhooks. They had pierced his clothing, stuck in the skin beneath, in his face and neck, and in his hands. He had managed to get his gun out before he had jumped, and now the pain and shock made him go wild. He was hanging in the air on the fishing line, but he began to fire his pistol rapidly ahead of him where he thought she still was and then around him into the brush and trees, up the trail.

Jane counted the shots. When she heard the tenth shot she began to move, but then her foot slipped and slid a few inches. The sound drew more shots that pounded into the ground and the trees around her. His magazine had held more shots than his friend's. She climbed uphill quickly to move out of his line of fire, and then ran hard the hundred feet back into the woods to her campsite.

Jane lifted her pack over her left shoulder and exchanged the Russian pistol she had left for her own Glock 17. She was more used to it and was probably better at reloading it quickly. Using the dead Russian's pistol was not as important as living through the next five minutes.

She could hear the man making little grunts of pain and assumed he was tearing the hooks out of his skin. She moved parallel to the trail, hoping to sneak up on him. As she made the last turn, she saw the glow of the headlamp and aimed her pistol at it.

"Drop the gun," the man said. "I'll say it only once more. Drop it."

The voice was coming from behind her. How had he pulled all of those barbed hooks out so quickly? She dropped her pistol.

She heard him crunching through the leaves toward her from behind and used the sounds to locate him precisely as she dipped her hand into her daypack. She grasped the pistol, pivoted, and fired through her daypack four times. He was so close by then that all four rounds put holes in his chest. He fell nearly at her feet and she pulled the gun out of the pack and shot him in the head.

Jane walked the rest of the way to the trap she had set. The man's headlamp had been hung on a tree branch at about his head height, and it was still turned on to make her think he was stuck there. She took it and used it to look at the places where she had tied the fishing line. The line was gone.

She brought the light to look at his body. She could see that the hooks were still in him. He had not even tried to remove them. He'd just cut the line with his knife, left the light, and gone after her.

Jane spent only a half hour dragging his body to the end of the stone section of the trail and then a hundred yards into the woods, then came back to get his pack and hide it. She put his pistol, his dead companion's pistol, the ammunition, his gear, and everything else of his into the pack. She returned her own belongings to her day-pack.

Jane walked steadily while the night sky slowly lightened. As soon as the world was bright enough to let her see the ground ahead of her she climbed up to the ridges above the trail and raised her pace to a run. She had not made much progress in the past twenty-four hours. Today she would try to make it to the end of the Hundred-Mile Wilderness. There were now five bodies along the hundred mile stretch of trail, and at least two of them lay unburied. She had to be gone before any of them were found.

26

Jane spent the hours of sunlight moving as efficiently as she could along the trail to the south. The trail to Monson took her two days instead of one. On the last day she was tempted to lighten the much smaller load that she was carrying to increase her speed, but she knew she had to maintain her discipline. Monson, Maine, was not going to be the end of her trip. She had to think about what she might have to do after that.

On the lower levels of the trail she saw chipmunks and frogs, and heard the calls of forest birds like nuthatches and warblers more often than she had on the ridges and peaks, where the cries of hawks were common. She saw the first northbound hikers that she'd seen in at least three days, but she decided to fade deeper into the woods until they passed to keep them from seeing her.

When they had passed, she hiked on until

she reached a pond, where she bathed and washed her clothes. She had allowed herself to become attached to the idea that she would reach the end of the trail, walk out of the edge of a forest, cross a street and step into a comfortable hotel where there would be a warm bath and a bed with clean white sheets. She had cured herself of that idea during the final two days. There undoubtedly was such a place, but for her it could easily be the most dangerous place of all. People would see her close up with a clean face and take an impression of one of her credit cards. It wouldn't have her own name on it, but it would be one of the precious fake identities she had planted and nurtured over a period of years. And within a few days there would be police officers asking the proprietors if anyone had just come out of the woods. There could also be Anne's ex-boyfriend Albert waiting for her nearby.

In the end she got off the trail as far as she could, hung her clothes on the branches of a pair of pine trees to dry, built a bed of pine boughs under her tarp, and used the poncho as a blanket. She made herself a meal of powdered soup mixed in water with various kinds of jerky. She wrapped herself in the poncho and the tarp to protect herself from the wind, and slept until the middle of the night.

She got up, verified that her clothes had dried, repacked everything, and began to walk in the dark. She made it to Monson well before dawn, and went straight through the little town. She thumbed her first ride on Route 6 after the sky was light enough to reveal to the driver and his companion that she was a woman. They were a college couple from Colorado who had done a short haul on the Appalachian Trail during their spring break. Kurt, the driver, was a geology major, and the woman, whose name was Amanda, was a computer engineer. They took Jane all the way to Waterville and let her off at the bus station.

Jane bought a ticket to Boston, and then spent the time before the bus was scheduled to leave by going into the ladies' room to make her clothes, hair, and skin look as though she had spent the past few days living in civilization, and then organizing the things that she had in her daypack and her pockets. She opened the Ziploc bag where she had put her phone and battery for the trip, reconnected the two, and charged the battery while she sat waiting for the bus. When she had hidden the last killer's body in the forest she had left with him all of the gangsters' remaining belongings except the money from the last man's wallet, which was just under four thousand dollars. Now she put together a paper bag of other things she wanted to discard — the hundred-pound test fishing line, the fishhooks, the bedding and tarp, the mosquito netting, the brimmed hat. When the bus was still a half hour away, she went to the dumpster in back of a fast-food restaurant and put the bag inside a thirty-three-gallon bag of garbage and pushed it near the bottom of the collection.

She still had some things in her daypack that might require her to answer some questions — the hatchet, hunting knife, and excessive sum of money — other things that were benign — food and water, clothes, poncho, watch cap, and gloves — and some things that would put her away — the Glock pistol, ammunition, and multiple identification and credit cards. She moved the money and ID so it was in her pockets, which meant that if she had to, she could just drop the daypack somewhere and keep moving.

When the bus pulled in, she went nearly to the back and sat in an empty aisle seat with her daypack occupying the seat by the window. She stayed away from the long, well-padded seat in the very rear of the bus because that always seemed to be plagued with periods of stagnant air interrupted by blasts of dragon breath.

It was early morning and most of the people who got on the bus after Jane were dressed as though they were on their way to work. The exceptions were a couple of women who had children with them. Two of the children were a boy and girl who looked about five and three. They had obviously traveled by bus before. They sat on either side of their mother in a seat, and kept looking in her travel bag to pick books they wanted her to read to them. The other mother and her kids were older. The two boys sat together talking conspiratorially, and the mother and the daughter sat together. Many of the other people on the bus were in late middle age, and there were several canes and a walker. They were who rode buses, she thought. It was the too old and the too young. Everybody between those ages was out there adding to the traffic jam.

Jane watched the five children, keeping her attention on one for a while, wondering what the little boy or little girl was thinking, what he or she thought about all of the other passengers, including Jane. Then she would pick another one and watch him. The older ones were less talkative but more attentive to what was around them. One of them, the boy in the aisle seat, kept his gaze on the window on the other side of the bus for a long time. He was watching her reflection in the opposite window. She knew because she was doing the same to him. "I know you," she thought, and it occurred to her that if she and Carey had been able to have kids, one would probably have turned out like that one.

The trip was punctuated by times when the bus coasted off the interstate and growled into the center of a town to the bus station. People would get off in small towns and the driver would open the outside compartment under the floor and retrieve their luggage. Jane always used this as a chance to get up and walk, and go to the ladies' room. In a couple of stations there were vending machines, and she bought bags of peanuts and cans of cola, flavors that she hadn't tasted during the time in the Hundred-Mile Wilderness. On the stop at the station in Portsmouth she considered calling Anne Bailey to let her know what had happened. She thought about it some more and decided that she was in no hurry to tell Anne. Telling her wouldn't serve to make her any safer at this point, since the four men were dead. All it could do was scare and distract her.

The bus came into the South Station Bus Terminal in Boston just before ten that night. Jane got off and slung her daypack over her shoulder. Adjacent to the bus terminal was the big transit center, where she got on an MBTA train to Quincy.

When Jane arrived in Quincy, she used her cell phone to call the number of the cell phone that she had left with Anne a few days earlier. She waited for a dozen rings and then hung up. She sat in a waiting area that was almost deserted until her phone rang.

"Hello," she said.

"Jane?"

"Yep. I thought I'd check on you."

"I'm so sorry. I keep this phone plugged in and charged in my bedroom, so I know it will be available and ready, but I was in the living room on another phone talking about a work project, and it took me too long to get here."

"That's fine. We're talking. How are you?"

"I'm still just fine. My job is going well, and the apartment is nice, and the car starts every morning. How about you? Are you okay?"

"After I left you I had some trouble. The car rental place where I got my car was somehow connected with the Russian gangsters. They used the car's locator to track me. I'm fine now, but I wanted to check to be sure you are too."

"Where are you?"

"Not far from you."

"Can you come and stay here tonight? I have a car now, remember? I can pick you up."

"No. I'll be at your door in a half hour."

Jane hung up and walked in the general direction of Anne's apartment. After all of the day's riding the walk was a pleasure. She walked around Anne's neighborhood looking at parked cars and trucks searching for people who were simply sitting and waiting, at vehicles with modifications intended to darken windows, hide the faces of drivers, for anything that might be equipment for watching or listening. She looked for apartment windows that had lenses mounted above the curtains or between them, for dark rooms with bare windows, and for any other pedestrians out tonight. A few times she stopped in shadowed, sheltered places to watch a window for movement or to follow a car's progress. Pedestrians were few after ten, but whenever she saw one as she neared Anne's apartment she made sure the gun she was carrying was where she remembered it, and then kept the person's location in her mind and studied him occasionally for unexpected movements or to see if he met someone else. In the end she arrived at Anne's door without seeing anything that worried her. She pressed the doorbell and Anne buzzed her in.

When she opened the door Anne's brows knitted. "You look different. Are you sick?"

"No. Never better, actually. I've been running every day for about ten days." She came in and closed the door and locked it. "Lots of fresh air and sunshine too."

"Come and sit down."

Jane stepped into the living room, but ignored the couch and the chairs. "I've been sitting all day. Have you noticed anything out of the ordinary since I left? Has there been anything that could have been connected to Albert McKeith?"

"I haven't seen any sign of him, or anybody else I'd ever seen in California. I've been trying to be careful in all the ways you taught me. I don't leave the apartment until I've sat looking out the window for five or ten minutes, seeing who's out there walking or driving by while I'm drinking my morning coffee. I always set the alarm when I leave, and when I come home I always drive past the building and around the block before I pull into the garage. I look — really look — at people on the street and near my job. Then I set the alarm again while I'm here. So far there's been no sign of trouble. I never go out to bars or other places where people meet, and never do online dating. I'm doing just what you said — concentrating on getting established in my new Anne Bailey life and work, and waiting Albert out."

"All of that is wonderful. It's exactly the right thing to do for now. Have you noticed any people who speak Russian, or English with a Russian accent?"

"No. I assume most of them would be at or near the places that attract tourists, or at the universities. Those just aren't stops on my itinerary right now. I work, I shop, and I come home. I hope that isn't forever, but right now it suits me. I was really tired of being scared. Now I'm making a lot of money — for me, anyway — and I'm making friends."

"Great. All of that couldn't be better. Don't let down your guard or get careless. And remember what I said. If anything changes, and you think it's possible you're being watched or stalked, just get in the car and go. Call me from the road."

That night Jane took a long, leisurely bath, and slept on the couch in Anne's apartment. It felt like such a luxury that when she awoke in the middle of the night, she thought for a moment that she was at home in her own bed. She had slept deeply in the Hundred-Mile Wilderness, but she had known at the time that it was happening because of extreme exhaustion. As soon as she realized that she was in the apartment she had rented for Anne, she fell asleep again and slept until she heard Anne's alarm.

After the two had breakfast, Jane gave Anne her spare cash, which was most of the four thousand dollars she had taken from one of the Russians. She also left most of the ammunition she still had in her daypack but kept everything else. On her way to work Anne drove Jane to the South Station transit center, where Jane got a seat on an Amtrak train called the Lake Shore Limited that was headed for Chicago. It was leaving an hour later and she didn't want to spend any more time in the station than she had to. She got onto the train and immediately went into a restroom and waited until she felt the train begin to move before she came out and went to her seat.

27

Porchen brought only three men with him to Maine. Four was a good number. Four men were more than enough to overpower and silence one woman and transport her. Four men all fit comfortably in the one car that he had rented in Boston, and the woman could spend the first few hours in the trunk. As soon as their work was done they could split up into two groups, and Magda and Albert could take the woman to California. He looked out the window while Yevgeny drove. Porchen had been in the Northeast before but never way out in the open country. He didn't like rain and he didn't like cold, and he didn't like being in places where there was nothing much to steal.

For much of his life he had felt the uncomfortable sensation of being the most intelligent person present. He was always the one who had to anticipate every change in advance so that the others would not get themselves arrested or killed by blundering and stumbling and reacting with violence instead of cunning.

He had heard the recorded cell phone call from Gregor Shivinsky. Gregor had said the woman had killed the other three men along the trail by various tricks and traps over several days and that he was going to be coming out of the forest at Monson alone soon. The minute Porchen had heard that, he had muttered, "No, you're not," handed the phone back to its owner and put his head down on his hands with his eyes closed tightly against the headache.

He had known at that moment that if Gregor was not dead already, he soon would be. He should have been silent, setting a trap to keep this woman from making him her fourth victim. Tcherinsky had assured him the four men were like wolfhounds. Porchen muttered, "Wolfhounds bark. Wolves don't." Porchen had already thought through the set of problems this caused. It had meant he couldn't simply stay in Boston talking with the other bosses and wait for his people to straighten out this failure and start the woman on the long journey to Los Angeles. He'd had to come all the way out here personally and pretend to care about four men who had been lured into the wilderness and defeated by a lone woman.

He would have to give their boss at least ten thousand dollars each, theoretically for whatever wife, girlfriend, or mother they had. Knowing Tcherinsky, he knew the money would not make it that far, but it was an easy gesture. In his mind he raised the payment to twenty-five thousand each. Some people would think he had overpaid, and some of them would think he was foolish enough to believe the money would go to survivors, but others would see what he was really doing. The real message was that California was the Golden State, a place where Tcherinsky's men might be happier than they were in the Northeast, and he was a boss who didn't keep everything for himself.

Yevgeny drove up to the motel and Porchen saw a door open and Magda appear. She held the door open and watched him. He got out of the car and went inside. When he stepped in he looked around, confused. "Where's the boy?" he said. "Where's Albert?"

"He's gone off after his girlfriend," she said.

"She's here too?"

"No," she said. "The woman we want

rented a car in Boston from a lot where a cousin of the Bolchevs worked, and he recognized her from the picture we sent out. Albert's girlfriend wasn't with her anymore. She had been with her in the park in Albany, in the hotel in New York, but a couple of weeks later, when the professional was leaving Boston, the girlfriend wasn't. So he figured his girlfriend was probably hiding in Boston."

"You let him go back to Boston?"

"Did I do wrong, Mr. Porchen? If I knew you didn't want me to I would never have done it. I thought he would just be in the way, and you would not want someone like him around."

Porchen put his hand on Magda's cheek and kept it there for a moment. "The professional killed all four of the men who went into the forest after her."

"Gregor Shivinsky called in as soon as he could get a signal on his phone. He said he was on his way here." She didn't move her cheek away from Porchen's hand. One didn't do that. She hoped he was just going to slap her, and not punch. She could tolerate the sting of a slap, but a punch could break a bone, dislodge teeth, even kill her. He was staring into her eyes and she didn't doubt that he was reading her mind.

"Magda, women are a gift from God," he said. "You must be disappointed in men so many times. We haven't heard from Gregor for two days. That means he's dead."

"Oh, no," she said. "I thought he must have just dropped me from the next calls because he had contact with Tcherinsky and Tcherinsky with you. I'm sorry to be so stupid."

Porchen said, "What do we do now, Magda? What's our next move?"

She said, "I'll call Albert McKeith and pick him up in Boston. His friend Jason De-Long followed his girlfriend to the place where she went to meet the professional. Somewhere in upstate New York, but he must know where."

"There," said Porchen. "See? This is why I love you." He moved his hand away from her face and patted her shoulder.

She went to the dresser and pulled her telephone out of her purse. She punched a number in and her voice changed. It became silky and soft. "Hello, Albert. Are you in Boston?" She looked at Porchen and nodded. "Have you found your girlfriend?" She shook her head to Porchen. "I'm going to come and join you."

28

Jane's train on the Lake Shore Limited pulled into the eleventh stop at the Buffalo–Depew station and Jane got off. She had been watching every person she saw for signs of trouble since Boston, but most closely since Albany. The closer she came to home, the more alert and careful she was about the chance that someone might be following her.

She used the app on her phone to call a rideshare car for Karen Sirino, one of her assumed names, and took it to a house near her old one. She walked around the house to be sure there were no broken locks or windows, then went into the garage and closed her eyes to listen while she turned the key in her car. She heard a pitiful ticking sound, but there wasn't enough of a charge to turn over the starter motor. She got out and went to the back wall where the workbench was and plugged in her battery charger. Then she opened the car's hood and looked at the instructions on the charger to remind herself where to clamp the two leads. She went into the house and walked from room to room looking at everything to be sure nothing had been moved or added. She looked at the carpet in the living room to be sure it still held the pattern of raised pile that she had created the last time she had vacuumed it.

While she waited, she made a shopping list, ran the water in all the faucets and flushed the two toilets, wiped down the inside of the refrigerator, and put in a fresh box of baking soda.

When she had done the small chores and checked to be sure the bulbs in the lights she had on timers were still alive, she locked up and returned to the garage. The charger's green light was on so she got into the car and started it. She removed the leads and unplugged her charger while the car idled. When it was warmed up she got back into it and backed out. She drove to the Wegman's supermarket a mile away.

She was surprised to see how incredible the displays of food and supplies looked to her after only a few days in the wilderness. She bought staples, luxuries, expensive cuts of meat, pastries, champagne, single malt scotch, gin and vermouth, and two bottles of a red wine she would have considered too extravagant a month ago.

When she drove in the driveway at the McKinnon house in Amherst she held her breath hoping that through some happy co-incidence his car would be in the carriage house, but when she drove into her space the one beside it was empty. As usual he wouldn't be home until he finished his rounds and made sure all of his patients were going to be alive in the morning.

She went into the house and put the groceries away and then performed her walk-around inspection. Carey was a sur-geon and was intolerant of microbes, so the kitchen and bathrooms were spotless and had been given frequent treatments with very strong cleansers. When she was not at home, he usually worked both early and late and ate at the hospital, so the refrigerator was practically empty before she filled it. She had stocked the freezer with food before she left, but he didn't appear to have cooked much of it while she was gone.

She saw that he had done laundry only a day or two ago, and that he had, as always, made the bed before he had left the house, which was a habit from his bachelor days. She walked around straightening things that didn't need it, changed a couple of towels, and then went back to the kitchen to cook. She worked out the specifics of her plan for the meal and prepped the vegetables and then got everything else seasoned and marinated and ready to heat.

At seven she texted his phone and said, "I'm home. Don't worry, you'll get used to it."

Two minutes later he texted back, "I'll be there in about twenty minutes to get started."

She decided that dinner should be ready in fifty-five minutes so they would have a half hour for a before-dinner cocktail. Carey had always been the sort of husband who loved her cooking but seemed always to be surprised. Probably that was because her movements had always been so unexpected and erratic. There were a couple of people that she had taken away from their troubles but felt she still had to check occasionally. People who used up their lives and needed to start over as someone else seldom made the transition easily or without emotional difficulty, and some of them had been unaccustomed to a life without certain shortcuts, such as stealing.

Jane wondered how her life was going to change from now on. She had made well over a hundred people disappear over the years, and she had always said that the last one to whom she would give a new life would be herself. She had not worked these things out in detail because what she did would have to be a response to the circumstances, but she had decided that the first thing that she would work at was her relationship with her husband. She was determined that if it was not perfect — if he did not get up in the morning happy to see her face and hear her voice, then it was not going to be because she had not tried as hard as she could. She was going to try to make up for every day and every night that she had not been here to devote her full attention to him.

She heard a car engine and recognized it was his BMW. She heard it go quiet and coast to the entrance of the driveway, heard the whisper of the tires on the pavement and the faint acceleration as it went up the gradual incline to the curve around the house and then to the carriage house. She felt her heartbeat quicken, and quicken again when the garage door hummed shut. She went to the back door and waited eight feet from it, smiling.

The door opened and he appeared in the doorway and stepped toward her. "Wow," he said. "You look better than I remembered you." He wrapped his long arms around her and pulled her gently into him. "You didn't need to lose weight." They gave each other a long kiss.

"Careful," she said. "This apron has probably got a preview of your dinner on it."

"I knew something smelled good. I thought they'd finally developed a beef-scented perfume."

"It's still in the research stages. But I brought home some single malt scotch and some martini ingredients if you'd like either one of those."

"Sure," he said. "I'll make us some martinis while you catch me up on what you've been doing."

"The girl is relocated, renamed, and employed in a new life. She's young enough to be flexible, and fortunately she has some talents and a quick mind. I checked on her a day ago and she was fine. So I'm home."

"How long?"

"How long will you have me?"

"That would be a long time."

"It will seem longer, probably," she said. "I expect all my overdue attention to wear on you."

"You're welcome to try that."

They finished their cocktails just as their

dinner was ready. Jane had set the table while she was waiting for Carey, and now they served the food together. Carey opened and poured one of the bottles of red wine Jane had bought. Everything was declared to be perfect, maybe because it was, and maybe because other things that were far more important than food were straining at the edge of perfection in Carey's mind.

It occurred to Jane that soon this would be a memory. She would see again the way Carey looked at this instant, and how tall and strong he was, and the open, happy expression on his face. You could see the sheer goodness that he exuded. She was afraid that the future couldn't possibly be as good as the present, and that when she remembered this she would feel the loss.

When they finished dinner, they went out to the refrigerator to look at the pastries she'd brought home, but they both agreed that they had no room for them now.

They cleared the table and sat in the living room on the couch in dim light from the kitchen talking and finishing their wine and setting the glasses down sometimes to kiss. After a while, Jane stood up and took both of their glasses into the kitchen and then reappeared.

She took Carey's hand, so he stood up.

"Where are we going?"

"It's bath time," she said. "Then it's bed-time."

"Now?" he said. "Isn't it kind of early?"

"Well, I'm going up there. The first man who comes in after me is going to have a very nice evening."

"Oh, yeah. I seem to recall some very big talk over the phone just before you stayed away for a few more weeks."

"I plan to redeem all rain checks and make good on all guarantees. In addition, if you've been having any fantasies in which I have played the lead female role, I intend to make them come true, just like the good fairy. Or the bad fairy — your choice. They're your fantasies."

They walked toward the stairs, and he said, "Do you have any fantasies?"

"Yep, I do. They're all pretty much like this."

They stopped on the first landing, and again when they reached the top of the stairs. They walked together down the hallway and by the time they got to the master bath they were naked. A moment later the oversized tub was filling, and they stepped into it together.

Jane and Carey spent that night exactly as Jane had suggested. At one point Carey said, "It's three o'clock."

"I know," she said. "I'm thinking that those pastries I showed you after dinner would probably taste really good about now."

He laughed. "You think so?"

"I do. Tomorrow they won't be as fresh, either. Not stale, but not as perfect."

"I wouldn't mind one of those napoleons. But there are still things I think we should try tonight."

"Write them down. It's pastry time. Come on."

They got up and put on robes and went downstairs to the kitchen. They sat at the kitchen table and ate pastries. Then they went back upstairs, and lay down on the bed, pulled up the covers and slept until noon.

After they got up and were drinking their coffee in the kitchen, Carey said, "If there is any time in my life that I could choose to live over again, it would be last night."

"How sweet," she said. "If that's true, you will. And more. Nothing held back. I was kidding last night, but not kidding. The reason I picked you wasn't because I needed a tall guy for my basketball team. You're the one for my life. I work because we work."

"I assume what you mean is that you're

still in love with me?"

"And I've told you about six hundred and eighty times, mostly over a pay phone or a throwaway cell, because I couldn't say aloud where I was or when and if I'd be home. It was true, but it sounded like empty bullshit even to me. So maybe I'm finding other ways to say it for a while."

The next day at 5:30 when Carey got into his car to drive to the hospital to prepare for the morning's surgeries, he found himself thinking about his own life rather than his patients'. He was pleased with it and allowed himself to feel grateful for the small miracle of meeting Jane Whitefield in Ithaca when they were both eighteen.

29

Albert McKeith stood on the street near the Lenox Hotel in Boston looking at the cars passing. He had spent the past few mornings looking for Sara in places where people went to have coffee, and afternoons in women's stores where somebody like her could have found a job in a short time. They loved to hire beautiful girls for those jobs, and beautiful girls came and went pretty quickly. The nights he had spent floating through the clubs and the trendy bars like a ghost, looking. Sara was the sort of woman who was always asked to dance, so he surveyed the dance floors. If there was a second floor or a balcony above, he would climb to it and stand by the railing looking down, searching for the corn-silk blond hair and the thin shape. A few times he had needed to come around to look from a different angle to be sure it wasn't her, and it always wasn't.

Magda had not told Albert much when she had called. The first time, when she called from the motel in Maine, she told him only to stay in the hotel where he was. He had allowed himself to interpret her intentions optimistically, and over time the optimism made him believe that Porchen had given up on finding the dark-haired woman, so Magda had decided to take a little break from being a *vor* and spend the next few days in the Lenox Hotel making Albert forget the things that were on his mind.

She had called him a day later and said, "We're on the way to the Lenox Hotel. Get packed and wait on the street near the front entrance so we can see you." There had been no chance of a mistake. She had said "we" twice. It wasn't over. They were just dragging him away from his own concerns into theirs again.

When he had thought of asking Cornell Stamoran for an introduction to some people who would be capable of helping him find and kill Sara, he had not imagined anything like this. He admitted to himself that he had hoped they would be such good friends of Cornell's that they would do it as a favor to him. Albert could thank them and be done with them, and the person he would owe would be Cornell. It wasn't like that at all. What Cornell had done was like giving Albert an introduction to the devil. Albert had a dim memory of Cornell giving him some kind of warning, but he couldn't bring back the exact words. No doubt it had been something like "Don't get too close to them."

He wished that Magda had told him what kind of car to watch for, the way the Uber and Lyft people did. It was still cool at night in Boston and he had been out on the pavement for a while. Then he saw the car. The car was a Chevy Tahoe, and it was black and it had tinted side windows in the back so a person couldn't see who the passengers were. The car glided to a stop at the curb and the side window slid down. He could see that the car had three rows of seats. Two of the seats behind the driver were occupied by Porchen and Magda, and the ones behind them by two men he had not seen before who looked like foot soldiers of the *Bratva.* The nearest seat he could get to was the seat beside the driver. He went to the door, climbed in, and untangled the seat belt so he could bring it across his chest to fasten it.

He said, "Hello, Mr. Porchen, Magda," and looked at the two stone-faced men in the back. "Hello," he said, and nodded to the driver, Yevgeny.

Porchen said, "Albert, we lost the woman who hid your girlfriend, but I remembered something you said the first time you came to see me."

"What was that?"

"You said that your friend Jason had followed your girlfriend from Utah and then all the way to New York State, where she met this other woman. Do you know where? What the address is?"

"No, I don't. He called me and I flew there to meet him. He didn't know there was going to be this other woman. There was a car Sara had bought and he had put transponders in it in Salt Lake so he could see where she went. He told me to meet him where he had followed it. I rented the same kind of car he had. They were SUVs, one black and one silver, and he and I kept in touch by phone. He said 'Turn here, turn there,' and I went expecting to wait, but Sara was already moving when I got there, and Jason said she had taken off and there was this woman with her. We started following Sara's car using the GPS."

"Okay. Call Jason now."

"Now?"

Porchen turned to Magda. "Is he deaf?"

He said more loudly, "Now!"

Albert dialed the number and then waited for Jason to take the call. He heard the ring signal three times, then a fourth, and he knew. Jason was looking at the screen of his phone and seeing Albert's name and number, and he was deciding that answering could only get him more deeply involved with the terrifying people who were with Albert right now. The phone rang again and Albert could see Porchen was getting irritated.

Porchen said, "What's the problem? Is his pocket a mile from his hand so it takes an hour to get to his phone?"

"I'm not sure what's holding him up," Albert said. "He could be asleep with his phone sound turned off, or just be out getting the mail or something. He'll see my name and call back."

Magda said, "Hang up for a few seconds and call again."

Albert shrugged, held up his phone and disconnected, and then redialed the number as she had asked. "What does this do?" He held the phone to his ear, but his eyes on her.

Magda said, "Sometimes you can dial the wrong number so a person who doesn't know you sees your name and doesn't answer. And if you did dial the right number, he'll realize you're going to keep trying until he gives in, because your life depends on it."

Albert didn't see Porchen look amused, so he kept the phone ringing. Then the ringing stopped. He turned it off. He saw that Magda's eyes were widening, and he knew it must be an attempt to warn him. This time he texted Jason. "I'm in a bind here. Tell me the address where you saw Sara leave with the woman."

A minute later, the answer came back. The text said, "I didn't see them come out of the house. I had put GPS trackers in her car in Salt Lake City, so I found her car and then parked a mile away. Her car was on Fletcher Street in the first block south of Franklin Street, and there were two big trees on the lawn."

Magda said, "Can you find it again?"

"I guess so," Albert said. "I wasn't there long because she had left, but I went past there and saw the place."

She only slid her eyes to the side toward Porchen and then focused them sharply on Albert. "Be sure. Whatever the answer is, be sure."

"I can find it."

Porchen reached up to tap the driver's

shoulder. "Take us to a hotel near the airport."

The man said, "Yes, Mr. Porchen," and Magda took her phone out of her purse as the man accelerated.

She said, "This is Magda Kaprovna. You remember me? All right. We will need five tickets from Logan Airport in Boston to Buffalo, New York, to leave tomorrow. One will be for me," then said, "Yes, Mr. Porchen is one. You have his information. One will be for Maxim Markarin, one for Yevgeny and Alexei, yes. There's only one you probably don't have. His name is Albert McKeith. Oh, yes, I forgot. So you have everyone. Those six. Please call me when you have our flight. Thank you."

The driver took them almost to the airport before Magda's phone rang. "Yes?" she said. She listened for a moment and then said something in Russian to the others, and said into the phone, "Do you have a hotel close to Logan Airport where you can get us four rooms?"

She listened again. "That will be fine. And while you're at it, can you get us another hotel near the Buffalo airport, just one night each. We can take it from there. Thank you."

This was the way that Albert knew where he was going and what he would be doing next. He thought about it and conceded that it probably didn't matter that he was being dragged away from his project of finding and killing Sara. His time in Boston had not resulted in any progress. The frustrating part was that he might have been twenty feet from her in a crowd at some point and never seen her, so there was no such thing as eliminating a district from his search. No matter when he came back to Boston, he would be starting over.

He felt a dozen contradictory emotions. For the first time in his life he had an alliance with powerful, intimidating people. This was a form of power. Even though the power wasn't his, it was frightening enough to protect him from people he might have been afraid of before. He also had them on his side to help him find his disloyal girlfriend and make an example of her. They didn't feel as much urgency about that as he had hoped, but why should they? And he had met Magda. She was beautiful, and she was, at least for now, interested in traveling with him, sleeping with him, and keeping him out of trouble. She had said this was a state of affairs that was sure to change at some point, but it didn't matter what women said to you. Relationships with any of them were day-to-day, often minute-to-minute. When they said now and forever, they meant now.

He had been satisfied with the situation, but the part that was happening today was changing the terms of their alliance. He hadn't been disturbed when his problem with Sara had been postponed. But now they were drafting him into their gang to kidnap the woman they were interested in. He had wanted their help in his affair of honor. He didn't recall agreeing to join in their moneymaking schemes. He thought about telling Mr. Porchen that he had already obtained for them the woman's location from Jason DeLong and that was all he could do for him.

He tried out the idea, saying it silently in a number of ways. He tried saying it in a friendly manner, smiling at their cleverness and audacity in cornering him this way. He tried the idea of using Magda as his spokesperson. He tried telling Porchen that although he had killed a man in LA he wasn't a killer, really. He was teaching a dishonorable woman a lesson, which he considered a duty. After he had run out of approaches, he knew that he would never use any of them.

Magda's phone rang and she answered it. When she had finished the call she said,

"We stay at the Holiday Inn near the airport. Our flight leaves for Buffalo at noon tomorrow."

When they got to the hotel in sight of Logan Airport, Magda gave Porchen his key card in the little cardboard folder, handed another folder with two keys to one of the two young men, one folder to Yevgeny, and handed a folder with two keys to Albert. Then she stood still and silent beside him for a few seconds and Porchen said to all of them, "You're free, but don't turn your phone off." He walked to the row of elevators while the rest of them waited until he had gone in and pressed a button and the door had rolled shut. Then they went to summon the next elevator. They all rode it upward together but the two men got off at the third floor, Yevgeny on the fourth floor, while Magda and Albert stayed on until the fifth.

Albert took her bag and his own and walked to the room that had been written on their folder, unlocked the door, and held it for her to enter. He was feeling good because she had made all the arrangements on the way and she had chosen to share a room with him. To Albert that meant, first, that she had no relationship with Mr. Porchen, meaning Porchen had no interest in her, and second, that of the four younger men in the party, he was the one she wanted close to her.

She went into the room and looked out the window, then turned on a light, closed the curtains, and went into the bathroom. She turned on the shower and took off her clothes while she waited for the water to warm up and stepped into it. She did not close the door or show any consciousness that he was still standing outside the door looking in. He was aware that if he had asked her about it she would say that it would be ridiculous for her to care about his presence. There was nothing that he had not seen and touched already, and she knew that he liked it and would wait to be invited to again.

When she finished her shower, she came out wearing the hotel's fluffy white bathrobe, which she cinched tightly around her waist. "You can take your turn in the shower," she said, sat on the bed, and used the remote control to turn on the television.

He said, "How do you know I want to take one now?"

"I know you don't want to sleep on the floor and if you don't take a shower you won't be in the bed with me."

He went into the bathroom and took a

shower. When he came back she stood up and let the robe slip off her shoulders, and then held her arms out for him to step between them. Tonight she was affectionate and passionate and he wondered if she was making up for her recent coldness. He was aware that there was nothing she did that wasn't practical and premeditated and it surprised him how little he cared about that.

The next morning Magda texted the other three rooms to wake the others in time to have breakfast and then she packed. The group met in the restaurant on the first floor and ate while they talked to each other in low-voiced Russian. Albert looked around him at the people at nearby tables and enjoyed the fact that they probably had noticed his table was speaking Russian, and would assume that he spoke Russian too. He wasn't sure why he liked misleading them when there was no particular advantage to it, but he did.

In another hour they were in the airport waiting and he felt again that other people assumed he was Russian but wasn't sure he was glad about it. In the past few years, he'd heard that there were always people from the government peering at travelers in airports through unseen cameras and recording what they said to each other. He only hoped that none of his companions was saying anything that would get him in trouble. Since he understood about four words of Russian, they might be saying anything.

A half hour later they were allowed to board the airplane. He was surprised to see that Magda's ticket put her beside Porchen at the aisle, Yevgeny had an aisle seat opposite, the other men's tickets put them in the A and C seats in the row behind, but he was seated in the B seat between the two large men. He waited until the airplane took off and then folded his arms, leaned back, and went to sleep, which wasn't difficult after his night being on the good side of Magda's disposition.

When they arrived in Buffalo, he expected to see more members of the *Bratva*. He had always heard that Buffalo was a place with a heavy organized crime presence, but there was nobody there to meet them. Magda had rented a seven-seat car in advance, and Yevgeny drove while Alexei sat in the seat beside him. Albert was seated by himself in the third row with the luggage.

They drove to the hotel near the Buffalo airport that Magda had told the brotherhood's travel agent to reserve, unloaded their luggage, and went inside. It was lunch time, so Albert's thoughts were beginning to move in that direction. He noted that Magda dealt with the front desk people and that she had four rooms again. He wondered if she was going to put him with one of the two big men and herself with the other, just to remind him that she wasn't his girlfriend, but she gave one of the envelopes to Albert and handed him her bag.

When they got to their room Albert set her bag on the folding stand and left his sitting on the closet floor. Then he sat on the chair that was facing the television set and watched Magda to see what was supposed to happen next.

She turned and looked at him. "What? You don't think I'm beautiful anymore?"

"I didn't want you to think I was treating you like a girlfriend."

"That was right, but I didn't want you to stop thinking like a man. We don't have to be anywhere until tonight."

He was up in an instant, kissing the back of her neck and unzipping the back of her dress so he could slip it down off her shoulders. The next two hours were better for Albert than he had ever dared to hope. As always, Magda seemed to shift moods, almost to be a different woman every few minutes, but today they were all pleasant, happy women, all wanting to stimulate Albert to desire them more.

Afterward, Magda said, "Are you hungry, baby?"

He knew that everything she'd been doing since she had called his cell phone in Boston was being done to manipulate and control him. He thought about it for a second and verified that he still didn't care. "Yes," he said. "Are you?"

"Yes," she said. "We can take a bath together and then go downstairs for a nice lunch."

While he followed her into the bath he studied her tattoos. She had told him that the big one on her shoulder of the Madonna and baby Jesus said she was a thief. The tattoo was a kind of good luck charm for the profession. The two pictures of American hundred-dollar bills below her hip bones and above her groin were so real they looked as though she could lift them off and spend them and didn't require an explanation. He had seen others on the arms or bellies of a couple of the men in the *Bratva*. It was typical that instead of the one-dollar bills on the men she would have hundreds. The two eight-point stars on the fronts of her shoulders were signs that the men all seemed to have. He supposed it meant that she was a member of the same gang.

When they were at lunch she said, "You seem fascinated with my tattoos. Do want to get a tattoo?"

"No," he said. "I just like to look at yours."

"They just say who I am. You already know who I am."

"I'll try not to be so obvious."

"It doesn't matter."

Her telephone buzzed and she put it to her ear. "Magda." She listened for about twenty seconds. "Da." She cut the connection and put her phone in her purse. "We go tonight at twelve. That means we check out of the hotel. We don't leave anything around, and we clean the room before we go."

"Do they know where we're going?"

"We're counting on you for that." She looked at him with her eyes to the side. "You said you knew where the house was."

"I said I knew the block. I didn't see the two women coming out."

"Albert," she said. "You must know this has been hard on all of us. If you don't really know, please tell me right now. Do not stand in front of Mr. Porchen later and say that you forgot, or all the houses look alike, or something. If you tell me right now, I might be able to get him to hold his temper and let you live. Please, please be honest with me. If we screw this up, he might not let either of us live."

"Don't worry," he said. "It's not that kind of problem. There are only about four houses on that block. Some of them will have people living in them that are not that woman. One of them is where she met Sara. How hard can that be?"

"I'm just trying to make sure this goes right. I know that you're a person who lives by your cleverness. You go from one person to another and give them what you have to and get what you can get. You're good at meeting people and talking people into trading things. That's okay. But we in the *Bratva* don't live that way. Everybody owes certain things to each of the others. If one of the others needs protection or money or food and I have it, I give it to him. That's why they call it a brotherhood. If you promise them something and don't give it to them, they won't understand it the way you do."

"I don't expect them to," he said. "I told them what I knew and I'll use it to find the right place. Then they'll be satisfied, right?"

"Right," she said.

That night at ten Magda called the bellman's desk and she and Albert went to the lobby with their bags. Porchen and his two men gave her their key cards in their little folders. Magda went to the front desk and waited until a young man came to the desk and said, "Are we checking out?"

"Yes," she said. She handed him the four folders.

He looked on his computer and said, "I'll get you your receipt." He typed something on the computer and turned away to see that the receipt was rolling off the printer. "Was your stay satisfactory?"

Albert overheard and watched her. She nodded. "Yes. We just have a flight in a couple of hours."

"I understand. Most of our guests are here for the airport."

The car was waiting in the circle in front of the hotel when they went outside. This time Porchen looked at Albert and pointed to the seat beside Yevgeny, and Albert took it. Magda and Porchen sat in the second pair of seats, and Maxim and Alexei claimed the third row.

Albert told Yevgeny how to get out of the airport and the rest of the drive from Cheektowaga, where the Buffalo Niagara International Airport was. The drive was the same one he had taken from the airport to get to the house before, following Jason DeLong's instructions. He took Genesee

Street to the west to the Youngmann Expressway to the Grand Island Bridge on the Niagara River and then along the east side of the river for about three miles. After dark the river looked black, but he could see the reflections of headlights on the road on the other side of the river. There were a few oil storage tanks on big empty fields along the river and a couple of concrete lots with big garages and trucks parked in front of them.

When they were just at the edge of the little town they went over a creek and past a park and then past the first houses. Albert said, "You can turn right on Wheeler Street."

Yevgeny said, "Weller Street?"

"I'll let you know where to turn when we get there."

He thought he remembered a stoplight at that corner and when he saw one coming up he said, "I think that's it right up there. Get ready. That's it. Turn here."

They went another three blocks and he said, "Turn left and go slow. It's in this next block."

Porchen said, "You didn't sound sure yesterday. Are you now?"

"Sure enough."

Porchen said, "No, you tell me you're sure, and I'll decide if that's sure enough."

Albert felt a sudden chill in his spine.

"Yes, sir. I'm sure that it's one of these four houses down here on the left. Jason gave me directions to where their car was parked. We were still on the phone when he saw the car pull out and went after her, and told me to go along the river to catch up. He said they must have come from one of those houses."

Porchen looked at Magda. She gave an apologetic shrug, as though to say, "I don't know what to think either," but what she said was, "If you want to let me out I can take a close look at the houses."

"Take him with you," Porchen said.

"Let me take Yevgeny. He's good with locks."

"So are you. Take Albert. He should be the one who shares the risk."

Yevgeny took them past the three houses and turned the corner. Magda and Albert got out and the SUV drove on. Albert looked at her and pointed. "The car was parked in front of the first one."

She walked past the first house without appearing to give it much attention. He said, "This one."

"Don't talk," she whispered, and kept walking to the second house. As she walked she looked over her shoulder at the street and turned her head at each house, clearly checking to be sure there was nobody look-ing out a window at them. She walked past all four houses and turned the corner at the end of the block. She walked about sixty feet and then went up a driveway.

Albert was disturbed that she had not stopped at any of the four houses he had pointed out as the possibilities. Had she not understood him, or had she just felt such contempt for his knowledge that she had assumed he was wrong? She seemed so certain of what she was doing that he began to question his own information. Had she seen something that made those houses im-possible?

As Albert followed her along the side of the house a dog began barking just to his left, and it surprised him so much that he jumped and felt the hair on his neck and arms rise, but Magda kept exactly the same pace without being visibly startled. He re-alized after a single growl-bark-bark the dog had stopped, and he tardily realized the dog was in the basement of the house and couldn't get out. When he passed the house he saw a doghouse in the yard. He realized that the dog probably slept in his doghouse when it was warm but it was still too cold for that in April. It reminded Albert that he felt a little cold right now.

Magda seemed impervious to cold. She wore her customary dark jeans and black pullover with a zipped-up leather jacket, so as she passed in and out of shadows it was hard to keep his eyes on her. When she reached the fence at the edge of the backyard of the houses, she hoisted herself up and over it to the next yard and kept going. He realized that this was the first of the houses he had pointed to. She was coming up on it from behind.

She moved close to a rear window and put her hands up to shade her eyes so she could see into the darkened room. Then she moved to the back steps so she could stand on the concrete landing and look inside from there. She came down and looked up at the second-floor windows, then walked backward for a few steps to get a better angle.

Then she went past the house to the next. This one was much like the last one. Albert hadn't seen any houses like this in California. It seemed to be only about twenty feet wide from the front, but was two and a half stories high, seeming to be a stone foundation that was about three feet high that was part of a full basement, a first and second floor, and a low attic. There was a detached garage near the back of the property, reached not by a regular modern driveway, but by a driveway that consisted of two parallel strips of concrete. Magda looked in a side window, so Albert did too. There was no car parked there, so he realized it was possible someone was out and might come home without warning when the bars closed or the party ended. There was also an unwelcome sight near the back of the house, a large dog bowl with water in it and a steel chain attached to a ring set into the concrete.

She stepped away from the house to look at the upper windows and then went up on the concrete steps to look in the kitchen, as she had with the other. Albert moved close to her and she looked surprised, as though he had interrupted her thoughts. "This is the one," she whispered.

"Are you sure?" He instantly wished he had not said that.

She merely nodded. Then she took a pair of small metal picks from her jeans and bent over the doorknob. He could see what she was doing — sticking the one he'd heard called "the tension wrench" into the key slot to turn the cylinder a little, and then putting the pick in to rake the pins into line. She opened the door and pushed him inside ahead of her, then closed it. She took a small flashlight from her pocket and turned it on.

She spoke in a natural voice. "While we're here, do not touch anything."

"How do you know it's the right house?"

"She and I have a lot in common. There's no burglar alarm because she's not sure she would want the cops to come and look around for clues or start identifying all the fingerprints. Instead she leaves a bowl and a chain for a very big dog that doesn't exist outside her door. She's good. This doesn't look like a safe house or a hideout or anything. It feels like your grandma's place." She ran the beam of her flashlight around the kitchen. "Somebody has done a lot of cooking here. See the old iron pans?" She moved the beam. "And look at that clock on the wall, with the red plastic case. I love that. Maybe I'll steal it when we've got her and hang it in my kitchen."

Magda walked to the refrigerator and opened it. He could see that the shelves had nothing on them except an open box of baking soda. She leaned in and sniffed. "A fresh box."

"What's it for?"

"It absorbs food smells. She's away a lot."

Magda closed it and walked through the doorway to the next space, a small hallway with a hardwood floor. To the right there was a narrow staircase against a wall, and ahead on the left was a living room. As Albert took his first step toward the couch she put her arm up like a traffic barrier. "Don't step on the carpet."

"What's wrong?"

"Do you see the marks from the vacuum cleaner?" She shone the flashlight on the carpet and the pattern appeared.

"Oh," he said. "I didn't see it."

"She knew you wouldn't. That's why it's there. Come upstairs with me. Don't open any doors, and look at the floor to be sure there's no powder to step on."

They climbed the stairs to the second floor and Magda went into the bedroom that from its position could be considered the master bedroom. Albert could see the house was old and it had been modest whenever it had been built. The bedrooms were all small. The master had a heavy bed and dresser but no clothes in the closet.

The second bedroom looked as though it had been the room of a couple. Things were tasteful and functional, but old fashioned. On one of the tables there was a photograph of a family that looked as though it had been taken in the 1980s. It seemed to be a husband and wife about forty years old, with a son and daughter that were both teenaged. They were dark skinned, Albert thought possibly Mexican or Central American. Magda looked at it hard, bending close to it, but not touching it.

In the third bedroom she looked closely at the top of the closet door to detect any hairs or slips of paper that might fall, then opened it. She smiled. "Hello, sister," she muttered. She moved some of the clothes on hangers a few inches so she could look at each garment. She stood on a chair to look at the shelf above the clothes, then came down.

She looked at Albert. "You said she looked a bit like me."

"She's nowhere near as good-looking," he said unconvincingly.

Without any warning Magda undid the button at her waist and stripped off her tight jeans. She took a pair of jeans off a hanger, stepped into them, pulled them up, and fastened them. She held her arms up above her head and joined her hands as Albert had seen ballerinas do on television, then spun around. The jeans fit. Magda lifted her right foot to the chair and examined the ankle. "She's about an inch shorter than I am. Otherwise, not much difference." She took off the pair of jeans and hung them on their hanger, which was still where she'd found it.

She put her own jeans back on and stepped into her boots, then took her phone from her back pocket. She punched a key on the phone. "We're in her house," she said. "She's not here."

Albert heard what he was sure must be Porchen's voice, speaking in Russian. She answered in Russian, went to the window, saw where the car was, aimed her small flashlight out the window at it, and then turned it on and off quickly. Albert heard the voice again, and she hung up. "They'll be here in a minute," she said.

She turned on the flashlight, looked in the mirror above the dresser, adjusted her hair with her hand, and then looked at Albert. "He's pleased. You may have saved yourself tonight. I don't think he would have been happy with you if this had gone wrong. And once he has her, he isn't going to need you, so you'll be able to be on your way." She waited for an answer, and then said, "Well? Nothing to say?"

"I understand," Albert said.

"Do you?"

"Yes. I didn't find it, I just narrowed it down. You found it." She shrugged. "Your girlfriend showed us where it is by parking in front of it. She's the one who's getting her caught. If you get around to killing your girlfriend, make sure you tell her she betrayed her last friend."

There were heavy footsteps on the stairs and then Yevgeny and Maxim came into the room. Porchen arrived in the doorway and reached in to turn off Magda's flashlight. "Let's not make it obvious we're here."

"Yes, sir," Magda said.

"The next thing we want to do is take some time learning about this place. If she's a professional she probably has some weapons hidden here, maybe money, identification, telephones, and whatever else she uses."

"I don't think she lives here," Magda said. "I wouldn't."

"I wouldn't either," he said. "This is something else. What I want is to use what belongs to her, so we don't let anybody know what happened. If we take things from here that nobody knows she has, it will help. It's even better to take her in her own car. Then no cops will say, 'Her car is still here, and her purse,' or whatever. Everything will just be gone, so maybe she took off herself. I want it to look to the people who know her that she did what she usually does."

"Yes, boss," Magda said. "I'll start in the attic."

"Good idea," Porchen said. "Don't leave prints, finger or foot, up there."

She went out to the hallway and began trying doors to find the one that went up to the attic.

Albert said, "Should I start with the other bedrooms?"

"Fine. We have to look everywhere and that's an easy start," Porchen said. "You're not dusty yet, so stay that way. Do this right. Put everything back where you find it. No prints."

Albert went out, using his cell phone for a flashlight, and started in the master bedroom. He supposed the *vory* would be better at searching than he was, because they had probably all done some burglary. But he had heard at some point that most people who hid valuable or important things hid them as close as possible to where they slept. A gun wasn't much good for protection if you couldn't reach it at night, and if you might need to get out of a place fast you had to be able to grab your money and go, not have to dig it up in the backyard.

Albert looked around the room with the idea that he was the person hiding things here. He tried checking the boards of the hardwood floor with his light and pocket-knife to try to find a loose one. He tried feeling the mattress and pillows for any hard or lumpy places. He pulled the mattress aside and then looked under the springs to try to see anything hidden there. He went into the closet and looked for clothes, then tried the floor and felt the walls to see if there was any surface that gave or sounded hollow. He stood on a chair and tried to find anything on the ceiling that had been plastered or taped over, examined the light fixtures and crawled along the walls to look for anything odd about a plug or fixture. He opened and removed every drawer and looked under and behind it for anything that might be attached. He scrutinized doors, cabinets, and bedding. He opened the window, hung the upper part of his body outside, and searched for anything that might have been stuck out there so a person could open a window and retrieve it. Finally he gave up and sat with his back against the wall for a while, thinking and waiting for the others to find something where they were searching.

This morning Carey McKinnon had gone to the airport to fly to a Cleveland hospital to take over a surgery for his colleague Mike Drooshin. In preparing for the operation Mike had asked Carey to examine the scans and X-rays, then to meet the patient, and then consult. Finally, he had asked Carey to do the operation while Mike assisted and learned the finer points of doing the procedure himself.

This was a big one, called a septal myectomy for a patient with hypertrophic cardiomyopathy. It had to be done with the heart motionless while Carey worked on it, which meant performing a cardiopulmonary bypass for an operation that could last three to six hours. When he had left for the airport last night Jane had hugged him for at least a minute before she let go.

She had planned and prepared for her day ahead of time too. She liked to stay busy with things that were routine on days when Carey was away. She was using this day to bring her safety and emergency preparations back to peak efficiency. Jane had been away for at least a month, so there were jobs that hadn't been done for a while.

Jane drove to a supermarket and a Target for supplies. She bought canned and frozen food, soft drinks, coffee, and tea. She bought cleaning supplies — Comet cleanser, disinfectant wipes and Lysol toilet cleaner, Windex, liquid hand soap, dust cloths, sponges, and brushes. She had a mop for the kitchen and bathrooms, and another mop for applying polish to the hardwood floors before buffing them.

She bought new matched towels for the bathrooms and dish-towels for the kitchen, a set of new curtains for the windows. She bought a supply of new light bulbs for the lamps she had on timers, and dust filters for the furnace and air conditioning intakes.

Jane had also brought replacements and new supplies for the part of the house that other people didn't know about. She was returning the now-cleaned special Glock pistol and its four reloaded magazines to the hiding place in the old coal furnace's round ducts. She also had some improved pieces of identification that Stewart Shattuck had included in the package when he had sent the identification for Anne Bailey.

She had also thoroughly washed the perfume bottle from her trip on the Appalachian trail and refilled it with her most recent batch of distilled juice of water hemlock, and a second perfume bottle with a second supply to carry in her purse, as always. Working with the water hemlock plants always required glass lab equipment, rubber gloves, masks, and protective clothing. The plants were beautiful, with a flat pad of bloom made of tiny white flowers, and tall stalks. Because they were so pretty there were occasionally women who picked a bunch for a bouquet and lost consciousness from touching them with bare hands. And of course, Jane brought money. This time Jane brought a few hundred dollars in mixed currency, and thirty thousand dollars in hundred-dollar bills. She also intended to return to the hiding place most of the identification cards and credit cards that she had brought with her on her trip with Anne Bailey.

The more problematic supplies she had hidden in the car before she left home, some in the car's natural hiding spots, such as the battery compartment her Volvo had under the spare tire beneath the trunk. The more mundane supplies had come in recyclable bags, and they were simply piled up in the trunk, with a few that didn't fit well there, like the mops, on the floor of the back seat area.

By ten forty-five Jane was driving past her old house looking attentively at the building, the yard, and the neighborhood for anything that might signal either of the two kinds of visitors — enemies or people who had been sent by someone to see her because they were trying to run away from the kinds of trouble that stopped a person's heart. There were no unfamiliar cars parked in the vicinity of her house. There were no trucks with people sitting in them and none with suspicious openings to the cargo areas, no vehicles at all that had opaque window tinting. The Buffalo area was famous for snowstorms, for occasional months when the sky stayed gray virtually all the time, not for annoying, blinding doses of sunshine.

She drove around the neighborhood a second time, looking again and looking farther out, and studying things that could be signs that someone was watching for her. The Russians worried her.

The Russians were professional criminals. The four men she had escaped on the Appalachian Trail should have been good enough to catch and kill her. If that had been their job, they probably would have succeeded. She was here and they weren't because they had been sent to take her alive. That requirement had made the difference. Being captured and tortured, forced into betraying all of her runners, was the prospect that she hated most. She had been willing to do anything to keep that from happening. From the moment when she'd realized that was what they must want, she had felt there could be no limit. Some people would call what she'd done self-defense, and some would call it murder. They could call it anything. She hadn't cared, and she didn't care now.

Jane had been caught once and made the subject of an auction, with a group of potential buyers drawn from some of the people who had known that she had stolen one of their victims from them. That was why she had made the decision to carry the bottle of deadly water hemlock for the rest of her life. Once she made the promise to one person that she would die rather than tell anyone where they were, she had the responsibility to have available the means of killing herself.

Jane pulled her car into the garage and

closed the big roll-down door, then opened the car trunk and put together her first load to bring into the house. She took the bags to the porch at the kitchen door and set them down, unlocked the door, and placed one bag against the door so it would remain open while she brought the other bags in and put them on the kitchen floor. She went back right away and stepped to the car trunk and lifted her next load. She walked in through the open door with the bags, and everything changed.

She heard a swish an instant before the first hard blow struck the side of her body. She knew she had been hit by a powerful force like a charging animal. It hit her so hard that her head snapped sideways and her body flew across the kitchen table and tipped it over, so her side slammed against the sink. When her body dropped to the floor, she landed on her face and shoulder, and for a second she thought her neck might have broken. A second collision occurred, and this time she had an instant to see a human shape flopping onto her and flattening her on the floor. The body was big, male, and heavy. It was on her back and pressing down on her, making it impossible to draw a breath into her with all that pressure on her lungs and ribs.

She felt at least three sets of strong hands and arms holding her still, and then pulling her wrists behind her body and twisting her arms together. There was the distinctive clicking sound of a set of handcuffs closing on both of her wrists.

At that moment Jane was powerless, unable to move, because the man whose body was crushing her was still there. She had some vague expectation that things were going to change, that they would lift her up or turn her over, but the expectation was wrong. The heavy body didn't move. It was a huge effort to expand her chest to gasp for air, but all she could get were quick, shallow puffs.

She felt as though she might lose consciousness and then she was dragged upward. She was aware of several kinds of pain at once. Her neck and shoulder and her right cheekbone were throbbing, and she could feel three or four sets of strong hands gripping both arms in a couple of places like clamps. They stretched her backward across the table, and as her eyes were aimed at the overhead light fixture, a person near her ankles moved toward her. It was a man and he punched her face, first the left side of her head, and then the right, and pounded her arms and ribs. She saw a flash as a punch landed over her eye.

He was beating her brutally, and she couldn't move because the others were holding her down. She tried to kick at them, but a new thing happened. Two more hands held her ankles, and some other person hit her legs with something. It felt long and fast, like a bat or a club. She could feel it hit her thighs and shins, but she could tell the person was aiming for her knees. She couldn't let that happen, so she struggled to roll to the side, and took a few blows against the sides of her legs and her hips. In a very short time they had her immobile again, and then something hit her head and she saw another flash and lost consciousness.

Jane woke. Time had passed and she had the feeling that she had been away somewhere. She tasted the iron taste of blood and could tell she must have been bleeding from her teeth cutting her lips and her nose bleeding into the back of her throat. Both her eyes and her lower lip were swollen so the skin was tight and tender.

As she blinked to see, she saw a face lean down into hers. It was the face of an older man, and his jaw was clenched and his eyes glowed in hatred. His hand streaked across the bottom of her vision on the way to slap her face so hard the blow spun her to the side. "Are you surprised we're here, you piece of scum? You cockroach?" The accent was Russian. They were going to begin the torture, the part of captivity she had been worrying about most.

Jane could feel her body manufacturing fear as a by-product of the pain his people had caused but, even more, a product of the pain he wanted her to feel, promising her was coming. He slapped her again, and she felt the sting of it as a token. She had already been hit many times, and she knew there must be damage because the hurt didn't seem to be fading. The slaps were nothing. It was as though the man was just waking her up.

"I sent my people to catch you. Don't give yourself some false hope that we don't know who you really are. I know if I burn or cut your body you can give me a hundred names for yourself to make me stop. What's your real name?"

She knew he must be aware that the name she grew up with was all over the house. It was on the mailbox. It was on the papers in her car. She knew he would have looked if he'd been here for more than an hour or two. She said, "Jane." Names were powerful things. In the old people's stories the witches and cannibals and monsters that infested the forests would try to find out people's names so they could control them. But Jane was an English name she shared with a million women, not the name that her Seneca relatives had given her, and not the name her father called her when she was young because her parents loved her and were proud of her. She had, over the years of using her English name, mentally removed all the power of that name and transferred it to her Onondawaga names.

"All right, Jane," he said. "Here is what I know. You are the same woman that was caught a few years ago because she made a business out of taking people who were being hunted and making them disappear. The people who caught you put you up for sale. Whoever paid the biggest price would be able to keep you and ask you questions. They had all spent time and money hunting for somebody that you had taken in and moved away. I remember hearing there was a man named Eckersley and you stole his wife from him. There was a man named Ronald Hanlon. There was a man named Phil Barraclough. You had taken somebody from his brother, and then nobody ever saw the brother again either. Isn't that right?"

Jane stared at him, silent. The man's right

hand shot out like a snake striking her face. She felt the blow both on her face and on the back of her head, where it had pounded against the hard table. "That's right," she said.

"Of course it is. I heard the bidding got up over a million dollars before it all fell apart." He hit her again.

Jane said, "It didn't fall apart."

He hit her again. "It did."

"They all had to bring the money they were bidding to pay for me, because none of them could trust each other. They were all so greedy they killed each other for that money."

"Some of them lived," he said. "Grady Lee Beard, Daniel Martel, a few others. They're still out there, looking for you. When they find out I've got you, they'll come to me."

"And what will you do?"

"You moved people and gave them new names and got them new jobs. I'll ask you what the person's name is now, and where they're living, and what they're doing to get money, and any other facts you know. You'll be able to keep on living for a long time on your memory. When you've sold each of the people you hid, I'll set you free."

"No."

"What?"

"I won't do it."

The old man turned and walked out of the kitchen. The four people who had been sitting on the kitchen chairs ranged around the wall stood up and converged on her and began to beat her again. Jane was shocked to realize that one of them was a woman. She was tall as the men, but thinner, with long black hair and very light skin that struck Jane as pretty, and then as corpse-like.

The ordeal went on and Jane lost track of time. She was in pain but beginning to feel numb, and then she lost consciousness again.

After some period of time Jane was awake again. There was only the woman and one of the men. Jane said to the woman, "Can you take me to the bathroom?"

The woman said to her, "You want everything to be nice and civilized but you didn't think that when you killed all four of the brothers who followed you into the woods." Her accent was less pronounced than the old man's.

"I have to go, and I don't see how it helps you if you have to step in my piss and shit."

The woman took her by the arm and then looked angrily at the man with her. He leaned forward and grasped Jane's other arm and the two of them guided Jane into the bathroom in the downstairs hallway. The woman went inside with her and shut the door. "Come on. Hurry it up."

"Isn't that man Albert McKeith?" Jane said.

"You don't ask questions. We ask the questions."

When Jane was finished, the woman pulled a pistol out from under her sweater and aimed it at Jane's head. "I'm going to take the handcuffs off for a minute so you can take care of yourself. If you do anything I'll be happy to kill you."

"Understood."

The woman unlocked the handcuffs behind her and let her wipe herself, flush, and wash her hands, and then put the cuffs back on. Jane saw in the mirror above the sink that her face looked much worse than she had anticipated. She had two swollen black eyes, lips split in a couple of places, bruises and lines where blood had dried in streams on her face.

When they came out of the bathroom all of the captors were in the hallway. The old man said to Jane, "We're going to sleep here and leave late at night. You'll be in the basement. You aren't going to be able to wait until we're asleep and come up to cut our throats, so forget that idea." He nodded to the two big men.

The two men took Jane down the wooden steps to the basement. As she went down she looked around her and saw things in a new way. The house was from the time when her great-grandfather was young, more than a hundred years ago. He and his friends had built the foundation out of big stones and mortar, but they had not been interested in putting windows in a cellar. The ground floor was held up by beams that had been whole trees and still had bark on them. The men sat her on the floor. The handcuffs she was wearing were not removed. Instead they ran a chain through the chain of her handcuffs and secured it with a padlock. They wrapped the other end of the chain around a pipe and held it there with another padlock so she couldn't go very far.

They set an old galvanized bucket on the floor. One of the men said, "That's for you. We won't be able to send Magda down here to take you to the bathroom again."

Jane remained silent, thinking about what she was seeing and what she could see. If she wasted herself making sarcastic remarks, they might do her more harm, and it was important that she memorize what was in the basement.

When they had finished tethering her in the basement, they began to walk up the stairs. The last man to the top left the stairway door open. From where she sat Jane could see the opening to the hallway by the pantry. She could see the upper part of the kitchen wall. She wondered what was going on. Why would they do that — so they could watch her?

The men went away, and then a few minutes later the two big men reappeared. One of them lay on his stomach at the edge of the top step and tied a rope to the board that formed the step. Then he got up and moved out of sight.

The second man lay on the same spot at the edge of the hallway. Someone Jane couldn't see who was beside the door pushed a carpenter's electric circular saw into the man's reach. He turned it on and spun the blade around for a few seconds. Then he went to work on the first of the two long diagonal boards that formed the frame of the stairway. He let the circular saw slice through one board, and then went to work on the second.

As soon as the blade sliced the last inch, the top step was severed and the whole stairway fell to the floor in one piece with a crash. Jane was shocked. The two quick cuts had disconnected the wooden steps. Even if she had been in perfect health she could never have lifted those stairs, much less reconnect them at the top and climb out of the basement.

The two men were on their feet again and standing in the empty doorway on the edge of the basement. "Nighty-night," one of them said.

Desperately, Jane turned her head and tried to look at everything she could see, at all angles. She tried to use the last seconds memorizing every shape that her eyes showed her. And then one of the men lifted his hand to the light switch at the edge of the hallway and the light went out. Then he shut the basement door.

31

Jane could see nothing but darkness, but she listened. She heard the voice of the woman above. The two big men were mumblers and mutterers, so she heard their voices but not anything that sounded like words. She assumed they were speaking Russian. When the voices were gone Jane slowly let her senses and her memory deliver their reports.

The pain was constant from her scalp to her jaw. She let her nerves feel each of the pains, moving from the tops of her feet to her ankles upward, keeping her attention focused on one area of skin at a time and thinking about what was under it.

Without deciding to, she was holding in her mind the big chart of the human body that hung in Carey's office. It had always looked to her like a person who had been skinned and was being gutted for roasting, so she had tried not to look at it, but she found it now intact in her memory and it helped her to verify a growing impression that while her wounds and injuries were painful, none of her major organs was damaged. Her heart, lungs, liver, and kidneys had not been hit with jabs that would reach and destroy them. Her muscles and head had taken the worst of it. If nothing else happened tonight she would probably not die.

Her mobility was very limited. She had no plan but she did have a step.

Jane lay on the floor on her left side, which was the one that wasn't as painful as the right when it touched the floor. She wriggled and stretched and flexed her leg muscles and fought the pain to bring her feet up behind her. She slipped her right forefinger into her shoe behind her heel to pry the shoe off, then used the left forefinger to pry the left shoe off. She pushed the shoes ahead so they would be against the wall where she could find them again.

Jane bent her knees, flexed her feet and stretched her arms under her all at once, and brought the chain of the handcuffs under the soles of her feet. After a bit of struggling she brought her handcuffed wrists to the front of her body. She lay in the dark breathing heavily. The strain of having her hands manacled behind her had been more and more uncomfortable. She felt glad for every minute she had spent doing yoga and Tai Chi to stay flexible and limber. The cuffs around her wrists even felt looser because her arms weren't pulling the wrists apart.

Jane didn't allow herself to assume that she had solved her problems by having her hands in front of her, but at least it was an improvement. She could move. She felt the padlock that held her handcuffs to the chain. She tugged it and wiggled it to get a sense of the mechanism, and lifted the chain and moved her hand along it. She walked tentatively, pushing her feet rather than lifting them, and pulling herself along the chain. The more of the chain she lifted the more respect for it she had, because it was very heavy. When she had still been able to see, it had looked to her like the sort of chain that people used for swing sets, but now her fingers and hands measured and judged it differently. She could feel each individual weld where each link was closed through the next. One by one she rejected each of the methods she had imagined might break it. Hammering, putting the links in the vise on the workbench and then bending and rebending the same link, sawing or filing it all seemed too weak. There were a few remnants of her father's old collection of household tools down here, but she would need some industrial version of them, and anyway they were too far away for her to reach unless she defeated the chain first.

When Jane got to the end of the chain with the other padlock, she touched the pipe, slid the chain up and down, jiggled it and strained against it. She spent some time feeling her way along the pipe. It was hard, immovable, and long. It had been the original pipe for bringing water into the house when it was built. Jane inched her way along it. There were a couple of places where there were T-shaped connectors that had once sent water toward the kitchen or bathroom so she tested her ability to turn the pipe to unscrew a connector. There were also right-angle turns, but she couldn't make any connection budge.

There had to be a tool that would do what she wanted, or some other way of doing things. She cautiously moved through the darkness along the wall to explore and expand the mental image of the basement she carried in her memory. She plotted courses. One took her along the wall of the basement to the current furnace, which had a hundred-gallon oil tank beside it and a couple of vents. It was more compact than the old coal furnace it had replaced when she was a child.

The old furnace was cylindrical with an iron door in its side for her father to shovel coal into from the coal bin. At the top it looked to her like an octopus because it had round ducts that came out of it like tentacles, went varying distances along the underside of the floor and rose to open under registers, brass grates set into the hardwood floors that let the heat into the house. Other tentacles continued to end under brass grates in the second-floor bedrooms.

Jane had used the decommissioned furnace ducts as hiding places since she was little, and even today she had brought money and forged identification cards and a gun that she had intended to put in one of the ducts.

Jane stopped and sat by the furnace and let her mind move along the floor of the basement to explore the mental images of it that she had memorized. There was the step-ladder Jane always used to reach the ducts. There was the other workbench, the one that her father had only used for the messiest projects. He had been good at taking old, painted-over furniture that somebody had decided was worn out and restoring them to a second life. He would strip all the old paint and stain so the chair or table or cabinet was pure bare wood. Then he would varnish it and sand and varnish again and polish it until it looked as though it had come from an extremely fancy antique store. The bench was still a place for his sandpaper and putty knives and brushes and strippers, solvents, and rags.

She let her mind range farther. Across the open space was a spot where Jane had stored equipment and supplies for outdoor activities, and most of the clutter was still there. Her memory showed her a croquet set, a picnic basket, a net for volleyball or badminton, a charcoal grill and a couple of bags of charcoal and starter, blankets, and lawn chairs.

Jane's mind kept working at her problem for a long time. She knew it was hours, but she had no clear idea how many. She was accumulating an unhappy list of the ideas she had found to be impossible and rejected. It was still pitch dark, she was still manacled and chained to a pipe she couldn't cut, separate, or disconnect. Her muscles were bruised and painful. It must be getting late. She had to start preparing herself for things other than finding a way to escape during the night. One thing that would give her another chance was to have a gun. There was still one gun hidden in the heating duct.

She tried to get to the stepladder, but she guessed before she tried that it would be impossible. She had always kept the stepladder on the wall farthest from the old furnace so an intruder would never think that the reason the stepladder was down here was so she could get up high enough to open the old furnace duct. She tried but she could not reach the ladder. She tried pushing the painting workbench under the duct but, after she had moved the bench, her chain would let her climb up there, but not let her lift her handcuffs high enough to get her hands up to the duct, let alone into it. The chain held her away by only a couple of feet.

She tried a dozen other methods, but then she heard the night train's whistle. The crossings where the engineer had to stop and whistle were only a few blocks away, but tonight the sound seemed distant. She had heard the sound every night of her childhood. Even when she was asleep the whistle must have been loud enough, but her brain would have heard and discounted it. When the train reached the crossing at

Kohler, then at Franklin, then at Wheeler, it gave that long, plaintive sound. Jane's grandfather had once told her it seemed to him to be the loneliest sound on earth.

Tonight the whistle froze Jane's heart. If the night train was crossing, that meant it was two A.M. In a couple of hours, the men would come to the door and pull up the wooden steps, nail them back in place, and take her to a building somewhere far from here to torture her. And because she was a human being with nerves and a brain, she would feel what they did to her in all its intensity. And because she had once been brought near that point, she feared that she could eventually be forced to tell them whatever they asked her. If she weakened, she would betray people she had spent her life trying to save. She had promised them she would die rather than do that.

The train whistle meant she had only a short time to do anything. She was in pitch dark, but her survey of the basement had shown her what she would have to do.

32

Jane crawled toward the place where she believed she had stored the portable barbecue grill in the fall. She had placed the grill just about halfway along the wall that had been under the stairs. It should be fairly easy to find because the fallen stairway was also about halfway. She crawled out onto the bare floor until her hand touched the foot of the disconnected stairs.

She felt the shape of the staircase, which was two long two-by-twelve boards on their edges placed exactly parallel and joined by fifteen two-by-twelve boards four feet long, all nailed there at the same angle so they would all be uniform and level when the staircase was joined to the first-floor beam. She used the stairway to guide her toward the other side. When she got there, she found her chain wouldn't let her get all the way unless she turned her body and held her wrists toward the pipe that held her chain.

Jane was determined to do whatever she had to do. She maneuvered her body until she was lying on her back with her hands extended in line with the chain. She used her bare feet to explore the space beside the wall. She felt the legs of the grill with her toes. They had little wheels on them, and she was able to hook her feet under the supports and draw the grill toward her until she could sit up and touch it with her hands. She pulled it close and felt the grate on top, then lifted it and felt around in the concave space below. At the beginning of the night when she had been trying to memorize everything in the basement she couldn't see inside the grill, but her memory was that late last September when she had carried it down here, she had put some things inside it so she only had to make one trip. She didn't dare even name them, just looked at the picture in her memory and felt for them. She got up on her knees. And then she felt them. She felt the set of long-handled barbecue tools — a fork, a spatula, and a pair of tongs. She touched and released them. Then she felt the second thing she had remembered. It was a quart can of charcoal starter, unopened, and left for next summer. She kept searching. Was she imagining she had put the other thing in the barbecue because she wanted it so badly, or because her memory was accurate? She patted the ash-soiled bottom of the grill, touching it everywhere. No. It simply wasn't there.

She began to think of other ways she might do this. There was electricity. She had seen the man turn the lights off, but he had done it with a switch, so the power was still on. Could she get to something that would make friction and sparks, like an electric drill? As she thought about it, the picture in her memory shifted. The first image had been wrong. She had not put a plastic cigarette lighter in the grill. She had bought a fireplace starter, a different plastic device that worked the same way but was longer, and left it on top of the grate over the grill. She felt for it and it was there in her hand. How had she missed it before?

Jane lay on her back again and extended her feet toward the wall. She was sure she was right about this part because she had noticed it when she'd taken her final look. Jane felt the crinkly paper surface of the bag of charcoal. She had bought two big bags of it on the same trip to the store when she had bought the new charcoal starter and the fireplace lighter. She pulled them to her one at a time with her bare feet. They were the largest size, full of charcoal briquets that she could feel with her toes.

Jane began to crawl again, pushing the wheeled barbecue grill ahead of her. She had a memory map of the basement that she had amended in the past few minutes to include the fallen stairway, and that helped her go around it and find her way to the big old-fashioned coal furnace.

When she arrived, she felt her way around the side of the furnace with both hands, trying to find the handle to the iron door. She pictured it clearly. The door was an iron piece, almost square but with a rounded front that made it fit the cylindrical shape of the furnace. The handle that opened and closed the furnace was a simple L-shaped latch, but the part that you were supposed to grasp and turn was loosely wrapped around with a single thick strand of wire that wasn't touching the shaft that it covered so the hand wouldn't be burned.

Jane stood and lifted the two bags of charcoal briquets off the grill. She found the string at the top of the first bag and tugged it so the bag opened. She opened the furnace and poured the bag inside. Then she lifted the next bag and poured that one inside too. She moved her fingers in the barbecue grill until she found the metal can of charcoal starter. Jane took slightly longer to figure out how to pop open the plastic top, and then she reached into the furnace and poured a generous quantity over the charcoal. It took some patience, because she didn't want the charcoal to smoke too much. She wanted the fire to start efficiently. When she believed she had done a good enough job she drew back from the furnace and felt for the fireplace lighter.

She held the lighter near the furnace door, pushed the button forward with her thumb and pulled the trigger. At the end of the starter a spark appeared and then a small flame, so bright that this much light seemed an impossible gift. She could see the charcoal in a heap, and she could see the inner surface of the furnace. She moved her flame into the furnace to the charcoal. It took only a touch before a blue ghostly aura rose from the charcoal and began to spread. Jane watched for a few seconds until she was sure the flame would not go out.

The furnace had been emptied and gutted when the new one was installed. The opening at the ground level for the coal truck driver to move his steel trough to pour the pieces of coal into the coal bin had been bolted shut and then covered on the outside with clapboards. The vent that had once allowed the smoke and gases to escape had been blocked in the same way so that rodents couldn't use it as a private entrance. This was the first fire to be built in the furnace since then.

As Jane watched, the flames in the furnace brightened into a yellow-orange color and flared up. The old furnace had been designed when people who made things had still been craftsmen. She remembered being a little girl coming out of the bath up on the second floor on cold nights and her mother wrapping her in a towel that went over her head like a hood and extended to her ankles and taking her out into the hallway to stand on the brass register set into the hardwood floor. She could remember feeling the warm air coming up through the elaborate brass cutout curlicues and circles and designs to warm her feet and make its way up under her big towel. It was one of the most comforting physical feelings Jane had ever experienced. As she sat on the hard stone floor she felt an outpouring of love for her mother. She remembered the soft graceful hands smoothing the towel against her to soak up the last of the bath dampness, and her mother's soft sweet voice.

The movement of the warm air was built into the design of the furnace. The heated air was less dense than the chilly air down here and, as it warmed, it rose upward toward the highest registers, the ones on the second floor. Ultimately the warm air found its way even higher, into the attic, before it cooled enough to begin to sink again.

Jane suspected that because the furnace was working perfectly, she had very little time. She had some dim memory of reading that carbon monoxide was slightly lighter than air, so a carbon monoxide alarm had to be mounted at least as high up as a person was tall. This old house didn't have a carbon monoxide alarm. The combination of warm air and light carbon monoxide would make its way to the upper floors quickly.

She had hoped that she would not have to do this, but they had chained her too well for her to escape the basement, and the contents of the basement had dictated what she could do. She noticed that the iron door of the furnace let some light escape, and she could see the shapes in the cavernous space. It was comforting, almost pretty, like candlelight.

She was not surprised to learn what her most painful feeling was. She loved her husband Carey so much that her throat felt swollen with regret and sorrow, and her tears were coming steadily. She knew she would never see him again. Carey had been her treasure, her spoils from the war she had always been fighting, the wish she'd granted herself. Now he was already in the past, a memory, a loss.

There was no question that she had to do what she was doing. Jane had promised all of those people that she would die rather than trade them for more life or even for an end to unthinkable torture. She had discovered some time ago why human beings were so good at dreaming up terrible things to do to each other. It was because they carried with them the knowledge of all the things they never wanted anyone else to do to them. The information was there in their minds, ready for when the time came. Most of what she was doing now was living up to her promise to kill herself rather than her runners. But there was more to it than that.

In the old times, when a Seneca warrior had been captured, as she had been, he would do anything he could to be sure he didn't dishonor his people by succumbing

447

to the tortures inflicted on him. But he would be especially watchful in the hope that one of his captors might get too confident as the Seneca captive appeared to weaken. What he wanted most was for an enemy to come too close, so he could overpower him and kill one last enemy before he could be stopped. Jane had good reason to hope that she was killing her enemies with herself tonight.

The air in the old furnace was filling with carbon monoxide from the charcoal fire, and the heat from the fire was propelling it into the heating ducts and upward into the rooms where enemies would be sleeping. The second floor would be the first to fill up with the carbon monoxide, because the fire-warmed air would push most of it up the duct to the highest register. Whoever was sleeping there would die first. Next the first floor would fill up, partly from the register at the spot on the first floor where the living room and the hallway met, and partly from the cooling air and carbon monoxide mixture flowing down the stairs from the second floor. The basement would fill up last, because it was the lowest.

Carbon monoxide was an odorless, colorless gas, and it was replacing the oxygen in the sleepers' red blood cells as the sleepers breathed it in. When the carbon monoxide reached a certain proportion in the air, they would die — the old man, the four younger men, the woman, and Jane. She thought she remembered from some pamphlet of Carey's that sixteen hundred parts per million was enough.

Jane sensed that it was time to give thanks. She spoke in a soft voice, because she did not want her words to reach the people with whom she was sharing her house and wake them up. Because she spoke in the Seneca language they would not have understood any of it anyway. But Jane had an important message to the universe. It was an ancient one, a product of the old way of thinking. The Seneca people's religion wasn't about asking for things. It was about being thankful for things they had received. They recognized that life was good, and that the world was good.

She gave thanks to every part of the universe beginning with the earth below her. She thanked the earth, the water, the fish, the plants, and separately thanked the edible plants and the medicinal herbs. She thanked the animals, the trees, the birds, the four winds, the thunders that announced the rains, the sun, the moon, the stars, all spirit messengers, and the Creator. Her life, she said, had been an exceptional one. She hoped that she had used it in the best ways she could each precious day. She was grateful particularly that she had encountered and received so much love.

Jane looked around and noticed a few things that might add some momentum to the final event. Her father's old refinishing workbench was within reach, and there were still some old rags from a project that Jane had started a couple of years ago. There were also cans of paint stripper. She remembered there was something about those. She made her way to the bench and picked up the can that looked the cleanest. It felt heavy and full. She held the back of the can up to the dim light from the furnace door and read it. "Warning. This product contains methylene chloride, which can cause carbon monoxide poisoning." That was what she thought she had remembered.

Jane took an armful of rags and the two cans of paint stripper and tossed the rags onto the fire. Then she opened the two cans of paint stripper and set them inside so gravity would empty them. The heat would send the fumes through the ducts, and maybe speed things up. She closed the furnace and crawled as far from it as she could, lay on the floor, and closed her eyes.

33

There was a noise, or there had been a noise, but Jane had been unconscious and had not exactly heard it. She had a vague impression of a bang and then glass breaking. She heard noise, clearly now, the sound of heavy, fast footsteps on the floor over her head. She opened her eyes with difficulty. She had a headache that felt as though something terribly heavy was pressing against her forehead. She tried to sit up, but a wave of dizziness swept her body to the side, so she tipped and fell again. She was confused and her heart seemed to be pounding as though she had run miles.

She heard the thumping feet, and then windows being slid open, and then "Jane!" and a few seconds of just the feet, and then "Jane! Where are you?" It was Carey. She caught her mind sliding into some complicated tangle of thoughts about how it was cruel to have her arrival in the afterlife greeted by the one she would miss so much it was like some animal tearing at her heart. There were a few more sounds of wood sliding, and then the hum of an electric motor. This sound was coming from close by. She located it at the modern oil furnace. Someone must have gone to the thermostat in the upstairs hall and turned on the powerful fan to vent the air from the house.

As she lay there, she heard more footsteps, and then the door opened where the top of the stairs used to be. "Jane?" Carey yelled.

"Here I am," she said. "I'm here. Don't come in, the stairs are down."

"I can see that. There's a rope."

About thirty seconds later he was beside her. He leaned over her and put a mask over her face and held it there. He said, "Jake is with me. This oxygen is from his house for his emphysema attacks. You have carbon monoxide poisoning, and this will help you a lot."

He suddenly noticed her wrists had handcuffs. He lifted them with his free hand. "What the hell is this?" His eyes followed the chain to the pipe along the wall.

It took a few minutes before Jane heard the voice of her elderly next-door neighbor, Jake Reinert, calling from the empty doorway to the first floor. "Carey?" he called. "I brought the aluminum stepladder from my garage. I'm going to lower it so you can reach it when you're ready."

"Thanks, Jake," Carey called.

There were sliding sounds and the rattling of the aluminum ladder as he lowered it into the basement.

Carey looked at Jane. "Just lie there, and don't move. Keep the mask over your nose and mouth and breathe. It's a hundred percent oxygen, and it's the standard treatment. We're also airing out the house. As soon as you feel better, we'll climb up the ladder out of here."

"Uh, Carey?" Jake called. "She's not the only one."

"What do you mean?"

"There are four dead men in the beds upstairs."

34

Three weeks later Albert McKeith woke up at nearly eleven in the morning. He had been hearing the swishing sounds of cars passing his apartment growing more constant for a while. He had gone to bed with the small, high upper window open. Los Angeles in late April was often hot, and he could feel the warm air and smell a faint scent of wisteria.

The nightmare set off by the betrayal committed by Sara Doughton was actually beginning to fade. He had only arrived home a couple of weeks ago, and his mind was beginning to feel almost completely different. His doctor had told him on his last visit that carbon monoxide poisoning sometimes caused delayed neurological symptoms like short-term memory loss, and even amnesia. Maybe some mild form of that had happened to help him get over the sting of her disloyalty. But whenever his mind passed across her on its way to somewhere else, she seemed only a momentary distraction. He didn't feel like wasting his time searching for her, and killing her somehow felt like too much work and too much risk when all it could accomplish was not seeing her again. She could take care of that for both of them.

He sat up in bed and opened his eyes in a squint to protect them from the first golden rays of the glorious LA sunshine. What he saw made him gasp and jerk backward away from it.

Standing about ten feet away in the middle of his living room was the tall, slender shape of Magda. "Stay still, Alberto," she said. Her right hand held a semiautomatic pistol. He could see that there was a silencer attached to the muzzle.

"What are you doing here?" He said, "I saw you and you looked dead."

"Well, I wasn't," she said. "I was lying beside you in the bed. You could have checked — felt for a pulse, at least. We were all poisoned with carbon monoxide, but I woke up when I heard you start the car and drive away. I got up and checked the others for a pulse. Mr. Porchen was dead. Yevgeny was dead. Maxim was dead. Alexei was dead. I even turned on the cellar light and saw the woman we caught lying on the floor, dead. She killed herself and tried to take all of us with her. And you ran away and left us there so she could."

"You can't blame me for that. I thought I was the only one alive."

"You don't understand. You came to us, to the brotherhood, asking us to help you as though you were one of us. That meant you had to live by the rules that we do. You can't run away and leave brothers behind to die."

Albert tossed the sheet off his legs, and stepped to the chair by his bed to put on the pants he'd left there.

"Don't," she said.

"What? Am I a prisoner?"

"Not anymore. Now you're a dead man."

She fired a shot into his chest and then stepped closer to fire the second shot through his forehead as he lay faceup on the floor. She unscrewed the silencer and put it with the gun into the purse that hung from her shoulder, and then stepped out the door and locked it behind her with the key she had known would be on his dresser.

35

It was almost winter again. The days were short, and when Jane woke up in the mornings to have breakfast with Carey the windows sometimes had frost along the lower panes, and most of the deciduous trees had only a few brown remnants of their leaves. This morning after Carey had driven toward the hospital for his morning surgeries, Jane learned something.

Jane looked out the window on the first landing as she climbed the stairs to the second floor of the old stone McKinnon house. It had been months since she had felt any shortness of breath climbing, which was why she had grown accustomed to stopping to look out the window through the trees. Now she did it to see the seasons changing.

When she was on the second floor, she went to the big cupboard in the second-best bedroom and took out the box she had stored there a few years ago. She had tightly sealed and wrapped it to protect the Ga-ose-ha from moisture and air, and inside it was packed with museum-quality nonacidic paper. She didn't open the box, just carried it down to the living room and left it on the big table on the end of the room away from the fireplace.

For the rest of the day Jane stayed busy doing chores. She drove to the biggest local supermarket to buy groceries. As the temperatures became cooler in western New York each fall Jane stocked up on food that she could make into good meals on the evenings she knew would come when she wasn't going to want to drive to a store. She also stocked up on general household supplies. On the way home she stopped at the Boulevard Mall to do a little bit of shopping, but it was mostly a scouting mission. She was planning to make some other trips to buy some things on other days, and today she was just getting a preliminary idea of what was going to be available this season.

When Carey came home after finishing his rounds in the evening it was already dark. She heard his car come in the driveway, saw the beams of his headlights illuminate the garage doors, saw the red

458

brake lights glow as he stopped and then got out.

The back door opened a moment later and he came in. He was smiling as he stepped to her and put his arms around her and held her there for a few seconds before he kissed her.

She kissed him and then pulled back. "Welcome home, Doc," she said.

"Thanks," he said. "It's good to be here. Wow, whatever that is smells good."

"It's that chicken and dumplings dish that my mother taught me when I was a kid."

"Great. I like that."

"I think she thought nobody would ever ask me for a date unless I could feed them."

"Not true, of course. I'm going to head upstairs to change. Come up with me, so we can talk. How was your day?" He started to walk through the living room toward the stairs, and she followed.

"Sort of surprising," she said. "I've been kind of waiting to check something out with you."

He stopped, and looked at the box she had brought downstairs. "Is that the, uh, the antique — ?"

"Well, yeah," she said. "It's the cradle board. I'm thinking of hanging it up again upstairs. But here is what I wanted to show you." She took a rolled-up paper napkin out of her apron pocket and handed it to him.

He unrolled it and saw the white plastic object, held it up, and looked at the plus sign on the side. "Really?" he said.

"I guess so," she said. "I know it's not really your field, but —" she shrugged.

"You don't have to be an ob-gyn to read a pregnancy test," he said. "That's a positive."

She reached into the apron pocket again and took out two other rolled-up napkins. "These too. I guess we shouldn't make any plans for the first or second week in August."

He took her into his arms again. "I can't believe it."

"Do you think we'll be any good at this?"

He laughed. "I'll do my best. And who the hell would be a better mother than you?"

ABOUT THE AUTHOR

Thomas Perry is the bestselling author of over twenty novels, including the critically acclaimed Jane Whitefield series, *The Old Man,* and *The Butcher's Boy,* which won the Edgar Award. He lives in Southern California.

The employees of Thorndike Press hope you have enjoyed this Large Print book. All our Thorndike, Wheeler, and Kennebec Large Print titles are designed for easy reading, and all our books are made to last. Other Thorndike Press Large Print books are available at your library, through selected bookstores, or directly from us.

For information about titles, please call:
(800) 223-1244

or visit our website at:
gale.com/thorndike

To share your comments, please write:
Publisher
Thorndike Press
10 Water St., Suite 310
Waterville, ME 04901